Don't Fall in Love

Editing by Allie Bliss from Blissed Out Editing

Proofreading by Sarah Baker from Word Emporium

Don't Fall in Love

BREAKING THE RULES
BOOK TWO

KA JAMES

Dedication

This book is dedicated to everyone who took a chance on me and read Don't Tell Anyone.

Each and everyone of you is the reason Don't Fall in Love is in your hands right now.

Trigger Warnings

To help you decide if this book is for you, I have included a trope and trigger warning outline below. Rest assured, there is a happy ending but to make it interesting for you, there has to be some turbulence on the journey.

This is a contemporary romance.

Tropes: Enemies to Lovers, Fake Dating/Engagement, Forced Proximity, Billionaire, Protective Alpha

Triggers: Anxiety and Panic Attacks

Playlist

Listen Here

Falling In Love With A Stranger - Song House

I Can't Swim - Ashley Kutcher

Head & Heart (Feat. MNEK) - Joel Corry

Movement - Hozier

Something in the Orange - Zach Bryan

Power Over Me - Dermot Kennedy

If I Showed You - Henry Verus

Break My Soul - Beyonce

Bad Memories (Felix Jaehn Remix) - MEDUZA

Devil in Your Eyes - CIL

Escapism (Sped Up) - RAYE, 070 Shake

30,000 Ft - We Three

Haunted Place (Turn Into Stone) - Kyndal Inskeep

Stand By Me - Florence and the Machine

Unconditional - Sinéad Harnett

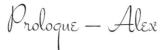

Prologue — Alex

I lost sight of Meghan about an hour ago. One second, I was chatting away with Maggie from the tenth floor about her two adorable babies, and then when I looked down onto the dance floor, Meghan was gone.

I figured she'd gone for a drink, or a dance or something, so I didn't start looking right away, but it's getting late now and she's nowhere to be seen.

This isn't like her.

I want to go home but I don't want to leave without her. Or at least without knowing that she's safe. My stomach churns with nerves as I stand at the rail that overlooks the lower floor of the club.

Taking my phone out of my black clutch, I send her a text.

ALEX

Hey, where are you? I can't see you.

It shows as delivered almost immediately but even staring at it, willing a reply to come, doesn't garner me one.

She couldn't have gone too far. I'll search the club and if I have no luck, I'll alert security.

Passion is an up and coming club. I've heard the owner has a few scattered around the world, and even at two in the morning, it's still bustling and doesn't show any signs of closing soon.

I take one last look over the balcony onto the dance floor before I turn and walk to the corridor that leads to the VIP restrooms. As I enter the dimly lit corridor, I notice four doors in addition to the restrooms.

No way she wandered into a supply closet. Unless... she could be getting laid. No, we're talking about Meghan, not me. With my mind set on my mission—find Meghan Taylor—I decide to test the handle of each door. Mystery door number one leads to the supply closet, stacked with cleaning products and smelling of bleach.

Next is the ladies' restroom. I go in and check each stall—luckily for me they're all empty so I don't have to stand around for too long. Moving back into the corridor, I go to the men's restroom next.

I may get unsolicited dick pics occasionally but I'm not actively trying to see some dick right now, so I knock on the door and keep my eyes scrunched closed.

Cautiously, I poke my head through the door and call out for Meghan.

Getting no response, I move onto the final three doors. Two of them are locked and after pressing my ear to them, listening out for any signs of distress, I move on when I hear nothing.

Maybe she is in there having the time of her life and they just have good sound proofing.

I smirk at the thought. As if Meghan would be getting it on with some random guy in a club. I'm lost in my own thoughts when I swing open the third door. In hindsight, I should have been paying more attention; who knows what I could've walked in on.

The most beautiful man I have ever laid eyes on is sitting behind a sleek glass desk with a laptop open in front of him. Behind him is a wall of windows looking out over the club below. His head snaps up as I enter, his brow furrows in question at my intrusion.

"I'm so sorry. I was just looking for my friend." I try not to stutter as I stare at him.

God, why am I so nervous? Butterflies take flight in the pit of my stomach and my skin heats under his assessing gaze.

He's set me on edge just by looking at me. It's intense. His full focus on me.

Watching like I'm his prey.

I can hear the dull beat of the bass in the club, but it fades away as we continue this silent staring... contest? He smirks up at me as he removes his glasses and reveals his dazzling eyes. They're kind of blue but mixed with the perfect hint of green.

Leaning back in his chair, he keeps his gaze trained on me. Like a deer caught in the headlights, I stay frozen in the doorway, unable to look away from him.

He's dressed in a crisp white shirt, which is sculpted to his muscular chest and arms. Navy-blue chinos encase thick thighs and navy-blue velvet Oxford shoes, that I can see through the desk, are on his feet.

A thought occurs to me as I take in his long legs that are crossed at the ankle—*what would it be like to sit under that desk and unzip him?*

My brow pulls into a frown at the confusing thought. He's a stranger and I've never had this almost instant attraction to someone that I don't even know the name of. I lift my eyes up his body, taking in his clean shaven jaw, full lips, and tanned skin tone. He has a straight nose and black hair, shaved on the sides but long on the top, that's neatly coiffed.

"That's okay, sweetheart. What does she look like? Maybe I can help?" he asks as he gestures towards his laptop.

Oh God, he's British.

I squeeze my thighs together and pray he doesn't notice the movement.

"Um, her name's Meghan. We work together. She was wearing a dusty pink dress. She's blonde…" I scratch my head as I try to think of more identifiable features.

He types away on his laptop and then his delectable

mouth lifts on one corner as if he's seen something amusing.

"She went home with somebody."

I stare at him for what feels like forever. With a shake of my head, I timidly move toward his desk, stopping next to him.

I need to see who.

He slams his laptop closed at my approach, and I frown at the action.

Oh my God, has Meghan been taken by someone?
Is he involved?

"I need to see," I state, looking down at him and trying to keep my composure. "No offense, but I don't know you and you could be in some conspiracy to..." I wave my arm around looking for the right words. "To kidnap her." I fold my arms across my chest in defiance.

"She left with someone from your party earlier. There is no conspiracy here, I assure you." He holds his hands up as he leans further back in his chair.

He returns my stare, but for some reason I feel like he's reaching into my soul and learning every facet of me.

Turning my head from his gaze—which is making me want to do things I never normally would—I stare out of the window at the clubbers below as I think about what he's said.

Meghan's a smart girl.

I'm sure she'll be fine. She's an adult after all.

Deciding to text her again and ask her to call me as

soon as she can, I make a plan to go home and get into bed. It's been a long week at work and I need to relax. Maybe I'll even drag out one of my much used toys and *really* relax.

I'm turning away from him when he grabs my hand and I stumble on my heels, falling back into his lap. He's all solid muscles and warm body. Even though we're both very much fully clothed, I still get wet from the contact.

Jeez, I need to get laid.

It's been months since I was with someone—the whole needing to have some sort of connection with the person I'm fucking really does screw with your sex life.

Turning my head to apologize for falling into his lap —even though it's kind of his fault—I suck in a breath as I realize just how close we are.

His mouth is inches from my own and it really wouldn't take much for me to close the distance and have a taste. I'm aware of his hands touching my body, one on my waist and the other on my thigh, stroking small circles.

Shouldn't he be helping me up, not holding me in place?

I wiggle my ass in an attempt to relieve the ache building in my core.

"Sweetheart, I wouldn't do that if I were you," he murmurs in my ear and I close my eyes at the rumble of his voice as it runs through my body.

Before I know it, our lips connect and his tongue dives into my mouth. He tastes like a combination of honey and mint. It's intoxicating. Moaning into his mouth, I wiggle my ass into his crotch again, this time eliciting a moan from him.

He lifts me from his lap and places me on the edge of his desk. His lips still devour mine even as he stands between my legs.

I should feel intimidated. He's all muscle as he towers over me. He must be at least six foot five. His hand skirts up the inside of my thigh and caresses my pussy through my G-string. I tear my mouth away from his to gasp in a lungful of much needed air.

My body feels like it's on fire and he's the only person that can temper the flames.

I've never been this reactive with a partner before... ever.

He sits back in his chair and lowers it so that his head is aligned to my crotch. And then with no warning whatsoever he buries his face in my pantie-clad pussy and inhales a deep breath. My eyes widen at his forwardness but, as if on instinct, I lean back and open my legs wider for him.

I don't know what's come over me.

"God, you smell fucking amazing." He moans, running his tongue over my underwear.

When he pulls away, I whimper at the loss of contact, and my eyes dart to his when he pushes my legs together. His features are dark with lust and they only darken further when his hands smooth up the outside of my thighs and under my dress to grab the top of my panties.

He removes them, and I spread my legs wide for him again as he throws my G-string somewhere over his shoulder. His eyes never leave my bare pussy as he trails a finger through my damp slit, and I moan at the contact, throwing my head back. Rubbing over my clit, he slides one of his long, thick fingers into my core, right to the hilt.

"You're so tight. I'm going to need to stretch you a little to get you ready." He groans as he brings his mouth to my pussy, covering my clit with his tongue and flicking the sensitive bud.

Slowly, he adds a second finger to my pulsing core and slides it in with ease, using my wetness as lubrication.

I don't think I've ever been this turned on, and with a stranger no less.

"I don't normally do this," I pant as his fingers begin to move.

An overwhelming need to make sure he doesn't get the wrong impression settles deep within me, even though I know he won't be bothered. Guys don't care about shit like that.

He doesn't respond to my comment, he just continues to eat me, bringing me to the edge before he pulls away and stands, causing me to let out a groan of disappointment.

"Take off your dress and put your hands on the glass," he commands.

I look up at him in confusion, my eyes moving back and forth between him and the window.

He wants me to do what?

I like to try new things as much as the next person, but I'm not an exhibitionist.

"It's a privacy window. They can't see you," he reassures me, tucking a strand of my straight, light brown hair behind my ear.

His words soothe me and for the second time tonight, I take what he has said as fact without seeing any evidence.

Standing from the desk, not daring to look back and see the mess I have no doubt made on it, I walk up to the window, my hips swinging with each step.

Reaching under my arm, I unzip my dress and let it fall to the floor until I'm left in nothing but my black strappy five-inch stilettos. I tentatively place my hands on the window, just as he's directed, throwing a questioning look over my shoulder at him.

He looks... *hungry.*

His gaze devours me like I'm his next meal and his tongue darts out to wet his bottom lip. *I need to kiss him.* I turn from the window and wrap my arms around his neck, pressing my lips to his, my tongue begging for entry into his mouth. He allows me to be in control for all of two seconds before his tongue is plundering my mouth and he's grabbing a fistful of each of my ass cheeks.

Dazed and confused, I pull back, returning to my position in front of the window. Even with my heels on, he still towers over me and, for a fleeting second, I wonder if I should be fearful of the power he's exuding and the control he has over both my mind and body.

The thought disappears as he moves his chair behind me and sits back down in it, pushing down on my lower back to urge me to bend over slightly. My flushed cheek rests against the cool glass and I watch the crowd. It's exhilarating to see the people below, oblivious to the pleasure I'm experiencing so close to them.

When he spreads my cheeks and proceeds to eat my ass, I tense initially at the unfamiliar contact before letting out a low moan of pleasure. My eyes close of their own volition and I enjoy the sensation of his mouth on the only virgin part of me.

His two fingers return to my soaked core and he slowly pumps them in and out, stretching me as he adds a third. I can feel my arousal running down the inside of my legs, and for a fraction of a second wonder what the view must be like for him.

"Such a good *fucking* girl, aren't you?"

I don't answer, unable to vocalize anything at this moment in time. His hand comes down on my ass cheek, filling the room with a cracking sound as it echoes in the confines of his office. I let out a yelp, the unexpected pain making me clench around his three fingers. He lets out a low moan as his palm soothes the spot he just spanked.

"You need to answer me, sweetheart," he growls.

"Yes," I rasp out.

"Yes, what?" he demands.

"I'm... I'm a good girl," I moan as he continues to pump in and out of me, almost punishingly.

"And what do good girls get?"

"Fucked?" I question a hint of desperation in my tone.

Please say they get fucked.

All over, the tingle of my arousal builds with every thrust of his fingers.

"Yes. Yes, they do, baby," he chuckles. He increases the pace of his fingers, moving his mouth back to the puckered hole of my ass.

My vision goes fuzzy as I feel my orgasm building and I let out a cry of release, clenching around his fingers while I come undone.

"Now is the time to get dressed and walk away if you don't want me to fuck you," he warns.

There's a hint of a plea in my tone that I can't quite hide. "No. I need to feel you inside me."

He stands. I hear the faint sounds of his fly unzipping and the foil of a condom wrapper being ripped. It feels like an eternity before I feel the head of his cock pushing into me from behind.

Stretching my sensitive pussy, his hands find my hips, gripping them roughly. In one smooth move, he's seated to the hilt and I let out a guttural sound of pleasure as an orgasm I didn't even know I was on the verge of having, sends spasms through my body.

Okay, what is he doing to me?

One of his hands moves across my stomach, past my breasts and up to hold my throat lightly, pulling me back into his embrace. With my body pressed between his and the window, he starts to move in and out of me.

His grunts of pleasure fill my ears as he slowly increases his pace. I'm in awe when a third orgasm starts to build with each stroke of his thick cock. Little whimpers fall from my lips—I don't feel like I can make it through this one. Each thrust has my body convulsing as if a current of power is electrifying my blood.

What is happening?

Moving the hand still on my hip to my clit, he rubs it in smooth, precise movements bringing me closer and closer to the edge. I try to wriggle away, but he holds me steady, murmuring words of encouragement into my ear. Before I know it, I'm coming again, and as I clench around him, I can feel and hear his own orgasm taking him over.

He pulls out of me, resting me against the window. When he's certain I'm able to stand on my own, he walks off toward a door I hadn't noticed when I came in, disappearing behind it and leaving me alone in his office.

Catching my breath, I take the opportunity to get dressed and sneak out. I hate awkwardness at the best of times, let alone after coming three times. I'm going to chalk this up to a wild, orgasmic experience with a guy I will *never* see again.

When I get home and I'm tucked in bed, reliving the events of the night, it dawns on me that I didn't even get his name. I suppose I could easily find it out by searching the club, but I'm not going to. There's no need.

It isn't until I see him again on another night out, that I realize he's friends with Cooper Jackson, one of the managing partners at the firm I work for.

This fact alone isn't enough to keep me away from him.

It should be, maybe then I could have protected myself better.

This is the start of our story; of how Sebastian Worthington barreled into my life and turned it upside down, because like a moth to a flame, I'm drawn to him.

Even if it ends in my own heartache.

ONE

Alex

TWO AND A HALF YEARS LATER

"**O**h, I didn't know you were still waiting out here," Meghan says as she walks into the hallway from her bedroom, adjusting her maternity dress around her bump.

Meghan and Cooper are throwing a housewarming party but were upstairs and because Lizzie, their daughter, had a fall I was tasked with getting Mom and Dad. I'm pretty sure I've interrupted them getting down and dirty.

"I thought I'd accompany my favorite godson downstairs," I reply.

Meghan lets out a low chuckle as she takes my offered arm. "You know it hasn't been decided yet, right?"

"As if you would choose anyone else," I scoff, leading her down the hallway to the staircase.

I'm not going to lie, I'm a little bit in love with their

new house. It's a classic New England Colonial, and with its white brick, green shutters and columns flanking the entryway. It reminds me of the house in *Father of the Bride*. It gives country vibes with its hardwood floors and three white and mahogany accented staircases. Modern gadgets fill each room, along with antique furniture and rugs that cost more than all of my furniture combined.

"I mean, there are at least six other people in the running. People who live in big houses, with equally big gardens," she jokes. "How is the new place, anyway?"

When Meghan moved out of our building, it made little sense for me to stay in our rundown neighborhood, so I found a new apartment in the Financial District in Manhattan.

"It's great. Much closer to work. It has a gym and the neighbors I've met have been great so far. You should come out with us one night when my little bambino arrives."

"That would be amazing. I know I didn't go out much when we lived in the city, but I'd love nothing more than to let my hair down and dance." Meghan sighs, as if going out dancing is one of her favorite pastimes and not something I had to drag her out to.

Meghan is content to fill the silence as we walk into the spacious kitchen. My mind wanders while I take in the grandeur of her home and the life she's built. The kitchen, like every room in this house, is spacious and light. White cabinets line two of the walls, a large range cooktop is built into the counter and a marble top island fills the center of the room. At the opposite end is a large dining table. Light spills into the room from the floor to ceiling windows and sliding doors that line one wall, giving a view of their perfect garden.

I'm so glad Meghan got her happily ever after.

Although I do have to wonder, how did we get here? I'm amazed at how much everything has changed in two and a half years. It feels like only yesterday I was sticking to my guns and forcing Meghan to keep her promise and wear the dress I chose for our Christmas party. Now my best friend is living a cozy life in suburbia, married to an incredible man. The same man that occupied her every thought for a whole year before they even hooked up.

Kind of how a certain man is occupying my every thought.

Cooper joins us as we stand by the backdoor. He hands Meghan a drink and puts his arm around her waist, dropping a kiss onto the top of her head. It makes me want to throw up because of how perfect he is for her and how much they love each other.

I want that.

I want someone to love me how Cooper loves Meghan.

I'll admit, it wasn't until I saw how happy Meghan is with Cooper, that I realized what true love looks like. Maybe I'm a little jealous of my best friend but I'd love to have someone to lean on when I've had a rough day. Deep down, I know the man I seem to be hooked on isn't the one for me and won't give me what I crave, but I can't seem to stay away from him.

"Have you seen what Cooper has done with the nursery?" Meghan asks, pulling me from my thoughts.

"No. Has he stocked it full of law books for his mini me?"

"Hey! There's nothing wrong with getting them started early," Cooper pouts.

A laugh bubbles from my throat. I enjoy teasing him and we seem to have fallen into an easy friendship, despite him being my boss's boss. "I'm just glad for my Godson's sake that Meghan is going to be home with him in his more impressionable years."

"Has she not told you? Susan across the street is going to be his Godmother." He takes a sip of his drink as his eyes twinkle with mischief.

I roll my eyes. "You and I both know——" the words die on my lips as the sound of the front door opening draws my attention away from the conversation. The hairs on my bare forearms raise and my stomach contracts as I watch Sebastian step through the threshold. Trailing behind him is a blonde woman in a dress far too revealing for a housewarming in the suburbs.

Even as my gaze roams over him, trying to take in all of his features, my throat becomes tight. *This is why I didn't want to see him*. I didn't want to be reminded of the fact that I was just another notch on his bedpost—just like I know she will be too. I feel sick at the realization that, even though I explode under his touch, I'm still just a number in a long list of women to him.

My gaze darts to Cooper, his features coated in apology and sympathy. I shake my head to let him know it's okay. I'd asked Cooper earlier if Sebastian was bringing anyone, and I'm certain he was being truthful when he reassured me that his best friend was flying solo. It's not like we had to RSVP, it's a damn house-warming for friends and family for God's sake.

I step away from Meghan with a mumbled apology and walk out of the patio door, heading toward the back of the garden.

They have a massive yard which is split up into thirds by rows of hedges. In the middle third is a vegetable garden and flower beds—Meghan joked about her lack of a green thumb and how the patch would be dead before long, but it's thriving as far as I can see.

The front third has a pool, BBQ area and lounge chairs scattered around it. This is also where most of the party is currently hanging out, enjoying the warm early September weather. The back third has a chill vibe to it with a hot tub, shed and a large daybed.

I'm dressed in ripped denim shorts, a white shirt tucked in at the front and a pair of five-inch stilettos, which I kick off as I reach the edge of the lawn. I carry the heels in my hand as I walk toward the back of the garden for some space. Pulling my sunglasses down from their place on top of my head, I fix my focus on making my escape.

The grass is bouncy and still slightly damp from the morning dewiness underneath my bare feet. I bypass the children screaming as they chase each other around the lawn and grab a beer from the table set off to the left of the garden. The daybed has been calling my name since I arrived, but even more so now. My usually warm skin color has been fading as we've left behind the summer months, so I'm going to make use of today's sunshine.

Just as I'm sitting down, Sebastian comes strolling through the gap in the hedge. I hate the awareness that ripples through me and how my nipples harden under his scrutiny. Even though he's wearing sunglasses, I can feel his dark gaze on me. I feign ignorance, settling back into the cushions as I unlock my phone.

I'm aware that it's just the two of us in this part of the garden and that the sound of the party is barely audible this far back. With my phone in one hand, I take a sip from my beer as I flick through social media.

Maybe he'll get the hint and go away.

We don't know each other well enough to make small talk—a few hook ups doesn't make us friends—and I certainly have nothing to say to him. At least not anything nice. I think the feelings I'd felt for him at one point have since morphed into... not hate, but certainly something close to that.

I'm aware of him moving to stand at the end of the bed, and I don't need to look at him to know his eyes haven't left me.

"Are you avoiding me, Alex?" he asks—his voice is

like honey as it caresses over my body—drawing my attention to him. Damn him and his sexy British accent.

A battle begins inside of me. I'm not sure if I want him to climb on top of me and claim me, or to throw a shoe at his stupid, handsome face.

I wish he didn't affect me like this.

Unable to ignore his presence any longer, I dip my sunglasses to the tip of my nose as I level my gaze at him over the rim, my eyes flicking up and down him with an air of boredom.

He's dressed in a pair of faded dark blue jeans, which he's paired with a white t-shirt and a black leather bomber jacket. A pair of black leather worker boots adorn his feet and the pièce de résistance is the baseball cap that he's wearing backwards, that with his Aviators on, has me practically weak at the knees.

"Shouldn't you be getting back to your date?" I shoot back, my brow lifting in question before I continue, "Who even brings a date to a housewarming party?" My tone betrays me and I pull my gaze away from him, pushing my sunglasses back into place so that he can't see the hurt in my eyes.

"I love how you've avoided the question." He chuckles as he sits on the daybed next to me, leaning back on his palms. He closes his eyes and lifts his face to the sun, as if he has all day to wait for me to answer.

I'm done with his games. I swing my legs over the edge of the bed, bending to pick up my discarded shoes and walk to the gap in the hedges. I thought I could do this, be civil with him, but I can't. It's impossible for me to be around him without emotions I can't quite identify being stirred up inside of me. I'm nearly at the gap in the bushes when he calls out to me.

"That's right, Alex, run away. You're good at that."

I roll my eyes as I turn to face him. He wants an answer. I'll give him one. "Yes, Sebastian, I am avoiding you. I'm not going to lie. When I fuck a man, I like to know that my pussy is enough for him. That *my* taste is the one that he craves. That he can only think about seeing me on my knees as I let him fuck my throat so hard, he bruises the back of it." My chest heaves, as I finally say all the things I've wanted to say to him for the longest time.

His eyes go stormy, and I can see the muscle in his jaw ticking, but I continue unfazed, "I don't need him to have a title; I just need him to not be fucking anyone else. I don't think that's too much to ask, and I'm *very* aware that I won't get that from you, so as far as I'm concerned, you've served your purpose. Somewhere out there will be a man that sets me on fire *and* whose thoughts *I* consume. Thanks for a good time, but I don't want or need you anymore."

Turning on my heel with my head held high, I walk back to the party, praying he can't see my shaking hands. I might have practiced that speech in my mind a thousand times but I never thought I'd have the opportunity to give him a piece of my mind like this.

I'm done with him, and it feels good to have gotten a

few things off my chest. He doesn't get to pretend we're friends when he's never treated me like anything but an available piece of ass.

"Alex, come and meet Ben," Meghan calls to me with a hint of mischief in her mossy gaze, as I step out of the house. "I think you guys will get along great."

I've spent the last half an hour fiddling around in the kitchen, trying not to watch Sebastian from the kitchen window. Despite my bravado earlier, I still find my gaze seeking him out, which only makes me more mad at myself.

Taking a detour to the drinks table, I deposit the empty bottle in my hand on the table with some others and grab a new one from the cooler, before walking over to Meghan and Ben. Taking a large swig from the bottle, I swallow it down as I pull my sunglasses from the top of my head and over my eyes.

I'm staying in one of Meghan's spare rooms tonight and my plan is to get drunk enough to pass out but not make a fool of myself. I'm going to need something stronger than beer if I want to succeed.

I pray to God that Meghan isn't trying to hook me up with someone. Even though it's not really her style, at this point it wouldn't surprise me. I'm not completely ignorant to the comments she's been making about my singledom—completely innocent comments, of course.

As I approach, my eyes coast over Ben behind the cover of my sunglasses. He's a good-looking guy. Like *really* good-looking. His features are striking, and with a straight nose, wide eyes framed by long lashes and high cheekbones, he could be on the cover of *GQ Magazine*.

His hair is shaved short and tight to his head, and a short beard covers what I'm sure is a strong jaw. He's dressed in a pair of navy boat shoes, tan chino shorts, and a short sleeve navy shirt showing off the tattoo sleeves on both of his arms. Standing in front of him, I can just about make out a rose tattoo on his neck.

"Hi, Alex. It's nice to meet you." Ben pulls me in for a friendly hug, and I get a whiff of his woodsy cologne. I return the friendly kiss he places on my cheek, before pulling back, with a genuine smile on my face.

"Hi, Ben. It's a pleasure to meet you too." I turn to Meghan as she squeezes my arm. She calls out to someone across the yard and moves away to talk to them.

Turning back to Ben, I take a sip of my drink, then ask him, "So, how do you know Meghan and Cooper?"

"I live about four houses down and ran into Meghan and Lizzie one afternoon about a month ago. We've been friends ever since." He throws a smile in Meghan's direction. "Apparently, you and I are very similar," Ben comments, his eyes scanning the backyard.

"Is that so?" I ask, my eyebrows raising in question as I wrap an arm around my waist, lifting my gaze to him.

"We're both stubborn." He laughs. "Have bubbly personalities, and like to push our friends to step out of their comfort zones," he declares with a wink.

I chuckle in response, knowing that he's heard all of that from Meghan. His gaze slides to something over my shoulder, causing his eyes to narrow a fraction. If I wasn't looking at his face—to avoid looking at a certain someone—I'd have missed it.

"We also like handsome men that appear unattainable. Although, I've never had one give the person I'm just talking to a death stare while another woman clings to him." There's a hint of curiosity in his tone as he flicks his gaze over my shoulder again.

My brow furrows at his statement and I glance over my shoulder to see exactly what he's just described. Sebastian stands with a tight grip on the bottle in his hand, his eyes focused on me and Ben while his date begs for his attention beside him.

With a shrug, I turn back to Ben and say, "He's nobody."

Keep telling yourself that, Alex.

"He's not looking at you like he's nobody to you. I mean, it's kind of hot. You know, he's got the whole alpha male, possessive thing down. I can practically see his white knuckles from here." Ben chuckles, pulling his gaze back to me.

"If you must know, we hooked up a couple of times."

I shrug, as if it's no big deal and take a sip of my beer. "Sorry to disappoint, but there's not much more to the story than that I'm afraid."

"Okay. I'm going to need more details. Especially because he looks like he's ready to come over here and beat the crap out of me." He leans in, his breath skating across my ear, as he asks, "Should I flirt with you to make him jealous?"

Throwing my head back, I let out a loud belly laugh, oblivious to the looks we're drawing. *Oh, God, that's hilarious. I couldn't make Sebastian jealous, even if I tried.*

As my laughter dies down, I look at Ben, who is staring down at me with a huge toothy grin spread across his face. "No, you don't need to do that. It wouldn't work, anyway." I smile back at him.

He holds out his arm for me, and I take it as he walks us toward the back of the garden.

"Come. Let's go out of earshot from little ears, and you can give me all the details. Emphasis on all," Ben mutters, as he leads the way.

And I do just that. I share all the details of my mistakes with Sebastian to a complete stranger. In my defense, he's very easy to talk to, and he gives me some brilliant advice. By the end of the afternoon, I've made a new friend and planned a night out the following weekend.

Ben and Meghan try to convince me that Sebastian's eyes haven't left me for most of the afternoon. Every time Meghan and Ben bring him up, I change the subject or reply with what I hope is a sense of indifference as I ignore the warmth that pools in the pit of my stomach at the thought of him being that obsessed with what I'm up to.

Truth be told, I'm exhausted with the up and down emotions he has me feeling whenever he's near or occupying my thoughts.

When they tell me he's put his date in a cab back to New York, I still don't bite. It shouldn't interest me what he does or doesn't do. No man, no matter how good he makes you feel in bed, is worth the headache or heartache he causes.

Or at least that's what I thought.

TWO

Alex

I t's been a long week by the time Saturday rolls around, and having worked at least sixty hours, I'm ready to let my hair down and party. On weeks like this, I question my life choices and why I chose to get into property law in the first place.

Being good at my job has its benefits, like the high salary I managed to negotiate when I took on additional responsibility at the firm I work for—Jackson and Partners in Lower Manhattan. The not so great aspect is the amount of clients that ask for you by name and refuse to deal with anyone else.

As I enter my apartment, I throw my keys on the small console table by the front door, kicking off my heels and breathing a sigh of relief. It's the best feeling in the world to take off a pair of heels I've been in since seven this morning. I live in a modest two-bedroom apartment in a building that has great security and, unlike my old building, a working elevator.

When you walk in the front door you step right into the living room that's decorated in mostly neutral tones. The kitchen is separated by a breakfast bar, and next to that is the hallway that leads to the bedrooms and bathroom.

Standing front and center in the living room, in all its bright pink glory, is my couch. As much as it's calling my name to lie down and binge watch a show, I've got to get ready. I dump my bag on the floor by the door and walk down the hallway to my bedroom, bypassing the family pictures that line the walls.

My gray, four-poster bed with a white fluffy duvet and a mountain of pillows, is the statement piece in my bedroom. White bedside tables sit on either side with a matching chest of drawers under the window on one wall and a small walk-in closet on the wall opposite.

Much like the couch, I feel like my bed is calling to me. With everything that's been going on at work for the last few weeks, I'm feeling both physically and mentally exhausted.

My hands are on the hem of my sweater when the sound of my phone ringing from my bag in the hallway breaks through the silence. With a sigh, I walk back to my purse, rummaging through its contents until my hand grasps my battered phone.

Meghan's name flashes on the screen and I connect the call with a smile on my lips.

"Well, if it isn't Mrs. Jackson. Has Mr. Jackson finally given you a break from all the fucking?"

I can picture the blush that will flourish her cheeks at my words. I've known Meghan for longer than I haven't, and with that comes the power of knowing exactly what makes my best friend blush.

She's thoroughly in love with her husband, and unfortunately for me, I've walked in on them a few times in some very compromising positions. So now I make it my mission, whenever she calls or I see her, to remind her of this. I'm just doing my duty as her best friend, really.

"Alex," she whines. "I called to see what you were up to, but I'm not going to talk to you if you're going to be like that."

I laugh, knowing she's all talk and no action. "I can't help it." I shrug, even though she can't see me. "I'm just about to get in the shower. I've got an hour until I'm going out with Savannah and Ben."

Savannah and I met in the elevator when I moved into the building. She's a people person and when she saw me hauling boxes, she offered to help. It turned out that she lives on the same floor as me with her brother's best friend. She doesn't like to talk about the events that led to her moving in with him, but in short; she broke up with her boyfriend and had nowhere else to go.

"Urgh, I wish I could come. Being pregnant sucks balls." The muffled sound of who I assume is Cooper draws Meghan's attention away from me before she continues, "Okay, I take it back." There's a pause. I assume he's left the room and then she whispers into the phone, "I don't really, Cooper said... it doesn't matter. It really sucks. I can't do anything fun."

"You never enjoyed coming out when you weren't pregnant." I laugh, reminding her of the fact that she's more of a homebody, anyway. "You're only saying that because you're about to pop and you're uncomfortable."

"That's true. And I guess I get a beautiful baby out of all of this at the end." She sighs dreamily. "So, tell me where you're going tonight. I need to live vicariously through you."

"I think we're going to start at Siren... and avoid Passion at all costs," I grumble.

Siren opened about six months ago and has old-school jams night every other Friday. Savannah and I have been a handful of times and it's always ended up being a good night out.

When Meghan lets out a breathy laugh, I don't think it's in response to what I've said, but when she moans, I know it's time for me to go. I swear, sometimes they do things like this just to rub their relationship in my face.

Even though I know she's not paying attention to me anymore, I say, "Okay... I'm going to go." Then I disconnect the call before I get drawn into some weird threesome over the phone with my best friend and her husband.

As I walk back to my bedroom, I undress from my work clothes, then wrap myself in my favorite white fluffy robe. With my work clothes in the laundry basket, I step into the closet and start combing through my dresses for an outfit for tonight.

My hand lands on a fitted white cut out dress that I know looks good with my golden skin tone, and, as I pull it from the rail, I know it's the perfect dress for tonight. I'll wear it with a pair of five-inch strappy gold heels that wrap around my calves and a gold clutch. Given the chill that seems to have creeped in as we get closer to October, I'll throw on my favorite white faux fur coat to finish the look.

I've only worn this dress once, but it makes my figure look like an hourglass and shows off my best assets. The dress comes to mid-thigh and has cut outs on either side of my waist, showing a very generous amount of cleavage through a lace up cut out that ends just under my breasts.

Leaving everything on my bed, I tie my caramel high-lighted, chest length, chestnut brown hair into a messy bun as I walk to the bathroom. With my thick and smooth hair, I only need to wash it once a week and thankfully today isn't the day because it takes hours, which I don't have. With the shower running, I take off my make-up at the sink, before holding my hand under the stream of water in the shower to test the temperature.

With it just right, I move under the flow of water and scrub my body twice with my favorite peach scented body wash, the whole time hyping myself up for tonight.

My plan consists of getting drunk, getting laid, and having as many o's as humanly possible. It's been... I don't even know how long since I last had sex. Even though I've dated, nothing has been serious because I've been too hung up on the man I've vowed to forget about.

Which I'm failing at miserably.

Once I've dried myself with a fluffy towel, I hang it on the heated towel rail. Naked, I stand in front of the mirror as I apply my makeup.

Tonight calls for me to whip out the skills I picked up during my brief stint in beauty school when I wasn't sure what I wanted to do with myself. I've always liked makeup so it made sense to go to cosmetology school, but I quickly learned that what I like to do for fun soon loses its enjoyment when you're doing it for a living.

For my eyes, I'm going to do a siren eye. It's only fitting after all, considering where we're going. Plus, it emphasizes my dark brown eyes, making me look like a temptress.

Checking that my body is dry—a single drip of water can give me the frizziest hair—I shake out my hair before moving into my bedroom to get dressed. My eyes go to the clock that sits on my bedside table, and I release a calming breath as I realize that Savannah will be here in about half an hour. I've got more than enough time to get dressed and make myself a strong drink. Emphasis on the strong.

Savannah doesn't know about me and Sebastian— and given that it's never happening again, I'd like to keep it that way. Should we end up at Passion, my plan is to be so drunk I either get turned away at the door or I just dance and completely ignore what we've done in his office.

I pull on my dress and sit on the couch as I strap on my shoes. With one last look in the mirror, I move to the kitchen and pour myself a two-finger serving of tequila. There's a knock at my door as I'm putting the bottle back in the cupboard. I hesitate for all of two seconds. Throwing back my shot, I leave the glass on the counter and walk to the door to answer it.

Savannah, the southern belle who loves her mama and papa but will go toe to toe with a grown man if needed, comes barreling through the door as soon as I open it. I've literally seen her try to fight a guy twice her size, both in height and width, all because he offended one of her friends.

I think she can be quite disarming, because she's absolutely gorgeous with a faint southern twang, but can bring a person to their knees. She has striking dark blue eyes with gold specks around her irises, and dark ginger-bread blonde hair that falls past her shoulders in bouncy curls.

Tonight, she's rocking a smokey eye which makes her blue eyes pop and a nude lip so as not to have too much going on. She's dressed in a backless, long sleeved, bright blue mini dress and white platform heels.

She looks... hot—like if I was into women, I'd totally

fuck her. Her six-inch heels only bring her up to my chin —sometimes I forget just how tiny she is.

Pulling me into her embrace, before leaning back to look me over, Savannah coos, "Hey darlin', you look gorgeous."

"Hey, thank you. You don't look so bad yourself." I wink. "I've got tequila in the kitchen; help yourself. I'm just going to grab my clutch and then I'm good to go."

"Take your time," she calls. "Noah and Sutton are going to meet us tonight."

Her back is to me so I'm not sure what to make of that statement. Noah is Savannah's brother's best friend from childhood, who Savannah is living with. Sutton is his girlfriend, and they all currently live together after Savannah moved in.

Savannah hasn't really gone into many details about her life, or what her relationship with Noah and Sutton is like, but I've got eyes, and I've seen the way Noah watches Savannah. I feel bad for Sutton because she's a great girl, but the brief glances he throws Savannah's way whenever they're in the same room as each other are very obvious. He probably thinks nobody has noticed, but he's not very good at hiding them. And I don't even hang out with him. It's like a puppy looking at you for a nibble of your food, except he's a six foot three mountain of a man.

I don't press Savannah on why they're joining us tonight. It's not going to impact my night.

With a head start on the shots, we grab a cab to Siren, where we meet up with Noah, Sutton and Ben.

It's one in the morning, and I'm with Ben on the dance floor in Passion dancing away to *Head & Heart* by *Joel Corry*. Despite my pleas to not go, we've ended up in Sebastian's club because Savannah said she had never been. Unfortunately for me, it's the best place to finish the night—according to Savannah and an article she read about New York nightlife. Stupidly, I agreed, because at the time I was too drunk to care. At this point in the night, I've sobered up enough that my eyes keep darting to the window above us.

Ben leans down to talk in my ear. "Do you want another drink? I'm going to the bar."

I shake my head in response and he breaks away from me to go. I just want to dance. I just want to forget. It was a bad idea to come here, especially after last weekend. As the bodies of fellow dancers close in on me, I contemplate whether I should have gone for that drink with Ben after all. At least then I could have worked on forgetting him and what I experienced upstairs. The song changes to another dance song that has me closing my eyes and swinging my hips to the beat, willing my mind to shut off and enjoy the music.

Strong hands land on my hips, gently squeezing

them for my attention, and, when I glance over my shoulder, as expected it's Wesley... I think that's his name. He's one of Alfie's friends, and I've seen him a couple of times since we first went out many moons ago with Meghan.

God, that feels like a lifetime ago.

His warm breath skates over my ear. "Hey, you remember me?"

I feel nothing.

With a nod of my head in response, I settle back into his arms. My mind takes this moment, and the lack of anything I'm feeling for Wesley, to remind me that I was fine before I met Sebastian. The thought is unwanted and has me faltering in my dance. *I'm going to be fine after him.* So what if every man I'm with since him doesn't ignite a fire within me?

It's not the end of the world.

I'm sure there are plenty of women out there faking their orgasms for a man they *feel* something for. In fact, I know there are because I was, once upon a time.

Forget about him!

Wesley is a good-looking guy. He's got to be around six foot four, with short ash blond hair, plump lips, mysterious brown eyes, and a sharp jawline covered with stubble. He has sleeve tattoos on both arms which are currently wrapped around me as he dances with me; his solid body pressed against mine.

Keep lying to yourself, Alex.

He doesn't compare to the man currently occupying

my thoughts and making me wonder what's going on in the office that overlooks the dance floor.

Is he fucking someone else?

Is he getting them all hot and sweaty while they're pressed up against the cool glass, looking down on us?

Like he did with me.

THREE

Sebastian

I've been sitting in my office watching Alex ever since she entered *my* club. The guys managing the door know her, and it's not worth them losing their jobs if they don't alert me when she arrives.

I don't know why I've resorted to threatening their jobs over a woman, other than it being a necessary precaution after she walked in on me with some nameless woman on her knees between my legs. When I'd looked up and seen her wide, dark gaze piercing me with a mixture of disgust and hatred, for a millisecond I'd felt something akin to shame.

Despite that, I refused to acknowledge whatever it was and carried on bucking my hips into the face of Suzy... Stacey... whatever her name was. I came with my eyes locked on Alex, and it wasn't until I looked down at the woman between my legs, breaking our eye contact, that she turned around and left.

I've tried my hardest to fuck her out of my system, but it's like she's taken root and I can't get her to fucking leave. No matter who I'm balls deep in, I picture her. These nameless women have all become *her*. So I tried to switch tactics and just fuck her, but even that's not worked because she still occupies my thoughts. She's like a fucking addiction.

Some might call me crazy, and they'd probably be right, because I could have swore I knew better than to connect with someone on an emotional level. Emotions are stupid, useless distractions. I've never had a need for them before and I sure as shit don't have any need for them now.

Tonight, she looks delectable as always, her body curving in all the right places, testing my resolve. For most of the night, she's been dancing with the guy from Meghan and Cooper's place the other weekend.

Cooper, despite being one of my really good friends, wouldn't tell me anything about the guy. Instead, he patted me on the shoulder and told me to leave Alex alone. As if it's that fucking simple.

As I watch her sway her hips to the beat of the music, my mind goes back to the speech she gave me last weekend. Everything she said was the truth. In all honesty, I'm surprised it's taken her this long to say it. She's right about it all; I can't give her more, and I'm only good for fucking. I'm not a man that's cut out for a relationship. If she was okay with that, we could give it a try. But she isn't, so I need to stay away. Despite knowing this, something pulls me to her and, no matter what I do, I can't get her out of my mind.

My focus returns to the CCTV image on the laptop in front of me. Alex is now dancing with a guy I've seen around here a few times; his hands rest on her hips as she grinds into his groin, swaying to the beat of the song. My fists clench involuntarily as an emotion I can't quite identify rolls through me, and I will myself to calm down. I'm not about to walk into the middle of the dance floor to drag her out to... to do what? Talk to me? To fuck me?

I roll my chair tighter against the desk, as if it's enough to keep me from storming down to her. With great effort, I stay where I am, watching her. Drinking her in as if it's been a lifetime since I last saw her. The guy dips his head to her ear, and she shakes her head in response to whatever he's said, their bodies still pressed together as they dance to the music.

Letting out a sigh of relief, I watch as she breaks away from him and moves through the crowd toward the restrooms. Before I can question my sanity, my reading glasses are tossed on my desk as I spring out of my seat and rush through the club. I'm oblivious to the party-goers as I walk downstairs to the lower ground. A sense of urgency and a need to talk to her drive me forward.

The club is a large open concept with seating areas on the two longest walls. The bar stretches the length of the back wall, with a collection of standing tables well-spaced in the area in front of it. There's a dance floor that takes up just over half of the room and the DJ booth is next to the stairs that lead to the VIP area.

Passion is my third club; I own four in total, but spend most of my time in New York as this is my biggest. I plan on opening my fifth in Chicago, but with a more exclusive vibe to it.

Bypassing the restrooms, I wait at the end of the corridor for her. Hidden in the shadows, I have a perfect view of the door. When she stumbles out, it's clear she's drunk.

For fucks sake, Alex.

She leans against the wall to keep herself upright, and without thinking, I stalk towards her. My arms wrap around her waist, and with little effort, I have her feet off of the ground and her back pressed to my chest. She lets out a squeal of surprise and thrashes in my arms, drawing the attention of a few people that are hovering in the corridor.

"Alex. Stay still," I growl, my lips brushing over the shell of her ear.

Her scent—I can only describe it as fresh peaches mixed with a fragrance that is all her—fills my nostrils. I close my eyes in an effort to fight against my rising desire. Fucking myself over yet again, the deep breath I inhale only serves to assail me once again with her scent, causing a visceral need for her to settle in the gut of my stomach.

Mine flits through my mind leaving me dumbfounded.

With a shake of my head, to clear thoughts that have no place being there, I turn my head sucking in another breath, this time of untainted air, in an effort to get some of my brain cells to function. With a somewhat clearer mind, I carry her down the corridor until I reach the room I'm after. Surprisingly, she doesn't put up a fight.

The private party room we enter is reserved for exclusive events, and since there isn't one booked for tonight, I know it will be empty.

It's just right for the conversation we need to have. About what, I haven't quite figured out. Not that she'll be able to hold a conversation with me if she's as drunk as I think she is.

"Put me down, Sebastian."

Right now, I'm not in the mood to listen to her; not yet anyway. I'm pissed at her, at myself, and at the man she's been dancing with. Opening the door and walking into the center of the room, I set her down next to the large oak table, before turning to close and lock the door. This room is soundproof, so she can scream and shout at me—*or for me*—all she wants.

The 'for me' is definitely wishful thinking.

Folding my arms across my chest as I lean back against the door, I ask her, "What are you doing here, Alex?"

"What does it look like?" she counters, mimicking my pose as she looks around the room avoiding my gaze.

The room isn't big, and the walls are painted an olive black color that makes it look dark and almost depraved.

Surrounding the oak table are ten high-back chairs, with a small bar in the corner. I wanted it to give off a dark but romantic vibe and with the dim lighting, it does exactly that.

"Stop playing with me, Alex. You've come to my club, dressed like that..." I gesture to her body that calls to me. "You dance with other men, knowing I'm going to be watching you."

She scoffs as she finally looks at me. "How exactly was I supposed to know you were going to be watching me, Sebastian?" I don't like the way she spits my name, like it's disgusting in her mouth and she'd rather not say it.

Moving away from the door, I shout, "Because I can't fucking stay away from you." Running my fingers through my hair, tugging on the strands, I turn away from her. I feel too vulnerable when it comes to her.

"Is that why you had a woman on your arm at Meghan and Cooper's last weekend?" she sneers. Her breathing is labored, and as I turn to face her I notice her fists clench and unclench by her side. She shakes her head and continues, "Get real, Sebastian. I'm just an available piece of ass to you. Don't insult my intelligence by pretending it's more."

I stalk towards her and for every step I take, she takes one back. For a second there is a flare of panic in her dark eyes before she masks it and lifts her chin in defiance. When her back hits the wall, I'm inches from her.

"What are you trying to do to me?" I whisper as my mouth crashes against hers.

Her hands go to my chest and I bring my own up to tangle in her hair. Grabbing fistfuls of the soft strands, I tilt her head further back so I can fully devour her mouth. She shows me all the hatred she has for me in this kiss and I drink it down like my life depends on it.

She moans into my mouth as I press my body into hers, pinning her against the wall. Coaxing her lips open, I tangle my tongue with hers, tasting the rum and strawberry from the daiquiri she's had tonight. Knowing she's had too much to drink doesn't stop my body from coming alive—after all, I've craved her for months—but I won't go any further than this kiss.

Just this one kiss.

I don't take advantage of drunk women.

Pulling away from her, she blinks up at me in confusion, a frown marring her beautiful features. As I untangle my hands from her hair, I take a step back in an attempt to compose myself. "I'm sorry. I shouldn't have done that."

Her hand comes up and connects with my face, catching me off guard. My head turns to the right with the force of her slap and the skin of my cheek stings from the contact. My eyes widen a fraction and my jaw goes slack as what she's just done sinks in.

I can't believe she just slapped me.

"How dare you!" she exclaims with venom in her voice.

Even though I know I deserve all of her wrath, it doesn't stop me from going on the defensive. *Anything to protect myself.*

My hand goes to my face and rubs my cheek to ease the sting from her palm. "You weren't exactly pushing me away, sweetheart." As my gaze flits up and down her body, a smirk graces my lips.

"Stay away from me, Sebastian. If you don't want me in your club, just say so. But don't accost me."

Her anger is warranted. I crossed a line. There's no two ways about it, but I can't think straight when I'm in her vicinity. Her eyes are burning into me, her anger and pain rightfully directed at me and if looks could kill, I'd be dead on the spot.

With a sigh of annoyance, I say, "I'm sorry." I hold my hands up in surrender as I back away towards the door. "I shouldn't have done that, not after... everything. You can come here as often as you like, and I promise to stay away from you. Take as long as you need in here."

I return to my office and as I take a seat behind my desk, my hand instinctively goes to the mouse sitting next to my laptop. I'm not sure how it happens, but the next thing I know, my screen is filled with images from the CCTV cameras again. She hasn't left the room, and I watch as she looks around. At the bar, she pulls out a bottle of something I can't quite make out—I'm guessing tequila based on the shape—before taking a deep drink straight from it.

She leaves the bottle on the top of the bar and exits

the room, looking as composed as ever as she walks back to the dance floor. It doesn't take her long to find the guy she came in with, or for them to get back to dancing and laughing.

I'm forgotten as if nothing happened.

As if I mean nothing.

Fuck this.

Phone in hand, I scroll through my contacts and dial the least problematic of the women listed. I don't understand why I can't seem to control myself around her but I know I need to occupy my thoughts with something else. Something like another woman.

This time I won't picture Alex when I'm balls deep.

Or at least I'll try not to.

FOUR

Alex

How dare he kiss me after everything? I thought after I'd made my feelings towards him clear, he'd leave me alone, but of course that's too much to ask.

I've had such a good night, aside from my run in with Sebastian—which has left me turned on, angry and confused. It's four in the morning; Savannah, Sutton and Noah left long ago and Ben and I are finally ready to go home. We're some of the last ones here, and if nothing else, that's a sign of a good night.

Ben has been a constant by my side all evening. He bought me more drinks when I came back from speaking with Sebastian and made sure I smiled for the rest of the evening because my mind was back in that room. It's like he could sense that something wasn't quite right.

As much as I tell myself that I didn't believe Sebastian when he said he couldn't stay away from me, something is niggling in the back of my mind. Despite my attempts to ignore it, it just grows as the night goes on and the same question I asked myself when he'd left me in that room, plagues me.

What did he mean when he said he couldn't stay away from me?

Walking toward the exit, I lean my head on Ben's shoulder as he snakes an arm around my waist. "Can you carry me home?" I ask, tilting my chin up to him.

His fingers flex on my hip as he tips his head back letting out a loud laugh that draws the attention of the nearby staff. "If that is what you want, I can."

"You're such a Prince Charming," I sigh dreamily.

I push out of his hold and collect my coat. I'm about to walk back to Ben, when Sebastian grabs my arm and pulls me into the alcove by the coat check.

Where did he come from?

My eyes dart around the space before going down to his hand which lightly grips my arm. Despite my gaze burning a hole into it, he doesn't relent, instead he commands, "I'll take you home."

It's an effort to not roll my eyes at the air of possessiveness in his tone. I can't comprehend the arrogance of this man. Instead, I look him in the eyes, willing myself to not react to his proximity.

"Sebastian, when I told you I want nothing to do with you, I meant it." Yanking my arm out of his grip, I fold my arms over my chest as I cock a hip, giving off an air of nonchalance. "No, you won't be taking me home.

Ben is going to take me, and you are going to respect my wishes and stay away from me."

"Alex…" he growls. There's a warning in there somewhere but I don't care to listen to it right now.

How dare he try to dictate what I do with my life?

"Alex, nothing. I've told you what I want, and you need to respect that. You don't get to tell me what I can or can't do." My eyes flick to Ben, who's standing by the door watching our exchange. "You don't get to tell me who I can or can't go home with. If I want to fuck every guy in Manhattan, then I will. Just like I'm sure you're fucking every woman in the city."

I briefly register the tick in his jaw and the way his eyes flare with anger at my statement as I brush past him. I know I shouldn't have implied I'm going to take Ben home and fuck him, but I couldn't help myself.

"Care to share what that was about?" Ben asks, his arm going around my waist pulling me into his side as we walk through the exit.

"Nope," I say as I rest my head back on his shoulder.

He leans down to whisper in my ear, "Okay, but if I'm going to die, I should at least know why." Turning my head but not lifting it. I frown at him in confusion, urging him to continue. "The look he gave me. It said, 'if you touch a hair on the head of *my* woman, you're a dead man'."

I can't contain the laugh that bursts from my lips. "No, it didn't."

"Oh, my dear Alex." He pushes a stray hair away from

my face, continuing, "Are you truly that oblivious? Yes, it did. Trust me. I've been on the receiving end of many looks like that. It was kind of hot. So... are you going to share the details?"

I think over Ben's question for a moment as we make our way down the sidewalk toward my apartment. Deciding I don't want to give Sebastian any more of my time, I shrug in the hopes that Ben will leave it be, before saying, "There isn't much to tell."

"Well, I don't believe that for a second. I guess, if you aren't going to tell me now, I'll just have to wait for you to be ready. But be warned, I'm a very patient man."

"You're just going to have to believe me, because there is *nothing* to tell."

Keep telling yourself that, Alex.

Deep down inside I feel a sense of failure just thinking about how I've let my desire for Sebastian control me. If he hadn't pulled away, I wouldn't have stopped him. That's the truth of the matter and the thing that brings me the most shame. I thought I had more self-control.

Apparently not when it comes to Sebastian.

Pulling my coat tighter, I loop my arm with Ben as we walk in comfortable silence the few blocks to my place. On the way, I decide to not tell him about what happened tonight. I haven't known him for long and, although I'm sure he won't judge me, I'm not quite ready to lay myself bare.

We're about half a block from my apartment when

we stop at the pizza place on the corner, grabbing a large pepperoni pizza to share. We take it back to mine and, as I let us in, I kick off my shoes and drop my bag on the console table by the door.

In the kitchen, grabbing some plates and drinks, I call to Ben as I peruse the refrigerator, "Soda or water?"

"Soda, please," he replies from the living room.

Removing two sodas, I return to find Ben on the couch with the pizza box open on the coffee table and a slice half eaten.

"You couldn't wait, huh?" I laugh.

A muffled 'no' and a sheepish pizza filled smile is the only response I get. Placing the drinks on the table, I sit on the couch, switching on the TV with one hand and grabbing a floppy, cheesy slice with the other. I moan around the first glorious mouthful as Ben chuckles at me. His long legs are splayed out in front of him, crossed at the ankles, as he leans back, chewing on his own slice with his eyes closed. He really is a good-looking guy, and I admire his relaxed features for a moment before turning to the TV.

It's crazy how comfortable we seem to have become in the short space of time we've known each other and although there are some things I'm not ready to share, I have no doubt that in time our friendship will blossom.

Since Meghan introduced us, we've hung out a couple of nights during the week as Ben works in the city and doesn't have anyone to go home to. Despite me asking, he hasn't given me an answer as to why he doesn't just live in the city and I haven't pushed him for one. I guess we both have things we aren't ready to share.

"What are you thinking?" he asks, obviously having noticed my dead stare at whatever show is playing on the TV.

"Nothing. Just thinking about how much fun I've had tonight." I grin, hoping to deflect as I take another bite of pizza.

Ben looks at me for a beat before going back to his own slice. For a moment, I think he's going to leave it be, but he speaks, his gaze trained on his pizza. "If something happened tonight, you can tell me. I'd like to think we're on our way to being really good friends."

I don't want to tell him what's happened and how close I was to giving in to Sebastian. I'm ashamed of my actions, and I don't need anyone judging me anymore than I am already judging myself.

"Honestly, it was just hard to see him again. It's always hard to see him," I lie.

"I get that. I really do. My advice still stands though…"

"Stop judging Alex of the past and future," we say in unison.

Ben continues, "Exactly. Sometimes in life there will be a person who will have a hold on your soul and, no matter how much you want to walk away, you'll keep coming back for more. Sometimes, the best thing you can do is just go with it and know that the universe has a plan for you and what you are experiencing is that plan."

I don't say anything, instead I think over his words, going back and forth about whether the universe has a grander plan or if she's just trying to fuck me in the ass for kicks.

It doesn't take us long to devour the pizza and, once everything is cleaned up, I show Ben to the spare room. Using the bathroom, I remove my make-up and brush my teeth. Back in my bedroom, I change into my PJs, which consists of an oversized t-shirt.

I haven't checked my phone all night, so before I climb into my bed, I grab it from my clutch in the hallway. I'm sure Meghan will have texted me at some point to tell me how much she hates that she can't come out with us and that pregnancy sucks. It's usually followed up by a text rubbing in the fact that she gets a gorgeous baby out of it.

My phone vibrates in my hand, and as I look at the message displayed on my screen, my steps falter.

SEBASTIAN

Did you get home okay?

I stare at the message for what feels like an hour, but is probably more like five minutes, debating whether to respond. On one hand, I've told him multiple times that I want nothing more to do with him. But on the other hand, I don't want him to worry about me. Not that he would, but still. Letting out a sigh, I open his message and type out a response, deciding to keep it simple.

ALEX

Yes.

There, short, to the point and doesn't lead to more conversation.

I continue my short walk back to my bedroom, climbing into bed and turning off the bedside lamp. The cool sheets chill me, and so I burrow further into them. A heavy sigh leaves me as I remember I need to charge my phone.

Puffing up my pillows, I snuggle down under the duvet again, closing my eyes as I will sleep to take me over. My phone chimes on the bedside table, but I ignore it. A million thoughts run through my head in the two minutes before it chimes again, reminding me I have a new message.

I should leave it.

Nothing I said needed a response...

Dammit! Reaching out of my warm cocoon, I blindly grab for my phone.

SEBASTIAN

I'm sorry if I ruined your night.

I'm at a loss as to what to say to that. He didn't ruin my night, but he also didn't make it a good one. I don't like that he has so much control over my body. That he can command so much of my attention by just being in my vicinity. Every time I see him I become a puppet on a string, ready for him to command. He's the only man that has ever had this effect on me.

Hell, this is how I want my future partner to make me feel. Like I can't breathe when he's near, yet when he's gone, I crave his touch. Wanting to burrow myself into his soul and never leave.

I type out a response, hoping it will be harsh enough for him to understand that I meant everything I've said.

ALEX

You didn't. You were barely a blip. Goodbye, Sebastian. I suggest you lose my number.

Laying in the darkness, I vow to put Sebastian Worthington behind me. To protect myself, because if I get anymore entangled with this man, I know that I'll end up falling in love with him.

FIVE

Sebastian

I left Passion not long after Alex. If I'd stayed, I would have just sat and stewed in my office, replaying the CCTV footage of her. After my second confrontation with her, I texted Tiffany to cancel our hook up. I'm in no mood for company, especially in the form of a bouncy, twenty-something year old.

I've never had this overwhelming need to... prove myself to someone. It should just be about fucking and satisfying my most basic needs. Instead, Alex brings out a feeling in me and I'm not entirely sure what it is.

Christ, what is happening to me?

My eyes roam over her message again.

ALEX

You didn't. You were barely a blip.
Goodbye, Sebastian. I suggest you lose
my number.

Rubbing my hand down my face, I rest my head back against the headboard of my bed. There's no point in messaging her back. She has been more than clear about her feelings, and deep down I know I should stop whatever this is. Even if it means ignoring the cravings that she brings to the surface. If anything, Alex doesn't seem bothered by what I'm feeling and instead hates me.

It angers me that she left with that guy. No, it doesn't just anger me; it makes my chest feel tight and causes a sense of panic to rise within me. She doesn't know him.

She doesn't really know me.

Tomorrow will be a fresh start. All my life I've been able to switch off my emotions and feelings; this should be no different. I should be a pro at detaching myself from someone.

Putting my phone on the bedside table, I switch off the lamp and roll over to sleep.

My alarm blares at eleven on Wednesday, and as I push the covers away, I scrub a hand over my tired eyes. I haven't had an ounce of sleep since I saw Alex in the early hours of Sunday. It's been three days since our last interaction and she's still filling my thoughts. My mind is a constant replay of the conversations we've had the last two times I've seen her.

Climbing out of the bed, my feet hit the cold hardwood floor as I make my way to the bathroom. I have a meeting at noon with Cooper that I need to get ready for. He's agreed to help with the purchase of my new club in Chicago. I wasn't overly impressed with the service I received from the firm I used to buy Passion, so my usual rule of not mixing business with pleasure has gone out of the window on this occasion.

Switching the shower on to warm up, I head back to the closet to grab something to wear. My apartment only has the bare necessities and people often comment on the show home vibe that it has. Cooper likes to joke that it's even worse than his old place, but unlike him, I'm only renting, so I haven't bothered to furnish the space. I won't be in New York much longer, so it doesn't seem necessary.

Showering in record time, I dress in a pair of navy-blue chinos, a white shirt, and a navy-blue blazer. A pair of tan derby shoes adorn my feet and I forgo a tie, leaving my shirt open at the collar. I'm aiming for some semblance of business wear for this meeting, but my usual outfit choice would consist of jeans and a t-shirt.

With the smallest amount of gel, I style my hair, slicking it back before spritzing on some cologne. My eyes look tired, and my lack of sleep is obvious, so I apply some moisturizer in the vain hope it will make me look less haggard.

With one last look in the bathroom mirror, I grab my phone, keys and wallet from the bedside table as I walk to the front door.

"Wow, you look... like crap," Cooper greets, a smirk on his mouth as I walk into his office.

"Thanks. You look... well, actually, you look great," I reply, unable to hide the jealousy in my tone.

Cooper chuckles, smoothing his hand down his tie as he sits back in his chair. "Thank you. What's kept you up? Too many flavors of the day?"

I take a seat in front of his desk, lifting one leg to sit on the knee of the other as I gaze out of the window. "Not many. Just one," I mumble, bringing my gaze back to him.

"Alex?"

I hate that he's hit the nail on the head the first time. That he knows me so well. Until I met Damien Houston, Jamison Monroe, and Cooper, I'd been a lone wolf. It's always been so much easier to keep people at a distance. I learned at a very young age, that you can't rely on anyone. Even to this day, the people I would say I'm the 'closest' to don't know everything about me. Especially my upbringing in England, and I prefer to keep it that way.

"Is it that obvious?" I ask, knowing full well it is that damn obvious.

"I'm not going to sugarcoat it for you because we don't have that kind of relationship and I know you put honesty above all else. You've really fucked up if you want to be with her—"

I cut him off. "I don't do relationships, Cooper. She's just a good pussy, that's all. I could walk out of here right now and find another woman that's ready and willing." I huff, unwilling to hear what he has to say.

Holding up his hands, he leans forward, resting his elbows on his desk. "Look, I'm not saying you have to marry her, but you clearly still want her. In all the time I've known you, you've never lost sleep over a woman. Maybe you should talk to her and see what she has to say. You never know, she could want the same thing."

I haven't told him about the conversation at his housewarming party and clearly Alex hasn't told Meghan either. For a brief moment, I wonder why that is. I always got the impression that Meghan and Alex tell each other everything.

I guess it wouldn't hurt to have some perspective on what happened the other night.

"She came to Passion on Saturday." I let my statement sit in the air.

Cooper's gaze is on me, searching my face for... who knows what.

When it's clear I'm not going to say anything further, he breaks the silence. "And?"

"She was with other people."

"You're going to have to give me more than one liners, Seb. I'm the lawyer here. I'm supposed to be the one who is evasive with the answers. We'll be here all day if you keep being so cryptic. Have you seen any of them before?" he asks.

I turn to the window, unable to face him as I replay the CCTV in my mind. "The women and one of the guys, I haven't. The other guy... he was from your housewarming. She was dancing with him." Facing him again, I can see his mind whirling. "Who is he?"

It's been eating me up, and the rage I felt when I saw them dancing in *my* club, did nothing to quell the feeling inside of me. And when she all but said she was going to take him home and fuck him, it was amplified.

"What did he look like?"

"Shaved head, beard, tattoos... his name's Ben, I think." I know it is. Her every word is ingrained in my mind—even the ones I'd rather forget.

Thanks for a good time, but I don't want or need you in my life.

Cooper lets out a loud bark of laughter, bringing me back to the present. His eyes crease in the corners as a huge grin spreads across his mouth. "Are you serious?"

"I don't think it's funny, Coop. Look, I didn't come here to talk to you about Alex. Let's just get on with our meeting."

"I'm laughing because Ben... is very much gay, but you're right, back to business. So, you need us to manage the purchase of a property in Chicago?"

He's gay. She was messing with me!

Fighting a smile, I reply to him, "Yes, if it's something you can help with."

I want to shout with joy from the rooftops, but I keep myself composed as if what he's just told me hasn't rejuvenated me and made this the best fucking day I've had in a while.

"What exactly is it you're going to need?"

"The works. I need someone I can trust, that will lay it all out for me. I'm leaving for Chicago on Sunday to meet with George Bennet and then on Monday, I have a meeting with Wilkins and Wilkins, a Chicago law firm."

"How long will you be out there for?"

"I imagine a few days. I have a return flight booked for Wednesday morning, but will stay as long as needed."

"Okay. I can't personally help you as I haven't taken the bar in Chicago, but I've got the perfect person in mind who can be a liaison with the firm in Chicago."

"I appreciate it. It's probably better not to have you involved, anyway. I'd prefer to keep business and our friendship separate."

A weird—almost mischievous—smile crosses his face as he picks up the phone from his desk. If I was a smarter, less distracted man, I'd demand he put it down and explain what the hell that look was. Instead, I turn to look back out at the view of Lower Manhattan.

"Can you come to my office, please?" Cooper asks whoever is on the other end of the line.

SIX

Alex

"Can you come to my office, please?"

My first thought when Cooper asks me that is, *what have I done wrong?* Despite knowing I've done nothing that would warrant being called to a managing partner's office, I still have butterflies in my stomach. My mind going over at least a million reasons that he would want to see me.

"Of course. I'm on my way now."

"Thank you," he replies before disconnecting the call.

Putting the phone back in its cradle, I save the report I've been working on and lock my computer. Around the time that Meghan left New York and Cooper went into a downward spiral, more work was shared out between the associates. It's been great for my career, and I've been able to take the lead with clients that I hadn't before. I thought that when Meghan and Cooper made it official, he might take back some of his clients, but that hasn't been the case... unless that's what he wants to talk to me about. Pushing away from the desk, I stretch my arms above my head, then check the time. I feel like I've been working for hours.

Jeez. It's lunchtime already.

It's no wonder I feel as stiff as a board. I got into the office at seven and have been hunched over at my desk all morning. I'll go see what Cooper wants, then grab lunch.

Walking to the elevator, I ride the five floors to the thirtieth floor. Jackson and Partners—the firm I work for and that Cooper is the managing partner of—is based over ten floors in a high-rise building in the Civic Center neighborhood of Lower Manhattan.

My best friend Meghan, before she became his wife, worked as Cooper's assistant. Although I rarely saw her during the day, if we could make it work, we'd always meet up for lunch. Since they moved out of the city and she now stays home to look after their gorgeous daughter, I don't see her as often as I would like to. Neither do I get out to lunch as much as I should.

"Hi Duke, Cooper called for me."

Duke is Cooper's new assistant and I love him... well, not literally. He really brightens up the office with his outlandish clothes and quick wit, but he is so young. In his first week here, he'd asked me out twice but, thankfully, as time's gone on, he's toned it down a bit and we keep it to once a month. The answer will always be no, because I'm nearly ten years older than him, but damn, does it make me feel good.

"Well, if it isn't the ever-beautiful Alexandra." He's also the only person—aside from my parents and Belinda—that still calls me by my full name. "Go on in. They're waiting for you."

They?

With a frown creasing my brow, I walk to Cooper's door, knocking on it. Not waiting for a reply, I twist the handle and push open the door. Despite his back being to me as I walk in, I know it's Sebastian. It's the way my stomach clenches in anticipation and my breath hitches as I step into the room. He turns to face me, and as is always the case, it's like I've been punched in the gut and the air is robbed from my lungs. Our gazes clash for a moment before I tear mine away and focus on Cooper. It's much safer.

Clearing my throat, I ask, "You wanted to see me?"

"Yes, please have a seat." He indicates to the chair next to Sebastian and I pull in a much needed breath as I walk toward it.

Would it be totally awkward for me to move the chair away from him?

Yes, Alex, it definitely would.

I sit as far away from Sebastian in my seat as I can. Turning to Cooper, I look at him expectantly.

With a mischievous twinkle in his eyes, Cooper speaks. "I have an assignment for you. You're the only person for the job, to be honest."

My stomach plummets as the realization hits me. He wants me to work with Sebastian. The guy I've told to stay away from me. Why else would he be here? It's not like Cooper would assign me work when he's in the middle of a catch up with his friend.

Fuck my life.

Sneaking a glance at Sebastian, I'm met with a ticking jaw as he focuses his attention on Cooper. My eyes snap back to Cooper so my mind can't focus on how badly I want to climb onto Sebastian's lap. I wonder what our kids would look like; with his dazzling bluey-green eyes and his paler skin tone mixed with my darker one.

Whoa.

Where the hell did that come from?

I don't even want kids, let alone with this man.

"... so you can see why I think you're the best person for the job. Especially when you have contacts at Wilkins and Wilkins in Chicago. It just makes perfect business sense."

"I'm sorry, I um... can you repeat what you just said?"

Cooper huffs out an exasperated sigh, as if he doesn't know how much I dislike this man. "In short, I said, with Seb wanting to purchase a property in Chicago and you having contacts there, I'm assigning you to be the liaison on this."

"With all due respect..."

"It's okay, Coop..."

We speak at the same time, both stopping to allow the other to go first.

"Please, you go first," I direct.

"No, after you. Ladies first and all that."

Damn him and his *Henry Cavill* sounding British accent.

"With all due respect, Cooper, I don't think I'm the best person for this assignment. Given our history..." My gaze darts to Sebastian, only to find his own intent on me. Shuffling in my seat, I turn back to Cooper, pressing on. "I can't guarantee that I will give my best for the client."

"I disagree with you. I know you both professionally and personally. You have exactly what it takes to put anything personal aside and focus on the job at hand."

We stare at each other for a moment until Sebastian breaks the silence.

"I was just going to say, it's okay, I'll find another firm. I don't want Alex to do anything that makes her feel uncomfortable."

Folding my arms over my chest and crossing my legs, I lean back in my chair as I look at him. What's his game here? He doesn't get a say in what I do or don't do when it comes to my career.

Maybe that's his game plan.

Stop being so paranoid, Alex.

Before I can stop myself, I blurt out, "I'll do it."

They both turn to look at me, shock clear on their faces, causing me to lift my chin in defiance. Cooper recovers first, smoothing his hand down his tie as he smiles at me.

"Excellent. You'll leave for Chicago on Sunday and be gone until at least Wednesday, possibly longer."

Shit.

What have I gotten myself into?

Okay, it won't be that bad. I'll just keep it professional and only talk to him when absolutely necessary. I'll have my own room and only need to see him during working hours. It should be easy. Yes, I can do this. It's going to be fine.

"Thank you." I turn to Sebastian and wipe my face of any emotion. "Do you have a property in mind?"

Pulling my phone from my jacket pocket, I pull up the notes app, looking anywhere but at him.

"Yes, it's currently owned by George Bennett. He's looking to sell, or so he says. The property has been on the market for nearly eighteen months. His real estate agent has said he's being very particular with who he sells to."

"Okay, I will do some research on him. What is in the building at the moment?"

"It's not being used, but he ran a successful club out of it about ten years ago. It was called Sanctuary. It's in the Loop neighborhood, so prime real estate. He closed it when he retired as none of his kids wanted to take over, so it's just been sitting there."

With enough detail to get started on my research, I give a nod to Cooper as I stand and walk out of his office.

I'm waiting for the elevator when Sebastian catches up to me. I know it's him before he even calls out to me. The hairs on the back of my neck stand to attention.

"Alex, can I have a word?"

I close my eyes, allowing myself a moment of calm, then when I'm ready, I turn to face him. *Get used to it, Alex*. My eyes land on his chest, counting down from three, I lift them to his face. Sometimes I forget just how tall he is. At five foot eight, I'm not short at all, but he towers over me at around six foot five.

"How can I help you, Mr. Worthington?" I ask, pasting on my most professional smile.

He chuckles and a dimple I've never noticed before appears on his left cheek. "Okay, I see how it is. For the record, I'd prefer for you to call me Sebastian or Seb. I just wanted to say thank you. I appreciate you agreeing to take me on."

"I'm only taking on your assignment, *Mr. Worthington*, because it's my job and I think it will be an excellent opportunity. If it were up to me, I'd never see you again." With that, I turn on my heel and walk through the door that leads to the stairwell.

When I return to my desk, I research all I can about Sebastian, his other clubs, and George Bennett. It doesn't come as any surprise to me that Sebastian is a hot topic in gossip magazines—I guess when you're an eligible billionaire bachelor it's bound to happen.

From my research on Mr. Bennett, he seems like a family man through and through, and if an article from five years ago is to be believed, he's not going to sell his club to a man like Sebastian.

I re-read the words again. *'I'm a family man, and would only sell this property to someone that holds my own values. It's the most important thing to me'.*

SEVEN

Sebastian

I don't know how long I stood in the elevator lobby after Alex left. Her words replayed over and over until Cooper came and slapped me on the back, pulling me from my thoughts. Alex has a way with words, that's for sure. Throughout lunch I'm distracted, but not enough to ignore the knowing smirk on Cooper's face the whole time.

I'm still in my head about it the next day when Alex waltzes into my office, looking cool and collected. As if our interactions have no impact on her. Leaning back in my chair, I feign an air of nonchalance. She's wearing a tight black dress that she's paired with an oversized blazer and shiny high heels. Her hair is down around her shoulders and her makeup is subtle but highlights her high cheekbones and dark eyes. She's the epitome of professionalism.

"Good morning, Mr. Worthington," she greets, a fake smile on her lips.

I feel the start of a headache coming on as I rub my temple and will myself to unclench my jaw. "Good morning, Alex."

She assesses me for a moment as she moves toward the couch, removing her blazer, taking a seat, and pulling some documents from her bag. I watch as she lays them on the small table in front of her before lifting her gaze to me, looking expectant.

She doesn't say a word, waiting for me to go to her.

My mind plays images of the last time she was here; I was sitting on that same couch, watching her and seeing the hurt she wasn't quick enough to hide. I couldn't help the bitter smile that fell on my lips or the way my hands instinctively tightened in the hair clenched in my hands.

She clears her throat when I take a seat next to her, shuffling away but coming to a stop by the arm of the couch. I'm probably too close, but it doesn't stop me from spreading my arms across the back of the sofa and playing with a strand of her hair.

Alex stiffens, leaning forward so her hair falls from my grasp. "We should keep this professional." After a long pause, she adds, "I meant everything I said to you." It's whispered and probably said more for her benefit than mine.

But my next words are said to reassure her. Even if they aren't true. "I am being a professional."

This gets her attention and as she turns to face me,

she folds her arms across her chest, leveling her gaze at me. "So you always play with the hair of your attorneys?"

She's got me there.

Holding my hands up, I say, "I'm sorry. No more hair touching."

"Good. So, I've done some research on George Bennett and the space you're looking to purchase…" Her voice trails off as a frown pulls on her brow. As if having won an internal fight with herself, she sits a little straighter as she asks, "Why aren't you using your previous attorneys?"

Alex shuffles the papers on the table as she waits for me to answer, and I watch, mesmerized by her slender fingers. My own fingers have gone back to the smooth strands of her hair, but she doesn't call me out on it this time. I feel relaxed and at peace; like all the stress has left my body.

"They didn't impress me with their service, and Cooper said he could help."

She turns to me, eyeing me suspiciously, folding her arms over her chest and tipping her head to the side. "Did you know he was going to assign me?"

"I didn't have a clue he was going to assign you. I didn't even know you specialized in property. In truth, I thought he would do it himself. You're full of yourself if you think I'd orchestrate this just to spend time with you."

Alex scoffs, leaning back against the arm of the chair as she shakes her head and says, "I don't even know what to say to that."

We sit in a comfortable silence for a moment, staring at each other, her gaze searching mine before she nods, and goes back to the papers on the table in front of her. She's decided on something and I don't like the fact that I'm not privy to it.

Our chemistry is undeniable and I can feel it crackling between us even as Alex talks me through her plan.

The soothing sound of her voice pulls me from my thoughts. "From all of my research—on paper—it doesn't look like Mr. Bennett will sell to... a man like you."

"What's that supposed to mean?" I know exactly what she means and apparently, I'm a glutton for punishment.

She squirms in her seat as she lifts her gaze to me and straightens her spine. "I just mean... well, you're not..." Pulling in a breath, she rushes out, "You're not exactly a family man."

"And?"

"Well, everything I've read—including an article he was featured in for *The Chicago Tribune*—said he would only ever sell to a family man."

"I don't foresee it being a problem."

"What are you planning?" She eyes me skeptically. "As your attorney, you should be sharing your plans with me."

"You'll find out soon enough."

The truth is, right now I don't have a solid plan, other

than using my British charm. And even though that works with the ladies, I don't think it will with George Bennett.

My fingers absentmindedly dust over the exposed column of Alex's throat as I try and sort through a plan of action. In the silence of my office, I don't miss the sharp intake of her breath. Grazing over the same spot elicits a slight tremor in her, and she lifts her eyes to mine. Our gazes lock and she clears her throat as she shifts as much as the arm of the couch allows her. She's still within reach, and I skate my fingers over the smooth expanse of her skin again. Her lips part, pulling my focus to them.

"I don't want to want you, and I really shouldn't because of..." She waves her hand as if signaling to the past. "... everything."

My own hand falls away, not wanting to put her in a position she's uncomfortable in. No matter how much I want her, if she says no, then it doesn't happen.

She's barely audible when she says, "But I can't help but crave your hands on my body or your cock buried deep inside of me."

"Alex," I moan, resting my head on the back of the couch, cause fuck if I don't crave her too.

I'm not entirely sure who moves first, but within seconds our lips crash together and she straddles my lap.

It's a hurried kiss filled with tongues tangling and teeth clashing. I will myself to slow down, enjoying the feel of her pillowy lips on my own as I take my time to explore her mouth. She tastes like coffee and the sweetness of caramel.

Biting her bottom lip, I smooth my hands up her thighs, pushing her dress further up around her waist. At the release of her thighs, she drops further onto my erection. The heat through her panties tempting me as my cock strains against the zipper of my pants.

"Just this one last time. Then we draw a line in the sand," she breathes against my lips, her voice thick with need.

Grinding her core onto me, I squeeze her thighs as I pull back from the kiss and press my forehead to hers. "Alex, it's going to be over too soon if you keep that up," I murmur through gritted teeth.

In answer, she tips her head back and grinds her hips even harder onto my now painfully hard cock, searching for her release. The little moans she elicits as she bucks against me and palms her breasts are nearly my undoing. *I think I might actually come like this.*

"Alex," I warn.

Her heady gaze meets my own, and a smirk graces her lipstick smeared lips as she continues her steady back-and-forth rhythm. She thinks she's in fucking control. And she just might be.

"You want to play, baby girl?" I growl, taking back the power she seems to have stolen from me. "Now you don't get to come until I tell you to."

A frown crosses her face, followed by a look of surprise as I grip her hands in one of my own and flip her off of my lap and onto her back on the couch. Hovering over her, I lift myself away from her; even in this position, she's trying to get herself off.

"Please…" she begs.

Leaning down to her ear, I whisper, "You had your chance. I'd have made you come until you couldn't remember your own name. Now you're going to be punished."

Letting out a whimper, she attempts to get out of my grip. Her eyes plead with me, and if it wasn't for the fact that her hips are trying to connect to my own, I'd have pulled away. With her dress lifted around her waist and a skimpy red triangle, the only thing covering her pussy, she looks delectable. As I run a finger over her pantie-clad slit, she lets out a guttural moan of pleasure.

The corner of my mouth lifts in satisfaction. "Tell me what you want," I command.

She holds my gaze, her own heavy lidded, before she captures her lip between her teeth. "I want you to make me come."

I don't answer her, instead I release her hands and pull her up to a sitting position so I can unzip her dress. Once it's discarded, I ease her back. Kneeling between her legs, I take in the vision in front of me. She wasn't wearing a bra, so she's spread out on my office couch in nothing but a red thong and her black high heels.

Leaning forward, I suck a nipple into my mouth, twirling it with my tongue before sucking it in deep. I love how responsive she is under my touch; even something as simple as me playing with her breasts has her moaning out for me. Moving to the next, I pay them equal attention until she's begging me with murmured pleas to make her come.

"Not yet. I told you; you don't get to come until I say you can."

My hand skates down the soft curve of her stomach, and I don't miss the slight twitch of her hips as I skate past paradise. Bringing my hand down to the back of her left knee, I lift it and drop it over the edge of the sofa, smoothing my hand up her inner thigh. My hand stops at the point where her thigh meets her pussy, teasing at the hem of her panties.

"Seb, please, stop teasing me. It's not fair," she whines.

I chuckle. "You want to know what's not fair?"

My hand moves over her stomach again, this time moving up toward her breasts. I catch her hand as she goes to move it into her panties, shaking my head.

"Maybe I should restrain you..."

Her eyes light up at the thought, and I loosen my tie, pulling it over my head and dropping it over her wrists. Pulling it tight to secure her, I tie the other end to the heavy standing lamp at the end of the couch. With her restrained and spread out, I don't quite know where to start. Leaning over her, I place a kiss on her lips, my tongue slipping through the seam of her lips to play with her own.

Placing gentle kisses from her cheek to her jaw, I

make my way down her breastbone. *I don't think I've paid her tits enough attention.* They're the perfect size for my hands—natural and perky. I take a moment to feel the weight of them in my hands before rolling her nipples between my thumb and forefinger.

My gaze lifts to her and I can only imagine the look of awe on my face as I really take in the woman splayed out in front of me. I've never truly appreciated her beauty.

I place a kiss on her breasts, reluctantly moving my mouth away as I kiss, lick, and nip my way down her stomach. My hands are still filled with her breasts, alternating between massaging them and tweaking her nipples.

Nirvana awaits me as I reach her pussy. I can't help but brush my nose over her core and pull in a deep breath, savoring her scent. At the contact, her hips buck. *She likes that.* I brush my nose back and forth over her pantie-clad slit, her pants and whimpers only serving to increase my need for her.

Releasing her breasts, I grab either side of her panties, pulling them down her thighs and putting them in my pants pocket. She's slick with her own juices, and I know it won't take her long to come undone. I'm not sure she'll even be able to hold off if I tell her to.

Unable to resist, I drag a finger through her slit. Her back arches and a moan slips from her parted lips. I'm fucking mesmerized, and the weight of emotions coursing through me nearly has me pulling away.

Unknowingly, she guides me back into the moment

as her heavy eyes meet mine and a silent plea is given. I don't want to play around anymore either. With my eyes still on her, I stand from the couch, taking my wallet out and removing a condom. Throwing them both on the table, I make quick work of my shirt and pants so I'm as naked as she is.

I remove the tie from the lamp and command, "Stand." My voice is gruff with arousal and her eyes widen a fraction at the tone.

I'm impossibly hard and want to be buried deep inside her. When she's standing in front of me, my hands dive into her hair, and I devour her mouth. There's nothing gentle about it, our physical need for each other showing in the way our tongues fight for supremacy. Her hands, still bound by the tie, are between us and as I lift the end, her arms come up. I wrap them around my neck and as I lift her, she's forced to wrap her legs around my waist.

Sitting on the sofa, I shuffle her back slightly as I sheath myself with the condom. Raising her hips, one hand guides my cock to the entrance of her slick core. Once I'm buried to the hilt, the sounds of our satisfied groans bounce around the walls of my office.

"I want you to ride me. Can you do that for me, Alex?" I ask.

She moans, nodding as she murmurs, "Yes."

It's the best and yet most torturous feeling in the world. With her bouncing on my cock and her tits filling the palms of my hands, I wouldn't want to be anywhere else. The walls of her pussy clench around me on every upward movement she makes, and it's taking an effort not to come. With one hand filled with her breast, I use the other to rub the bud of her clit, matching her pace.

Flipping her onto her back, I take over the movement, my thrusts sure and measured as I try to keep myself back from the edge.

"Fuck, princess, you feel so fucking good."

I don't let up the pace, not even when she starts clawing at the skin at the nape of my neck. If anything, it turns me on even more. My eyes roam over the perfection that is her body, greedy to remember every last inch.

"Seb... I'm so close."

Her lips part and I drop down onto one elbow, grabbing a hold of her chin as I capture her lips, my thrusts becoming almost frenzied. I feel like a man in the throes of desperation; my heart is racing and a light sheen of sweat coats my skin.

"Fuck, me too... You can come, baby," I rasp, even though we're so past that game.

At my words, she explodes, setting off my own orgasm. A wave of ecstasy rolls through me as my balls tighten and my thrusts are an almost jerked frenzy as I find my release. I collapse as much as the couch allows to the side of her, still connected as our breaths even out and everything around us comes back into clarity.

When I feel like I can stand, I lift off of her and make my way to the bathroom attached to my office to dispose of the condom. When I come back, she's zipping up her dress, with her back to me. I lean against the doorjamb—naked as the day I was born—as I wait for her to tell me this was a mistake. Because by the energy that's rolling off of her, I can tell her guard is back up and she regrets what just happened. *And I fucking hate it.* The irony of it all is that I don't regret anything I've ever done with her.

"Let me guess... What just happened shouldn't have?"

She whips around, lifting her chin as she maintains eye contact with me. "In a nutshell, yes. I don't want to compromise myself as your counsel, and everything I've said to you previously still stands." She picks up her bag, moving to the door before she stops and turns to address me again. "I guess I'll see you on Sunday at the airport."

"I can pick you up."

"I'd rather make my own way."

She looks as composed as when she walked in and as she turns to grab the door handle, I call out to her, "I'm looking forward to working with you, Alex."

Pausing momentarily, she replies, "As am I, Mr. Worthington."

When the door clicks shut and I'm left staring at it, with the smell of sex and her perfume filling my office, a tightness pulls at my chest. My muscles are tense as I walk to the couch to get dressed. It annoys me that she can be so blasé about everything and shrug it off as if it's nothing. *As if I mean nothing.*

If today has proven anything, it's that she wants me, but she's fighting herself on this.

87

Now dressed, I sit at my desk and try to concentrate on the work I need to get done before my trip, a headache threatening to end my day earlier than expected.

These next few days in Chicago will be the perfect opportunity for me to see how open she'd be to having something casual between us.

Before I even broach that, I need to decide if I'm ready for it. To be casual with her would most likely mean only her.

EIGHT

Alex

After leaving Sebastian's office, I all but run back to Jackson and Partners. Even now, an hour later, I can still feel him inside of me. It's like he's stretched me out and my body is still adjusting. I hate that, yet again, I have given into my most basic of desires with him.

Why do I do this? It's like every time I see him, I drop my panties.

I'm not going to do it anymore. I'm going to keep things on a professional level because I can't be his legal counsel if I'm sleeping with him. Most importantly, I need to be strong and stick to my guns.

On Saturday, Savannah, Meghan, Ben and I are going for lunch, and I'm going to tell them everything that has happened. And I mean everything. *The good, the bad and the ugly.* I clearly need someone holding me accountable for my actions if I'm going to stick to my plan.

I'm too caught up in giving myself a pep talk that I don't hear my boss, Belinda's approach. When she speaks, I all but jump out of my chair, placing my hand on my chest over my now racing heart.

"Alexandra, do you have the Ainsley file?"

"Sorry, Belinda. Let me just get that for you."

She looms over me as she lets out a sigh and taps the toe of her *Manolo Blahniks* in annoyance. I barely resist the urge to roll my eyes at her. Not two seconds into my search and she taps her toe harder with impatience. *God, she can be such a bitch.*

"Any day now would be nice, Alexandra," she huffs.

Breathe, Alex.

Typically, the file is at the bottom of the ones piled high on my desk, but a quick look through shows my notes stuck inside. I breathe a sigh of relief as I hand the file over, a serene smile on my face.

"Here you go."

Her eyes narrow at me when she takes it. She flips through it, and then turns on her heel to walk away. No 'thank you', but that's just typical Belinda. My focus goes back to typing out the report I was working on before she interrupted me.

The sound of my phone buzzing in my bag has me looking over the partition of my desk like a meerkat. I'm not expecting any work calls and Belinda is a stickler for making sure cell phones are *only* used for business purposes during working hours.

With no sign of her, and certain it's going to be a message in the group chat about brunch tomorrow, I enter stealth mode and pull my phone out of my bag. I keep it hidden under my desk, as the screen lights up, showing the trail of messages in the group chat. There's another text on the screen from an unknown number, so I click in to read that one first.

> UNKNOWN
>
> I've booked your flight and accommodation. We're departing from terminal 4 at JFK. I will see you there at midday on Sunday.

I know exactly who this is from, even though I deleted his number just last week. He clearly didn't heed my request when I suggested that he lose mine. I'm tempted to ignore his message and make my own arrangements, but he's a billionaire, so I'm sure what he's booked will be ten times nicer than what I would.

> ALEX
>
> Thank you, Mr. Worthington.

Polite yet professional. Exactly how I need to keep all of our interactions going forward. I move from his message to the group chat, where they're arguing about where to go for brunch. I shoot off a quick message with the one spot I know they'll all love.

The Atrium is a beautiful restaurant, popular with the influencer types for their aesthetic and fantastic food. It helps that they also serve crazy potent cocktails. It doesn't take long for my suggestion to be met with an influx of gifs and cheers, just like I knew it would.

Despite it being a Saturday and a day I could be sleeping in, I've been up since six am, with too much energy coursing through my body. My suitcase is open on my bed, half packed, as I rummage through my closet for outfits that scream 'professionalism', cursing myself as I come up short. *I've got to have something in here that's at least past my knees.*

I thank God when my hand lands on a long dress. Plucking it off the rail, I hold it to my body as I walk to the mirror in the hallway. It's a knee-length black power suit dress with a blazer and sensible pumps. I think it could work.

Now to find something to wear for the rest of the trip.

A knock on my front door has me hanging the dress over the mirror as I move to answer it. Looking through the peephole, I'm greeted by the bundle of energy that is Savannah. I throw the door open as she raises her fist to knock again.

"Jeez, give me a chance to get to the door. I could have been getting serviced."

I close the door behind her. She gives me a pointed

look as she breezes past me. "We both know the only person servicing you is the one man you keep pushing away, and it's very unlikely you'd let him into your apartment."

"I'm keeping healthy boundaries," I say, aghast.

"Really?" she asks, taking a cup out of the tray and handing it to me before removing hers and taking a sip.

Not one to pass up free coffee, I take the cup from her hand, savoring a drag of the caffeinated nectar before responding, "Yes, really." Well, no, he's the last guy I was with, but I'm putting boundaries in place. Or at least trying to.

"I don't want to mess up my career or get entangled with a guy that has no interest in being monogamous."

She shrugs, walking toward my bedroom, calling over her shoulder, "Come on, let's get your bags packed, then we can go to lunch."

"I don't need your help packing, Savannah. I can just do it when we get back," I call after her, but she ignores me, and so I follow her.

As I cross the threshold, my gaze lands on my now empty suitcase, which is sitting on my bed. My brow bunches as I try to piece together what is going on. I was literally seconds behind her. How did she get it empty so fast?

Savannah walks out of my closet with an arm full of clothing, placing them next to the open suitcase. Picking up a dress and folding it up, she puts it in my luggage.

"What are you doing?" I ask, approaching her timidly as if she's a wild animal and I don't want to startle her.

She turns to face me but continues with folding *my* clothes. "I'm helping you pack. What does it look like?"

"I can see that, but you've taken out the things I've already packed. You know, my business suits and—"

"*Bridget Jones* style underwear?" Savannah raises a brow at me, scrunching her nose in disgust, as she holds an offending pair of underwear up on one finger. "Last time I checked, you can still wear good lingerie even when you're trying to repel a man."

"But I want to feel comfortable. I don't need a string up the crack of my ass."

"Trust me, when you feel sexy, you act more confident, and you can't do that wearing ugly ass granny panties."

She turns away from me and starts humming along to a song I'm sure I heard on the radio the other day but couldn't name. I throw my arms in the air in resignation as I turn on my heel. There's no point in trying to negotiate with her now. When I get home, I'll repack and make sure my clothes are appropriate for my trip.

"Do you want a glass of wine?" I call out to her from the hallway. The coffee Savannah brought, no longer appetizing.

"When have you ever known me to turn down wine?" She chuckles in response, and a smile forms on my lips because I've never known Savannah to turn down wine.

My mind whirls as I walk to the kitchen. If I'm being honest with myself, I'd love nothing more than to be myself on this trip—kicking ass in the day and letting my hair down at night—but when it comes to being in the same vicinity as Sebastian, I can't seem to say no. It doesn't matter how much I don't want to give in, when he touches or looks at me with lust filling his gaze, I all but beg him to fuck me. Just like I did on Thursday when I went to his office.

Having busied myself with pouring out two *large* glasses of wine, I head back to my bedroom only to walk in on Savannah zipping my case closed.

"That was quick. I'm guessing I'm going to need to add a couple of things?"

"Nope." She pops the p, grabbing a glass from my hand and breezing past me into the living room.

Trailing behind Savannah, I take a seat on the couch across from her, resting my feet on the oak coffee table as I eye her curiously. She purposely avoids my gaze, and I know her well enough to know that she's up to something. However, I'm too distracted by Sebastian to dig any further.

Instead, I change the subject. "So." I take a sip of my drink. "How is it living with Noah and his girlfriend?"

"It's... fine. I've mostly been keeping to myself, so I'm not really aware of them."

Jokingly, I tease with a laugh, "Except for all the hot sex they must be having." Savannah looks at me with what looks to be tears in her eyes, and my humor dies immediately. I reach across the sofa and pick up her hand, pulling her under my arm as I ask, "What's wrong?"

She shakes her head and looks down at the wineglass in her lap. "I'd rather not talk about it, if that's okay?"

"Of course. I totally get that."

We sit in a comfortable silence for a while before I speak again. "More wine or shall we head to the restaurant?"

Savannah pulls away from me to push her glass onto the coffee table, and as she sucks in a deep breath, she runs her now empty hands down her thighs. "Let's go."

With a nod, I stand and carry the glasses into the kitchen, putting them in the sink to clean up later. Meeting Savannah by the door, I grab a light jacket, my purse and keys, ready to leave.

As we make our way to the restaurant, I replay our earlier conversation. I don't like that Savannah didn't feel comfortable enough to open up to me, but I guess that's what I get for not opening up either.

It's a two-way street, after all.

It's on me to show her that she can confide in me and it's this revelation that tells me I'm doing the right thing in coming clean today.

The cab pulls up outside of The Atrium. While I hand over the fare to the driver, Savannah steps out onto the sidewalk. My nerves have hit, and I'm in desperate need of some Dutch courage.

I have no doubt my friends will be supportive and non-judgmental. Even though on the ride over here I thought I was ready to tell them everything, now I'm not so sure I am. They all know to some extent that something has been going on between Sebastian and I, but I've always kept most of the details to myself in my poor attempt at self-preservation.

In a daze, I follow Savannah into the restaurant. I'm a step behind as she talks to the maître d', too up in my own head to engage in conversation. Maybe it wasn't such a good idea to do this today, not with going away with *him* and having to spend at least four whole days together. In a daze, I follow along behind as the host shows us to our table.

"Oh my God, it feels like forever since I last saw you," Meghan squeals, practically leaping from her chair to body check me, bump and all. The action pulls me back into the moment.

A smile spreads across my mouth as she wraps her arms around me, and I can't help but laugh at her excitement. "It's literally only been a week."

"A week too long. I used to see you every day and now it's like I never see you," she pouts as she pulls away and rubs at her bump. I swear it's grown even more in just a week.

I brush a strand of her hair from her forehead before squeezing her shoulder. "Maybe you should have a word with that husband of yours and get him to give me more vacation days." I wink.

Ben moves away from Savannah and pulls me into a hug as he addresses Meghan, "Hey, why are you hogging our girl?"

"I knew I should have never introduced the two of you," Meghan huffs, turning away and greeting Savannah.

With my arms wrapped around Ben's waist and my head tucked under his chin, I give him a final squeeze before taking a seat next to Meghan. Savannah sits opposite me, and Ben takes the seat on my other side. While I look over the menu, they talk amongst themselves.

It doesn't take long for the waiter to return and take our orders. In what feels like a matter of minutes, he brings our drinks and I practically snatch my glass out of his hand as he lifts it from the tray and hands it to me. Taking a deep swig of my Negroni, I brace myself for what's to come.

Advice. I need advice, I remind myself. After Thursday, it's become increasingly clear that I don't have a handle on this situation.

At all.

"I had sex with Sebastian. Again. On Thursday," I blurt out and the low murmur of chatter at our table dies down.

Three sets of eyes turn to me, and my gaze bounces

from one familiar face to the next, looking for any kind of shock etched on them. None comes. Instead, three near identical 'I told you so' smirks grace the faces of my friends as they stare at me.

Ben takes a long pull of his drink through his straw, his gaze not leaving me even as he puts the glass back down on the table. "So." He drags out the word, adding, "Was it good?"

I roll my eyes, huffing, "Of course it was, but that's not the point or why I'm telling you guys."

"In the nicest possible way, why are you telling us?" Savannah asks, a look of curiosity on her face.

My focus drops to the napkin in my lap as I fiddle with the coarse fabric. "I need some advice and... help." I lift my gaze and look each of my friends in the eye before continuing, "I don't want to keep sleeping with him, but I can't seem to stop myself when he's near. It's like he's got me under some kind of spell. One minute I'm telling him to get lost and the next I'm begging him to take me. I want to have more willpower when it comes to him because I don't like this hold he seems to have over me."

Savannah and Ben look at me with matching masks of sympathy filling their faces. When Meghan sniffs, my eyes dart over to her, finding tears welling in her moss green eyes.

I reach out my hand to take hers on top of the table, giving it a gentle squeeze. With concern lacing my words, I ask, "Why are you crying, Mama?"

"You've..." She hiccups as a tear slips free and falls down her cheek. "You've... been dickmatized."

I truly love my best friend, but right now I can't take her seriously. I belt out the laugh that bubbles its way up my throat. Savannah and Ben join in while Meghan wipes her cheeks with her napkin and we draw attention from the surrounding tables.

"It's not funny being this hormonal, guys. Plus, I'm worried about my friend..." she trails off.

I hold my hands up as my laughter dies down. "I'm sorry, but dickmatized? Really?"

Meghan shrugs, looking away sheepishly.

"I mean, it's actually a really good description for whatever the hell kind of spell he has on you," Savannah pipes up. My head whips to her and one of her shoulders lifts in a carefree manner before she takes a sip of her drink.

Ben leans forward and rests his elbows on the table, balancing his chin on his closed fist. A look I can't quite decipher fills his eyes. "Not to make it all serious again, especially after Meghan made the mood so much lighter, but what's going on?"

Blowing out a breath, I start at the beginning. "There's just something about him and I'm drawn to him like a magnet. It started at a Christmas party, nearly three years ago, when I was looking for Meghan." My gaze flits to her before I look away. "I practically barged into his office. He checked the CCTV, I went to leave and literally fell into his lap. Next thing I know, he's kissing me and one thing led to another.

"I didn't think it would be anything more than that one time, but it's like he's crawled under my skin in the most deliciously infuriating way possible. Nearly every time I see him something ends up happening. And in the moment, I give myself up to the feelings he ignites. But when I'm alone, that's when I start with the regrets." I blow out a breath as I look at the faces of my friends.

Ben is the first to speak. "I'll be honest with you, I've never experienced anything like that."

"You slept with him the night of the Christmas party?" Meghan asks, a look of hurt on her face. "And you didn't tell me?"

I open my mouth to say something, but Meghan holds up her hand, halting the words on my tongue. "Sorry, it doesn't matter. You're coming to us now. That's the important thing."

"Exactly," Savannah soothes, drawing the attention of everyone at the table. "This is a very unique set of circumstances. What's stopping you from letting him satisfy your needs and leaving it at that? You don't need to make it into more."

All eyes are now on me, and I don't have an answer I want to voice. I drop my chin and straighten my cutlery as I think of a response. It would be a slippery slope, that's why. Look what happened to Meghan and Cooper when they started hooking up; they ended up with their happily ever after, because people catch feelings, that's why I don't fuck around.

But you want that, right?

Not with him, he's not the right man. At least, I don't *think* he is.

"It's not as simple as that." Ben fills the silence.

With a shake of my head, I lift my chin and say, "You're right, it's not as simple as that. With sex comes emotion, and I'm not immune to catching feelings. I'm not like him, I can't just switch it off and feel nothing. Doing anything with him isn't an option. Yes, I have to help him with this property purchase, but once that's over, I can go back to having nothing to do with him. I think it will be for the best."

"What about when Cooper and I want to do things with you both?" Meghan asks.

"Well, of course I would still be there." I squeeze her hand to reassure her. "And I'll be civil to him, but I'm going to be guarded, because at this point, I don't want to keep being in this cycle. It's not healthy."

I suck in a deep breath as I prepare to drop the biggest of bombshells, because of their misconception of me being a free spirit when it comes to sex. On a shaky exhale, I say, "Despite trying to, I haven't been able to have sex with anyone else but him."

My gaze passes over each of their stunned faces. They're well within their rights to be surprised, especially seeing as I've dated two guys in the nearly three years since Sebastian Worthington and I first slept together.

Savannah is the first to come around. "What do you mean you haven't slept with anyone else?"

"Just that." I shrug. "I've tried, but anytime I've tried to go beyond making out, I've clammed up and had to put a stop to it. It's why Deacon and I broke up. He said I was being frigid, and he had needs that weren't being met."

"Well, you are just full of surprises today," Meghan murmurs.

"I'm sorry. I should have told you all about this a lot sooner. I thought I could handle it myself, but I'm coming to you now, because I need your help. I'm going to be stuck with him for this assignment, and I need someone to break this spell he has me under."

Even though I haven't known him long, I've come to realize that Ben is a fountain of wisdom. He proves this yet again when he says, "Sometimes the best thing you can do is give yourself some space and time to be out of that person's orbit, and there's nothing wrong with doing that. It's okay to put yourself first, and I'm sure Cooper would understand if you stepped away from this assignment."

My focus moves to Meghan looking for confirmation —he's her husband after all and she used to work directly for him. Her response is a simple shrug of her shoulders.

Very helpful, Meghan.

"I know there is no shame in saying no and putting myself first, but this is my career, and I'm not going to let him have me stepping back from what could be an otherwise amazing opportunity." With a shake of my head I continue. "No, I'm going to work on his case and make sure that whatever has happened between us in the past remains in the past. Once it's over and done with, I'm going to be cordial with him and make sure I am never alone with him again. That's when I seem to give in, so that should stop anything more from happening."

Meghan stands from her chair and pulls me into her chest. "And we have your back. You want someone to check in with you every day while you're away, we've got you. You want someone to intercept if he tries to get you alone, I'm your girl. Whatever you need from us, just say it and we will do it."

"Thank you," I whisper, my voice shaky.

"You know you could always just have a bit of fun with him, exclusively of course. Get him out of your system, then you can walk away and find someone to settle down with," Savannah suggests, taking a sip of her drink, her gaze fixed on me over the rim of her glass.

When I don't answer, Ben chips in. "That's not a half bad idea, to be honest. And you know we'll have your back whichever choice you make."

"I tried having some fun with him and then I walked in on him getting a blowjob, so no thank you."

Silence falls over the table and I think about how supportive my friends are and that deep down I knew they would have my back. "You guys are the best, and I'm sorry I didn't speak up sooner," I reply sheepishly.

Our food arrives, perfectly timed, and it doesn't take long for us to move onto happier topics. Even though the drinks flow and the chatter is easy, my mind can't help but think over the suggestions from my friends. Do I use Sebastian to scratch my itch—even though it didn't work before—or protect my feelings and cut him from my life as much as possible?

NINE

Alex

As I wake up, nausea rolls through me. Even with my eyes closed, it feels like I'm at sea while being spun around at speed. My head pounds, reminding me of the choices I made yesterday. Bad, bad choices.

With a groan, I roll over onto my stomach and bury my face into my pillow, hiding from the intrusive daylight peeking into my bedroom. That's the last time I let Ben and Savannah talk me into going out after brunch.

After we left The Atrium, Meghan went home and the three of us went to a bar and drowned my sorrows. Savannah and Ben were more than happy to come along for the ride and what a ride it was.

I turn over onto my back and throw my arm over my eyes as I recount the events of last night. *Oh God*, we got kicked out of one place because I hopped on the bar and danced like a loon. A giggle slips through my lips before I groan at the pain the sound causes.

Why did I drink so much?

With my arms over my head, I stretch out, twisting and turning to wake my body up. My eyes land on my bedside clock as I move to lie on my side, trying in vain to find a position that doesn't make me want to barf. I blink almost comically as I try to make the numbers on the digital display make sense.

Shit.

How is it ten thirty already?

I was supposed to be up an hour ago so that I could repack, shower, put on my armor, and make it to the airport with enough time to give myself a pep talk before I see *him*.

Now, I only have thirty minutes to get my ass out the door.

I grab my phone from the bedside table and bolt out of bed, ignoring the raging hangover that protests with my every move. My stupid phone alarm glares up at me mutely, and as I clear the screen, I see messages pop up in the group chat.

SAVANNAH

O.M.G! Why did we drink so much?

MEGHAN

LOL!

BEN

It's not funny, Meghan! We're suffering over here!

MEGHAN

Never have I been so grateful to be unable to drink. You guys gave me enough material to embarrass you ten lifetimes over!

BEN

Don't you dare, Meghan Maria Jackson!

MEGHAN

Maria? LOL, that's not even my middle name!

The messages continue on and as I put my phone on the bathroom counter. I make a mental note to check through them on the subway. With the shower heating up, I undress and throw my hair up into a bun. I don't have the two hours required it takes to wash and dry it. I don't even have the thirty minutes needed to straighten it.

Under the warm spray of the shower, I scrub my body with my favorite body wash and loofa, then rinse off. Everything is going to be much more rushed than it normally would, and I hate it. There's nothing worse than being late.

After washing my face, I step out of the shower and pat myself dry, mentally going through my wardrobe for an outfit to wear. Casual should be okay. Maybe jeans, t-shirt and a sweater to cover up, what with the cooler weather we're getting.

With a light dusting of makeup and my hair tied into a high ponytail, I make my way into my bedroom to get dressed.

God, I'm so annoyed with myself.

Why did I go out and get drunk last night?

Especially since I knew I needed to be prepared to see him, considering this isn't just a quick meeting. I'm going to be stuck, for days, with the one man that seems to have a hold over me and who I can't seem to resist.

Within minutes, I'm dressed in a pair of skinny navy-blue jeans and a white t-shirt. I'm going to have to make do with whatever the hell Savannah packed for me. My only saving grace is that she knows this is a business trip, but to be on the safe side, I grab the suit I originally packed, stuffing it into my case.

With my luggage trailing behind me, I pick up my phone charger from my bedside table and walk into the hallway. My handbag is knocked over on the side table by the door; I must have left it there when I came stumbling home.

From the hallway closet, I grab my sneakers and walk over to the couch to put them on. I have one shoe on when there's a knock on my door that has my brow pulling into a frown.

I pull on my other sneaker as I contemplate who could be there. All my friends know I have a flight to catch and probably think I've have left by now. I'm not expecting any packages, plus it's a Sunday, so they aren't likely to be delivered today.

With both sneakers now firmly on my feet, I walk to the door and pull it open. I don't bother to check the peephole, which in hindsight was a stupid thing to do because I'm greeted by the beautiful face of Sebastian Worthington.

Our gazes roam over each other as if we haven't seen each other in months. He too is dressed casually, wearing a pair of black ripped jeans, a plain black t-shirt that stretches across his taut chest, and a leather jacket. His clean, woodsy fragrance assails my senses, and I'm seconds away from grabbing the front of his t-shirt and pulling him into my apartment.

It annoys me that he looks *and* smells so good.

Pulling my focus away from his chest, I ask, "Why are you here?"

"You asked me to pick you up," he says with a question in his tone and a furrow to his brow.

"No, I didn't. How did you get my address?"

We've only ever hooked up in his club. I've always kept him out of my personal space.

"You texted me your address. Last night. When you asked me to pick you up." He looks down at me like I've lost my mind, and maybe I have.

"I'm telling you now—" My words trail off as I remember sitting in a booth in a club texting him.

Fuck! What the hell was I thinking?

He pulls his phone out of his pocket and taps the screen a couple of times before turning it toward me.

I shove his phone back to him, not wanting to see the evidence of my drunk texting. "I don't need to see. I remember now. Thank you for collecting me, Mr. Worthington. I'll just get my things."

"You're welcome, Alex." He puts the emphasis on my name then continues, "If you're going to work for me, you're going to have to call me Sebastian, or even Seb, but this Mr. Worthington crap has got to stop."

There's a gruffness to his voice and a hint of a threat, that if I do it one more time, I'll be over his knee. Which doesn't actually sound that bad. Maybe I should keep calling him by his last name.

Oh, my God. What the hell is wrong with me?

Using his last name isn't supposed to be some sort of foreplay, but a reminder for myself that he is a business associate and *not* someone I can fuck. Again.

I feign nonchalance and shrug as I turn away from him to grab my bags.

He doesn't enter my apartment, which I'm grateful for. I'm not sure I could handle him in my space, behind a closed door where *anything* could happen. I need to get my mind off of sex with him, before I end up doing just that. It's already too much for me to spend the next few days with him.

The door shuts as I let go of it and I take the reprieve to drag in some much needed, untainted air. Two rounds of deep breaths in and out, I spring into action and collect my things. I pause at the mirror, smoothing a stray strand of hair back into my ponytail. I dust my finger under my eye to wipe away a speck of mascara and then run my eyes over my outfit.

Why am I checking myself out? It doesn't matter what I look like, I'm not trying to impress him. With a shake of my head, I turn away from my reflection, resisting the urge to mess up my appearance to prove a point to myself.

With my hand on the doorknob, I suck in one last lungful of Sebastian free air, trying to calm the nerves racing through me at the thought of facing him. When I tug it open, I find him leaning against the wall directly in front of my door, and of course, he looks like a damn model. I hate that he looks so effortless and that I don't seem to have any effect on him.

He straightens and grabs my suitcase from me. The look he gives me has my protest dying on my lips and my thighs clenching together. *How can one look have such a powerful effect?* I turn to lock the door before following him down the corridor to the elevator, berating myself for getting all worked up over a look.

Miraculously, the elevator is there waiting when Sebastian presses the button. As he steps in I follow, moving to the corner—as far away from him as possible.

There's humor in his tone as he turns to face me and says, "You do realize you're going to have to be in my vicinity for the next few days, right?"

With a heavy sigh, I lift my chin. "Seeing as I love my

job, and this is one of the many hoops I'll have to jump through to get a promotion, I'll suck it up and be cordial. I'd rather I didn't have to be in your vicinity ever again though, to be honest. As soon as we get out of this elevator, you're nothing more to me than a client."

Perfectly timed, the doors open on a ding and I brush past Sebastian. Our hands touch and a current of electricity passes through my fingers. An involuntary gasp slips through my lips and has me turning away from him so he can't see the way a simple brushing of our hands has affected me.

A dark chuckle falls from his lips before he says, "Right. Whatever you need to tell yourself, Alex."

God, he annoys me. Him and his stupid, sexy accent.

As I step out onto the sidewalk, my gaze goes up and down the street, unsure of how we're getting to the airport. I imagine he'll have a driver rather than driving himself. People don't really drive themselves in the city, it's like the hunger games in metal death traps.

"The car's over here," he murmurs in my ear, causing a shiver to run down my spine.

Thankfully, he doesn't say anything else, instead he steps past me and leads the way to a town car parked a short distance from my building.

A driver climbs out and holds the door open for me as I approach. Sebastian hands him my suitcase and waits for me to take a seat in the back. Once inside, I buckle myself in and turn to face the window, intent on ignoring the man filling the space next to me.

The drive to the airport is uneventful. When we check-in it appears Sebastian spared no expense in booking our flights and we're seated in first class. We pass through security quickly and find a seat at the bar of a restaurant near our departure gate.

Sebastian has left to go to the bathroom and I'm grateful for the break it gives me from him. It feels like my posture has visibly relaxed now that I don't have to be on my guard. His stupid aftershave has been enveloping me in a calming blanket since he picked me up. I need to get a handle on the effect he has on me.

"Mind if I sit here?"

I'm pulled from my thoughts by the owner of a deep voice and turn to face a guy who can't be much older than thirty. At my lack of a response, he takes Sebastian's seat and holds his hand out.

"I'm Ryan. You going far today?"

I blink in confusion at what is going on right now. I think he's... hitting on me. He's a good looking guy; his hair is a dark brown mop of thick curls and he has a strong sharp jaw that's clean shaven, emphasizing his full lips. Dark blue eyes twinkle at me with a hint of amusement in them.

"You don't get many guys approaching you, huh?"

At that I finally find my tongue and reply, "Not really. Don't most people meet online nowadays?"

A rich laugh belts from him, and he tips his head. "I guess so, but not to sound conceited, I'm not most people. When I see a beautiful woman sitting all alone, I can't help but make conversation."

"You sure are a rare breed then, Ryan. I'm Alex, nice to meet you."

I hold my hand out and his warm, large palm slips into mine. For a moment, we just hold hands and I can't help but wonder what else might be big on this man.

"It's nice to meet you too, Alex." His gaze lands on my lips and unconsciously, I dart my tongue out to wipe across it.

"Care to introduce me?" Sebastian's gruff voice bursts the bubble that Ryan and I were in and my focus goes to him as I pull my hand out of Ryan's.

With my chin lifted in defiance I say, "Of course, Ryan, this is Sebastian, my—"

"Her husband." Sebastian cuts me off as his arm goes around my shoulder and he levels a hard gaze at Ryan.

For a moment, I stare at him dumbfounded. *What the fuck is going on?* The word *husband* repeats in my mind.

Husband.

Sebastian. My husband. Married. To Me.

I can't help it. Like a maniac, I burst out laughing, right there in the middle of the airport bar.

Ryan turns to Sebastian and says, "Sorry man, it was, uh, nice to meet you both."

I don't miss the way his eyes widen a fraction, probably at my craziness, as he vacates Sebastian's seat and scurries away.

Oh, my God.

"You do realize you look like a mad woman, right?" Sebastian asks, his tone full of authority. I never thought I had a thing for accents, but there's just something about the British one that does something for me.

It has *nothing* to do with the man himself.

He takes a seat and acts as if he didn't just say the most out of this world thing.

When my laughter finally dies down, I point to my chest. "Me? In what world would you be my husband? Scratch that. In what world would you be *anyone's* husband?"

"I don't think it's that far out of the realms of possibility," he says, sounding offended. Although that can't be right, because I'm certain that this is the same man who has a different woman for each day of the week.

His hand rests on the back of my high-backed stool, and for a moment, I wonder if he's going to play with my hair. Images play through my mind of the last time he touched me. It's dangerous when I'm the subject of his attention, because he makes me want things that he's made clear I can't have.

Images of the last time his hand rested behind me run through my mind and I clear my throat to dispel them. "It doesn't matter whether it is or not, you shouldn't have said that to him."

His response is a shrug, and I could slap him for it, but instead, I huff out a breath of annoyance at his complete non-answer. "The least you could do is apologize"

"I would if I felt I did something wrong, but I don't, so I won't."

"You are unbelievable." I down the rest of my drink and swing my chair around ready to leave.

"Where are you going?"

"Away from you." I glare at him, pasting a probably creepy smile on my face as I say, "Dear *husband*."

I already can't wait for this trip to be over.

TEN

Sebastian

I didn't bother following Alex out of the bar. It seemed pointless, seeing as we're in an airport and she can't go anywhere. Instead, I finish my drink and ordered another one as I thought about why I'd just told some guy I was her husband.

Seeing her with her hand enveloped in another man's had made feral feelings ignite inside of me. I'd watched as I made my way across the room, waiting for her to steal her hand back, but it never happened. Barely talking myself down from laying the guy out, I settled for the one thing I knew would have him running.

Calling myself her husband.

It felt like a kick in the dick when she said she couldn't see me being anyone's husband, and I'm not sure why. I've never wanted that, and I still don't, but my chest ached at her comment.

I spent the time finishing my drink, rationalizing that

it only hurts my pride because she holds so much more power than she realizes. A knot of worry twists inside of me as I contemplate whether or not I'm making a mistake. This was nothing in comparison to the grand plan that starts when we meet George Bennett.

I've done my own research of Sanctuary and it's very apparent that I'm not the man George Bennett would sell to. It will be much easier to convince him I'm the man to sign on the dotted line with when I have a fiancée on my arm.

A very fake fiancée.

Alex was sitting at the gate when I arrived. She gave me a look of frustration when I sat down next to her, ignoring me as we waited to be called to board the plane. Being seated next to each other on the flight didn't get her talking. In fact, she put in her earbuds and stopped any attempt I made at conversation. She's ignored me in the car the entire journey to the apartment I've rented and even as we've collected the keys, she's remained silent.

I wanted to afford us some privacy, so instead of booking into a hotel, I've rented an apartment in a central location for the meetings we will be having.

As the elevator doors open on our floor, she follows behind me to the door of the penthouse apartment. Once this door closes, we aren't leaving until she tells me what's caused her mood.

I mean, I have an idea, but I don't think it warrants this kind of reaction.

With a turn of the key, I push open the door. As I step through and hold it open for Alex, my eyes don't leave her as I take in her reaction. There's a hint of disbelief mixed in with the evident awe on her face.

She walks further into the space, stopping as she reaches the threshold of the open plan living room. It's sunk into the floor and you have to step down three marble steps to reach the two large couches which face each other in the middle of the room.

"Wow, this room is bigger than my whole apartment," Alex murmurs.

I've got to admit, it's a beautiful place, but it doesn't distract me from the woman in front of me. Neither do the floor to ceiling windows that run along the entire wall of the room as you walk in. They give a fantastic view of downtown Chicago.

I stand behind her as the sweet scent of her peach perfume—or body wash—settles over me like a comforting blanket. The urge to touch her is strong, but with my hands fisted at my sides, I ask, "Care to share why you've felt it appropriate to ignore me since the bar?"

Alex doesn't say a word, so I walk to stand in front of her. When she drops her head to avoid my gaze, I lightly grip her chin between my thumb and forefinger, lifting it so that she has no choice but to look at me.

"Let me be clear, Alex." Her lips part and I struggle to keep my focus on what I want to say. "If you're going to be working for me, you need to understand that when I ask you a question, you fucking answer me. Understood?"

Her eyes darken and I'm not entirely sure if it's from anger or lust. I want to believe it's lust, but I'm certain that's a tall order at this point.

When her tongue darts out to lick her lips and her gaze slides down to my mouth, I know it's lust. As if on fire, I release her chin and take a step back.

Unable to hide my frustration, I run a hand through my hair. I turn away from the temptation that she is because when it comes to her, I have no control over my actions. I could spend an eternity buried inside of her, breathing her in... holding her to me.

I'm almost dismissive when I say, "Go and get settled in and we'll leave to meet George. He's expecting us at four, so you have some time."

The sound of her sneakers and suitcase moving across the white marble floor echo around the spacious room.

Jesus, I need a drink.

I'm not quite sure how I'm supposed to get through the purchase of this club if she's going to be so... present.

In lieu of hard liquor, I walk to the kitchen and grab a cold bottle of water. Like the living room, with its sleek lines, the kitchen is filled with modern appliances that make it feel remarkably similar to my apartment back in Manhattan. The privacy we're afforded by having our own space was a good call.

As I lean back on the counter, I drink down half of the

bottle in one go. Pulling out my phone, I scroll through the messages Alex sent last night.

The fact that they started at one in the morning was enough to tell me she wasn't sober. And yet, I couldn't help but see what she had to say. When she'd said good-night, I read through the messages over and over again until I couldn't keep my eyes open and sleep overtook me.

ALEX

Did you know I don't like you very much?

SEBASTIAN

I had an inkling. You haven't exactly been subtle about it.

I'd sat with my next message for a while before I pressed send, the urge to know greater than the urge to not.

SEBASTIAN

Why do you think that is?

ALEX

Because you're too good at sex.

And I don't like that you make me feel so good yet so bad at the same time.

I'm addicted to you.

You've dickmatized me, Sebastian.

SEBASTIAN

Dickmatized?

It felt like the least dangerous part of her messages to pick up on. Even though I wanted to know more about her addiction to me and if it meant she was affected by me like I am by her.

ALEX

I'm hypnotized by your dick.

Dickmatized. Duh!

SEBASTIAN

Well, I'm sorry. I will keep my dick away so that you can come back around to the world of the living.

ALEX

I'd appreciate that.

Can you pick me up in the morning?

SEBASTIAN

Sure.

Alex coughing brings my attention back to the present and I look up from my phone to find her standing in the doorway of the kitchen, looking at me expectantly.

Fuck me.

She's dressed in a black knit dress that stops at the top of her thigh, knee high boots and a khaki belted overcoat. She looks fucking stunning. Her hair is down and atop her head is a black fedora.

"Are you ready?" she asks.

123

I clear my throat as I straighten from my position leaning against the counter and reply, "No, I was just grabbing a drink, but I will go get changed myself. Help yourself to anything you want."

Before we arrived, I had the place stocked up. The fridge holds water, beer and soda, as well as an array of veggies and meats. In the pantry we have crisps and candy. My guilty pleasure and the reason I spend so much time in the gym.

"Okay."

As I walk past her, it takes all of my strength to not pull her into my arms, bend her over the kitchen island, and fuck her senseless.

This should be an interesting few days.

It doesn't take me long to get changed and meet Alex by the front door. She throws a small black bag with a chain strap over her shoulder as I slip my wallet into the pocket of my navy-blue chinos.

Because this my first face-to-face meeting with George Bennett, I've attempted to look semi-presentable. I need him to believe I'm the person he's been waiting for, that I'm a respectable, committed business man. That's why I've opted to pair my pants with a white shirt rather than wear my usual, much more casual fare of jeans and a t-shirt.

In the days since my meeting with Cooper and then leaving New York, I've formulated a plan that might just work. It's pretty much the only plan I have.

Normally, it wouldn't be necessary for my legal counsel to meet the client I'm buying from, and certainly in the US, I would use a broker, however I have an ulterior motive bringing Alex with me today. I'm grateful that, so far, she hasn't questioned why she's coming.

I need this club.

And I need Alex to get this club.

Just not in the capacity of my legal counsel.

I'm wholly aware that what I'm about to do is underhanded, and if anything, incredibly stupid. Especially given her reaction to me calling myself her husband at the airport. But I'm hoping that she keeps her cool—at least until we get back to the apartment—and doesn't throw a fit.

"You're being awfully quiet." She breaks the silence that's blanketed over us in the back of the cab.

If I was a better man, which I'm not, I'd bring her into my plan, but it's too personal and there would still be the possibility that she'd walk away. I can't have that happen.

Instead, I just smile. "Just going over the points I want to discuss with George."

"Okay." She eyes me for a moment, shaking her head as she continues, "I'm not sure why you brought me to this meeting, but tomorrow I'm meeting with the firm that will be hosting us when we close. I think it would be a good idea for you to come along. To get to know them."

"Sure," I reply, looking out the window as the streets of Chicago pass us by.

I wonder briefly if I should back away from this club and the plan I'm about to initiate. I rub my sweaty palms on my thighs, berating myself for letting my nervousness take over. So much is riding on this and if it blows up in my face, I could ruin my reputation and I've worked too damn hard for that to happen.

Meeting George for the first time is a huge detail and as my heart races, I try to prepare myself for the conversation that's to come. As if sensing my need for quiet, Alex is content to look out of the window.

It doesn't take long for the cab to arrive at the club. Even at four in the afternoon, the neighborhood is bustling with patrons filling the high end restaurants and tourists coming and going from the hotels. High-rises fill the skyline of downtown Chicago, and I pull in a deep breath of city air as I step out of the cab. I turn and hold a hand out for Alex as she follows.

Of course, she doesn't take it. I don't know why I expected her to. This is the guarded Alex. The Alex that texted me last night is a side I doubt I'll ever get to see in the sober light of day.

My steps are confident as I walk to the entrance of the two story building. The exterior has a warehouse vibe to it. Small windows are dotted around and the walls are white-washed brick. If I didn't already have a plan and was really going to turn it into another one of my clubs, it would be the perfect location and vibe. I would turn it into an exclusive club, tailored to Chicago, with a nineteen twenties speakeasy style club.

I just need George Bennett to sign the place over, then everything else will fall into place and I can walk away knowing I got what I came for. *Revenge.*

I hold one of the glass fronted double doors open for Alex and she breezes past me, leaving a hint of peaches in the air behind her.

"You're being quiet. Disturbingly quiet." Alex's eyes are squinted at me as we stand in the lobby of the building.

"I'm in business mode. I like to take in a property without noise," I say almost pointedly.

My gaze roams around the room. It will need some work, but nothing that previous buildings haven't needed. Sometimes people can become complacent with their properties, especially when they've owned them for as long as George has.

As if reading my mind Alex says, "It's going to need some work."

"That it is, I'm afraid," a booming voice calls from the door that I assume leads to the main space of the club.

George Bennett reminds me of Colonel Sanders and Santa if they'd had a baby. He looks a lot different to the pictures I've seen of him; older and more weathered. His rounded stomach and cheeks match perfectly with his pure white hair and handlebar mustache. A beaming smile graces his aged face, and as he approaches, the laughter lines tell a story of a life well lived.

He envelopes my outstretched hand in his own and gives me a strong, sure shake. Reminding myself that I need to play nice and not let my personal feelings toward this man show, I lift the corner of my mouth into some semblance of a smile.

No time like the present to throw the grenade down, I guess. "It's nice to finally meet you in person, George. This is my fiancée, Alexandra."

If I didn't have so much riding on this very moment, I'd have laughed at the comical nature of it. Alex's eyes practically bug out of her face, but the smile doesn't leave her lips as she simultaneously greets George and throws daggers at me.

Oblivious to my impending doom, George fills the silence. "It's so nice to finally meet you both. Let's get on with the tour so you can enjoy the rest of your evening." He turns to walk into the club, leaving Alex and I to follow behind.

"What the hell was that?" Alex whisper-shouts, her eyes ahead on George.

"I'll explain later. Preferably when he's not within hearing distance."

I'm sure she'll get over it. There are more important things at stake than her hurt feelings.

"I can't fucking believe you, Sebastian. You're in a whole heap of s—" Alex's words die on her tongue as George turns to speak to us.

"This is the main—" George narrows his eyes at us, before asking, "Is everything okay?"

Alex steps up beside me and wraps her arm around my waist and instinctively, I do the same before resting my chin on the top of her head.

"Absolutely perfect. We are just so gosh-darn excited to see this space," Alex blurts.

Gosh-darn? Who even says that nowadays?

"If you're sure."

He's turning away when Alex speaks again and I could murder her. "Well, if I'm being honest, George, Bastian here..." She pats me on the chest as she rests her cheek against my chest. "He surprised me this morning when he knows how much I *loathe* surprises."

With a chuckle and a knowing look, George replies, "Oh. My advice, young man, is to do whatever makes your lady happy. If she doesn't like surprises, don't surprise her. It'll make for a much easier life."

A goofy grin spreads across her mouth and in this moment she's never looked more beautiful. She actually looks free and happy. Everything inside of me is telling me to push her away and get the fuck out of here, but I fight through the urge and paste what I'm sure is a crazy looking grin on my own face.

George frowns slightly—probably wondering why he met up with two clearly crazy people by himself—before the corners of his own mouth tip up.

Great. Now we're all smiling like *fucking* loons.

Although George's seems to have a hint of concern within it.

"You were saying?" I ask, in an effort to ease the awkwardness that's settled over us.

Ever so slightly flustered, George looks away as if to find the words he was going to speak. "Oh. Yes. Well. This is the main space. There are two function rooms, a large one and a smaller one. The VIP area is on the lower floor, just over there." He points to a red velvet curtain at the opposite end of the room. "Just behind that curtain. I tell you what, why don't you two go and explore and I will wait here."

"That sounds like a great idea," I reply, a more natural smile now on my lips.

We're no more than ten paces away from him when Alex asks, nostrils flaring, "Are you going to tell me why I came here as your legal counsel but have somehow become your fake fiancée?"

For a fraction of a second, I wonder if I can distract her with sex, but the look of anger on her face tells me that won't work this time. This isn't the place for that either. A quick glance behind me tells me George is busying himself by the bar and not intent on listening to me being ripped a new one by Alex.

With a hand on her elbow, I guide her to the opposite end of the club. "Look, I will explain everything when we get back to the apartment and have some privacy. Just, please, don't make a scene here."

Her head is turned away from me, and I watch the

grinding of her jaw as she processes what I've just asked of her. She draws in a slow, steady breath, blowing it out and repeating the process. Her anger is palpable. I'm not sure how I can get her to go along with my plan, not when she's so clearly furious with me. Maybe this was a bad idea. Maybe I should have left Alex back at the apartment. There wasn't really any need for her to be here today.

She pulls me from my thoughts as she sighs softly. "Fine. I won't make a scene, but don't take that as me agreeing to go along with this stupid farce in the long run."

She walks away from me, looking around the space and effectively shutting me out until we meet back up with George half an hour later and have to play pretend again.

This was a bad idea, but at least it's only for this trip, which will be over in a couple of days. It's not like we'll have to spend long with George in that time anyway. I'm sure we can make it through a couple of meetings and maybe one dinner.

When we approach him, George ends the call he's on with a whispered, 'I love you', before asking us, "What do you think?"

Some of the concern seems to have left him, and with my arm around Alex's waist, I give him an easy smile. "It's great, and with a little bit of modernization, I can see the space working for my next club. I'll have my legal counsel draw up the paperwork."

His eyes dart to Alex at my last statement and I wonder if he knows. A sense of unease washes over me and I tighten my grip on Alex as if that can somehow make him believe my lie any more.

"And what do you think, Alexandra?"

"Please, call me Alex. I love the club and the old charm of Chicago you have running through the features. I think Bastian will only add to that charm." She turns into me and presses a palm over my racing heart. "Don't you think, baby?"

Her chin is tipped up to me, and as if it's the most natural thing to do, I cup her cheek with the hand not around her waist, dropping a soft kiss to her plump lips. As I pull away, my gaze drops to her mouth. I watch as her lips part as she sucks in a breath and the slight widening of her eyes tells me she wasn't expecting it.

Neither was I, Alex.

George clears his throat, forcing my focus back to him.

"I couldn't agree more, princess," I murmur.

Her nails dig into my chest punishingly as she grabs at my shirt, and I know there will be hell to pay later.

"Look at you two. I remember love like this, and let me tell you, it just gets better as time goes on," George says gleefully as he clasps his hands in front of him. "Now before you get anything drawn up, there is one thing that is very important to me."

With a bow of my head, I assure him as I say, "Anything, to make this transition smooth for you, George."

A grin stretches across his mouth. "Fantastic. So a week in Lake Geneva with my family is doable for you?"

Where has he pulled this crap from?

It's the selling of a property, not a fucking cult sign up. Jesus. I scrub my hand over my jaw as I consider how to answer him.

It's not really a question I can say no to—no matter how much I want to—because if I want this property—which I do—I'm going to have to go on this trip.

I look down at Alex as she looks up at me, searching my face for who knows what, and looking away when she can't find it.

"I can make it, but I'm not sure Alex can. She's very busy at the firm." I'll have to do this without her because she's only mine for a few days.

The smile falls from George's face as he looks at us. "This may be a problem. One of my stipulations is that I get to know the family taking over my property."

My mind lingers on the word family and I fight to not let my *disgust* towards him show on my face. It's laughable that *he,* of all people, thinks family is important. I want to give him a piece of my mind, his words nearly pushing me over the edge, but I can't blow this deal.

No. My time will come. For now, I'll stick with my belief that the only person you can rely on in life is yourself. Even now, with this situation I've put myself in, I know I can't truly rely on Alex to go along with my charade. Hell, after today she probably won't.

Alex rests her head on my shoulder before she

speaks. "I'm sure we can make it work, George. Bastian has your number. He'll call you for the details later once I've called my work."

"Of course. Let's talk later, Sebastian."

We leave George and as we climb into the cab and drive further and further from the club, I know deep down that I won't be getting it, not if Alex doesn't want to go along with my plan.

What will I do if Alex wants nothing to do with my lies?

I'm quiet on the ride back to the apartment, my mind whirling through plans I've already discarded once before.

I fear I may have to let this club go and find another way to get my revenge.

ELEVEN

Sebastian

Neither of us has spoken a word since we left George. I hold the apartment door open for Alex and can feel the restless energy rolling off of her in waves as she walks in. She at least waits until I've closed the door and turned to face her before she speaks. With the fedora she was wearing now discarded and her overcoat hanging open, she looks ready for battle.

In my mind, I imagine crashing my lips to hers and finding out what she's wearing underneath that dress. I swear I saw a hint of lace when she was sitting in the car earlier.

Jesus, I need to get laid.

And not by Alex.

With my hands raised in surrender, I say, "I know, I owe you an explanation."

"You owe me more than that, but it's a damn good starting place. What the hell were you thinking?"

She doesn't raise her voice, instead she's cool, calm and collected. It's unnerving that she's acting as if I haven't just roped her into my ridiculous plans.

"I'll explain it all, I promise." I brush past her to the kitchen and the sound of her heels clicking along the marble tell me she's following.

I find the cabinet with the glasses easily enough, pulling out two tumblers before I swipe up the bottle of whiskey that was sitting on the sideboard when we arrived. With a generous pour in each glass, I hand one to Alex before I bring mine to my lips and take a sip. The full bodied smoky flavor goes down smoothly and eases some of my tension.

As I lean back against the counter, crossing my legs at the ankles, I allow my gaze to roam over Alex freely.

She shifts under my assessment. Slamming back her drink and walking out of the room, she calls over her shoulder, "I'm going home, Sebastian. I've had enough of this shit."

I let her go, at least until I finish my drink. She's not leaving. I need her to see this through.

On the way back to the apartment, I came to the realization that there is no other plan and I'm not walking away. I'll do, or pay, whatever it takes to get her to do this.

With no plan, I put my empty tumbler in the sink and

walk to her bedroom. She's throwing her stuff into the case haphazardly but freezes when I knock on the doorjamb.

"I'll start with the explanation, and then we can negotiate."

"Negotiate? What exactly are we negotiating, Sebastian?"

"You know, I preferred it when you called me Bastian. It's a new one, but I liked it."

She cocks a brow at me, and when I don't say anything, turns back to stuffing things in her suitcase.

"Okay, I'm sorry. I should have clued you into my plan."

"You shouldn't have had the goddamn plan in the first place." She's starting to lose her cool, and I'd be lying if I said it didn't turn me on.

Focusing back on what she's just said, I hang my head because she's right, I should have found a better plan, like maybe hiring someone to buy it under a shell company.

But it has to be me that does this. My plan doesn't work unless I can throw it back in his face at the end.

"I don't know what else I can say aside from I'm sorry."

She folds her arms over her chest and cocks her hip. "Really? You can't think of a single thing you should say or do?"

When I don't answer she continues, "Because I think

something along the lines of 'you're right, Alex, I shouldn't have lied to George that you're my fiancée. I'll come clean to him and back out of the purchase.' I think that might be a fantastic place to start."

I scrub a hand over the back of my neck. Doing that isn't an option. If I do, then he won't pay for his sins. "I can't do that, Alex."

"If you can't, then perhaps I should. Maybe I should call him right now and tell him everything that you've lied to him about."

She moves to her phone resting on the bedside table. My stride is longer and I make it to her before she can pick it up, my arm banding around her waist as I lift her up, and place myself between her and her phone before putting her down. She lets out a squeal of surprise, spinning to face me when I let go. Her eyes are murderous.

"How dare you!"

"I'm sorry."

"You sure are doing a lot of apologizing. Did you ever think that maybe you shouldn't be such an ass and then you wouldn't have to?" Her eyes widen as she looks at me for an answer.

I fight the smirk that's trying to spread into a full on grin. I'm a smart enough man to know that would send her over the edge.

"Look." I squeeze the bridge of my nose, the beginnings of a headache forming. "Whatever you need, I will do or pay. Money is no object."

She turns away. Picking up a t-shirt, she folds it and puts it in her suitcase. I'm left wondering if she's going to say anything as she packs up her luggage.

A sigh slips from her lips and she carries on folding her things, refusing to make eye contact with me, even when she speaks. "I have my student debt." She shifts uncomfortably, her hands fiddling with one item.

"I'll pay it off. How much?"

"It's a lot."

"How much, Alex?"

"If you pay it, I'll pretend to be your fiancée for as long as you need, and *if* I can get time away from work, I'll come with you to Lake Geneva."

I move to stand in front of her, lifting her chin and forcing her to look at me. "How. Much?"

"One hundred and fifty thousand," she breathes.

"Consider it done."

Stepping back from her, I slip my phone out of my pocket and pull up the text chain with Cooper.

SEBASTIAN

I need to borrow Alex for a week or so.

COOPER

What do you mean 'borrow Alex'?

SEBASTIAN

Just that. We'll be back in the City in about a week. Speak soon.

COOPER

What do you mean?

My gaze lifts to Alex as I slip my phone back into my pocket. It buzzes incessantly and I can just imagine the shit I'm going to be in with Cooper when I see him next. Perhaps I could have just said that it's to get to know George, but it doesn't hurt to mess with him a little.

"It's sorted. You can come with me."

"Excuse me?" Alex's eyes widen and her brows inch towards her hairline.

"I've cleared it with Cooper." Sort of. "You can come to Lake Geneva for the week and be my fiancée."

"Fake fiancée, Sebastian."

I stalk toward her like a lion stalking its prey. My hands cup her cheeks, my lips inches from her own. "I need you to play make believe and convince the Bennett's that you are madly in love with me and I with you. When George signs on the dotted line, you can walk away and in return, I'll make sure your student debts are paid off."

She looks like a deer caught in a headlights and I don't miss the way her gaze drops to my mouth. I can feel the heat from her body and smell her unique scent as it wraps around me.

She still wants me, and based on how dismissive and guarded she's been, she doesn't like that.

"Don't fall in love with me," she blurts out. Her breathing is labored, as if it's too much to be this close to me.

The laugh that falls from my lips can't be contained. To think of me falling in love with someone is ludicrous.

Love is for the weak. It's for people that want to lay themselves bare and be ripped to pieces when the person they think they love walks away. Love is just a feeling, and feelings are fickle.

"You don't ever have to worry about that with me, sweetheart." I brush a strand of hair away from her cheek, continuing, "I don't do love."

My lips brush over hers and as I pull back she follows me. I see the moment what I've said registers and the questions that come to the front of her mind as she searches my face for answers she isn't going to get.

A look I can't quite decipher flits through her eyes. She averts her gaze, hiding from me as she takes a step back, forcing my hands to drop. She wraps her arms around her waist as if trying to comfort herself. As if my words have somehow hurt her.

"Okay," she whispers.

If the room wasn't so quiet, the sound of Chicago traffic a distant murmur, I might not have heard her or the sense of defeat in her tone.

Watching her, stood at the end of the bed, a cloak of sadness wrapped around her, causes a niggle of something that feels suspiciously like guilt to settle into the pit of my stomach.

I have two options.

I either let her go back to New York and clean up the fallout that will come from my lie, or—and this is where I should be a gentleman and go with the former—I force her to go along with my lie and get the property I need to exact my revenge.

The silence is thick in the air. Before I can do anything stupid, like tell her that for her I'd try, I walk to the door, pausing just outside the room.

I never claimed to be a gentleman and I sure as shit am not going to start now.

"Great. I'll call George and we can head up in the morning."

I leave her standing in the room, not missing the look of disbelief that washes over her face. Buying this club is more important to me than protecting Alex's feelings. She's a big girl, she'll get over it. And if she doesn't, she can go back to avoiding me like the plague.

In my own room, I call George. He answers on the second ring, clearly expecting my call. "Sebastian, it's good to hear from you so soon. I trust you have good news for me?"

I can hear the smile in his voice. It irks me that he always seems so happy; that he's a man that 'has it all', whatever that means.

My tone is perhaps too gruff when I speak, but I don't bother to bring it down a notch. "We'll be there. Just send me the details and we can leave first thing in the morning."

It's as if he's oblivious to my mood. "Oh Sebastian, that is perfect. I will let Miriam know. She's been asking to meet you since I told her about your interest in Sanctuary. My middle child is visiting with his wife, so you can get to know at least one of my brood." He laughs as if he's just told the funniest joke. I don't react.

We iron out a few of the details and confirm that Alex and I will take the two hour drive and should arrive by noon tomorrow.

Now all we need to do is iron out the plan of our backstory, because for the next week, we're going to be under a lot of scrutiny.

Sitting on the end of my bed, I finish up emailing my contact at Wilkins and Wilkins to cancel our meeting tomorrow. I'm contemplating how long I can stay in my room and avoid the inevitable awkwardness with Alex when my phone buzzes in my hand.

Oh, shit, I forgot about Cooper.

To say he's not pleased would be an understatement.

COOPER

What do you mean?

Hello?

What do you mean?

Sebastian?

You can't send me a cryptic message like that and not tell me what you mean.

Answer me.

Great, now Meghan wants to know what you meant.

Sebastian William Worthington, I swear to God, if you don't answer me there will be hell to pay.

From my wife.

The bubbles on the screen are still going, so I type out a quick reply.

SEBASTIAN

Mate, you are so easy to mess with. The old boy wants me to go and stay with him and his family for a week.

I need Alex as a buffer. She's agreed to go, if she can get the time off, which you have done. You and Meghan don't need to worry about it.

COOPER

Fine, but you owe me when you get back. Dinner is on you.

Meghan is going to call Alex.

Not bothering to respond, I laugh at the angst evident in Cooper's texts. He'll get over it. He's just so fucking pussy whipped by Meghan. She's an amazing woman, but ever since she walked into his life, he's been under her thumb even when they weren't together.

I guess I should go and update Alex on the situation.

She's sitting on the large gray sofa in the living room, her feet are tucked under her as she flicks through a magazine about things to do in Chicago.

"I didn't think you were going to come out," she says, not looking up from the magazine.

With perhaps too much defensiveness in my tone, I reply, "I was making a phone call."

She looks up, her eyes searching my face for something. "Was the call to Cooper?"

"No, it was to George Bennett, confirming our plans. He's expecting us to be there around noon tomorrow, so we'll need to leave around ten."

Alex doesn't say anything for the longest time and I can see the internal battle that she's having with herself, even from my place behind the couch. After a moment, she turns back to put the magazine on the coffee table, standing as she does.

She still doesn't say a word until she's at the entrance to the hallway that leads to her room, "I'll be ready to leave in the morning. Goodnight, Sebastian."

It's like seven in the evening. Surely she can't be going to bed yet?

I don't question her, instead, I'm grateful for the breathing room it will afford me.

However, no more than thirty minutes later, as I'm watching *SportsCenter*, she comes waltzing into the living room looking like every man's wet *fucking* dream. She's wearing a dress that I can only describe as bondage, heels that would be more at home in a strip club, and her hair seems to have grown at least ten inches.

"Where are you going?"

Alex rolls her eyes before saying, "Out."

"I can tell. But where?" I growl, every ounce of possessiveness I feel for her barely under wraps.

"Well, *Daddy*—"

My eyes flick up and down her body. "I'm not adverse to being your daddy."

She rolls her eyes again, flicking her ponytail over her shoulder. "Not that it's any of your business, but I'm going to a club."

Jesus, she's acting like a child.

"Don't play dumb, Alex. It's not a good look on you. Which club are you going to and who are you going with?"

"The last time I checked, I was an adult and didn't need to tell anyone what I was doing or who I was doing it with."

"You're in a strange city. You shouldn't be going out by yourself."

"It might be strange to you, but it isn't to me." She turns and walks to the door, calling over her shoulder, "Anyway, Meghan knows where I'm going and who I'm going with."

As soon as the door clicks shut behind her, I grab my phone from the cushion beside me.

SEBASTIAN

Where has Alex gone?

COOPER

You've lost her?

SEBASTIAN

I haven't fucking lost her. She's gone out. Ask Meghan where she's gone.

COOPER

Meghan said she doesn't know.

SEBASTIAN

What do you mean she doesn't know?!

Alex said Meghan knows.

COOPER

It's Meghan. I don't know where she's gone, but she's a grown up and knows the city. I'm sure she'll be fine.

I'm two seconds away from asking Meghan to check in with her and find out where she's gone, but instead I chuck my phone onto the couch and go back to watching the TV.

That lasts for all of two seconds before I snatch up my phone and text a buddy of mine that works security at a few clubs in the city. I type out a message, then delete it. Scrubbing my hand over my jaw, I put my phone down and walk into the kitchen. I pour myself a drink of whiskey, throwing it back as my heart races, worry taking me over.

I can't just do nothing.

What if something happens to her?

My feet carry me back to the living room and when I swipe up my phone, my fingers fly across the screen. I don't hesitate when I press send. The response I get back is almost immediate.

JONAH

Leave it with me.

I pace around the room as I wait. My eyes going to the clock on the TV as each minute ticks by. It's no more than five minutes when Jonah texts me back, but it might as well have been five hours.

JONAH

She's in Vixen. We'll keep an eye on her.

SEBASTIAN

Thank you.

I collapse onto the couch, relief causing me to sag. As I rest my head on the back of the couch, I berate myself for being so obsessed over this woman. Fuck. Alex and Meghan were right. She's an adult and doesn't need to tell me where she's going or who with, but I can't help but be concerned.

That's the problem.

When it comes to her, or any woman for that matter, it's not my place to be concerned.

She's burrowing under my skin and making me feel things for her that I shouldn't. I've never had this overwhelming feeling before. I should be pushing her away, not trying to pull her in.

She shouldn't come to Lake Geneva with me.

But I need her.

I pinch the bridge of my nose, the pounding from earlier returning with full force.

Despite going to bed hours ago, it's not until I hear Alex getting in at four in the morning that my shoulders relax and the knot that formed in my stomach eases.

With frustration at the situation I find myself in, I punch my pillow and turn over to try and get some sleep.

TWELVE

Alex

Sebastian knocks on my door at nine am and it sounds like a swat team is trying to get through. When I only groan and roll over—not because of the alcohol but the lack of sleep—he opens the door and sticks his head in, calling my name.

"Alex, you have an hour until we need to leave."

"Just leave me to sleep," I whine.

"I've got you a caramel latte and some eggs and bacon on cooking. Come, eat and then you can shower."

Urgh, I hate that he's being so nice.

Why is he being so nice?

My brow tugs into a frown, trying to remember when I told him what my go to coffee order was. I'm certain I haven't.

Last night, after he all but dictated that I was going to go to Lake Geneva with him, I called my friend Winnie. We were roommates in college and became fast friends when we ended up having most of our classes together. She also just so happens to be my contact at the firm Sebastian's using in Chicago.

I thought we would have plenty of time to catch up while I was in town, but that obviously isn't going to happen now. I'll admit, I felt a little guilty agreeing to go along with his lie if he paid off my student debt. It's a lot of money. But then he was an ass, and it made it a little easier.

Despite not drinking much, I had the best time and spent most of the night trying to convince Winnie that she needed to come and visit me in New York, or you know, move to New York.

The smell of bacon wafts in—thanks to Sebastian leaving my door open. I think I'll sleep in the car—I'm so tired. As I push the covers off, goosebumps prickle my skin, the cold air outside of the comforter drifting over my skin. Not too different from a zombie, I trail my way down the hallway, salivating at the smell of the perfect breakfast food.

My eyes go wide as I come to an abrupt stop in the opening to the kitchen.

Have I woken up in an alternative universe?

I rub my eyes in an effort to clear the mirage standing in front of me.

Sebastian stands in front of the stove with his back to me. This would be a completely normal thing to walk in on if it wasn't for the fact he has no shirt on.

Who cooks food half naked? And bacon, no less!

He's just standing there looking all tempting, with a pair of gray sweatpants hung low on his hips and his bare chest on display. The muscles in his back ripple as he moves what I assume, based on the lack of sizzling, are eggs around the frying pan.

Jesus.

I rub my thighs together to ease the ache that's building between them. *Get your shit together, Alex.* A whimper slips through my lips and Sebastian turns, his gaze finding mine before it drops down my body. It's then I realize I'm still dressed in my oversized t-shirt and nothing else. Not even underwear.

My gaze drops to his chest and over the ridges of his abs. His waist is tapered and I realize that this is only the second time I've ever seen him without a shirt on. My greedy eyes drink him in like I'm dying of thirst and he's a cool glass of water. His muscles ripple as he turns to face me. I knew he had them. It's obvious even with a shirt on, but they are magnificent.

Would it be weird if I licked his six pack?

He's fucking perfect.

Of course he is.

"Alex," he growls.

My head snaps up to focus on him before dropping down his body again. There's a sternness in his tone, but not like I'm in trouble; it's just how he speaks. It adds to his sex appeal and right now, I'm finding everything about him so hard to resist.

For a split second, I lift my focus back to his face. I've

never had an impulse so strong, and before either of us know it, we're moving toward each other. Our lips crash together, his tongue invading my mouth. As my arms wrap around his neck, he grabs the back of my thighs, lifting me up as I wrap my legs around his hips.

My back slams into the wall of the kitchen as his hands roam under my shirt. Finding nothing underneath, with a growl I feel vibrating in his chest, he breaks the kiss and asks, "You're naked underneath this?"

I can only nod, as my own hands skate over the muscles in his shoulders and down his back as I take him in greedily. Every time we've been together, it's been rushed and I don't think this time will be any different.

He brings me back to the moment as his mouth finds my neck, sucking on the sensitive skin at the base, working his way up with nips and licks. Instinctively, I tip my head back to give him more access. I need more.

As his lips coast over the shell of my ear, he murmurs, "I'm going to fuck you so hard that even when I'm no longer inside you, you're still going to feel me there." He dips his fingers into my already drenched pussy. "I'm going to fill up your perfect little cunt until it's stretched around my cock and you're begging me to stop because you can't take anymore."

The heat of his body pressed against mine through the t-shirt I'm wearing and the dirty words he's just spoken are like a match to a flame, igniting a fire inside of me.

"Bastian," I moan.

His voice is gruff, as if his own words have turned him on. "I know, princess."

With me still in his arms, he carries me out of the kitchen, down the hallway and into his bedroom. He sets me down on the bed and I scoot into the middle as I pull off my t-shirt and throw it on the floor. I'm completely naked for him. His eyes darken as he looks down on me from his spot at the end of the bed. Sunlight beams in through the open curtains and casts a bronze glow over his skin.

In a matter of seconds, his sweats are gone and his delicious cock is jutting out proudly. My tongue comes out to swipe across my lips when he grips the base and strokes himself.

"Spread your legs and show me how you play with your pretty pussy, baby."

Without question, I widen my legs and slip my hand between them. I'm soaked for him and the first swipe of my fingers over my clit has me moaning.

"Do you do this when you're home alone?"

Words won't form. I can only nod as my eyes feast on him.

"Do you think of me when you're finger fucking your-self, princess? Do you imagine it's my fingers filling you up?"

Oh God, yes.

My head falls back as my fingers, alternate between rubbing my clit and dipping into my tight channel. When his big hand grips my ankles and he tugs me closer to the end of the bed, I yelp in surprise. My hand pauses, unsure what to do.

"Don't you dare *fucking* stop."

"Bastian, please," I beg.

I need his hands on me. I need him to fill me. Now.

"I know. Just play with that pussy until you come. I want to see how you get yourself off." His voice is a rasp that casts over me, heightening my desire.

With the heat in his gaze spurring me on, I feel sexy and confident, even spread out on full display for him. It's just another thing he does to me that nobody else ever has. I like it when he watches me. Just like when I'm with him and we have sex in places we might get caught.

It doesn't take long and I'm coming, my fingers rubbing over my clit as I watch the most beautiful man I've ever seen stroke his cock. He looks like *Michelangelo's David*—but his cock is much, much bigger.

As I'm coming down from my high, I hear the tearing of the condom packet and then the bed dips as he climbs between my legs. The tip of his cock rubs against my sensitive clit as he cups my breasts, pulling one nipple into his mouth. His tongue twirls around before flicking it, then moving onto the other one. He spends equal time on each one until I can't take any more.

When I'm close to begging him to fuck me, he drags a hand down my stomach until his thick fingers are filling me. My hands rest on his shoulders as he starts at an agonizingly slow pace.

"Please, Bastian. I can't take it anymore."

"I think you can take so much more," he murmurs.

His teeth graze over my nipple and the pain mixed with pleasure has me nearing my climax again.

"More. I need more."

With that, he lifts himself off of my body and thrusts into me.

It's the most wonderful feeling as my walls stretch around him. He gives me a minute to get used to the feeling of him inside me before he starts moving. I teeter on the edge of my climax, and with two hard thrusts, I come again.

My legs are lifted onto his shoulders and he increases his thrusts, almost punishingly pounding into me finding his own release. With a roar, he comes. His chin drops to his chest as it rises and falls with his labored breaths.

As he collapses on top of me, I drop my legs to the side, brought back to reality with a bang.

What the fuck am I doing?

I push him off of me, ignoring the look of confusion that pulls his brows together, and climb from the bed. Swiping up my discarded t-shirt, using it as a barrier as I back up to the door.

"Alex, what's wrong?"

Oh, God, he looks so fucking hot. Naked with a slight sheen of sweat over his body and his softening cock resting on his stomach. It takes everything in me not to run back into his arms and beg him to do it all again.

To own me.

Instead, with as much cool indifference as I can muster, I say, "I don't know what that was, but it won't be happening again. When we see George and his family, that should be the only time you touch me." I motion between us with my finger "This was a mistake and I'm going to say that in my sleep deprived state I didn't know what I was doing. I'm going to get ready."

I practically run back to my room, not giving him a chance to respond. We both know I'm right. With my back to the door, I pull in a deep, calming breath before blowing it out.

So much for keeping my distance from him.

After a moment of meditation, I push away from the door and go about getting myself ready. If I wasn't going to be debt free at the end of this, then I'd have left by now.

Neither of us has said a word since we left the apartment. I'm tempted to ignore him for the whole journey, but then we'd be under pressure when questions start flying at us.

At first, I tried to sleep, but now that I'm awake, I can't. Whenever I close my eyes, I see him above me, as he thrusts in and out.

Sebastian drives the rental car and I stare out of the window as the bustling sidewalks and gleaming buildings turn into less densely populated areas with more greenery than buildings.

We've been driving for around half an hour when I decide there's no time like the present to break the awkward silence.

"So, I guess we should get a couple of things worked out before we arrive."

He flicks his gaze over to me for a moment before going back to the road. "Such as?"

I throw my hands in the air and blow out a breath of frustration. "I don't know, Sebastian. How about how we met? When did you propose? Do we live together? Are we in love? Things like that."

Calm as ever, he answers, "We met when you came to my club for a Christmas party. I proposed on Meghan and Cooper's wedding day. We were on the dance floor and I knew at that moment I wanted you as my wife. Yes, we live together. No, I don't do love."

Wow. Okay, so he's really thought about this.

Hold up. "I would be so pissed if you proposed to me on our best friends' wedding day. It's selfish. I wouldn't have said yes."

"I didn't get down on my knee. I just whispered it into your ear as we swayed to a song."

My voice is scratchy as I ask, "What song?" I clear my throat. "They'll ask."

He lifts one shoulder in a shrug. "I don't know. Maybe that one... What's it called? *Unconditional?*"

"Really?" My eyebrows reach for my hairline.

"I don't think it really matters, but if you do, you can choose what you want it to be."

Going back to the thing he'd said earlier, I say, "You know, I wouldn't marry you if you didn't love me. You're going to have to pretend you do, because nobody willingly gets married to someone who doesn't love them."

"Fine. I will pretend. What else do you want to cover?"

"Okay, we met just over two years ago. When did we start dating?"

"Straightaway."

"Why did you propose?"

He thinks on this one for a while, before asking, "Will they really ask that?"

"I would." I shrug.

"Fine. I proposed because you captured my attention from day one. You're nothing like anyone I've ever met. You're committed to your job, independent, and yet not afraid to ask for help when you need it. You're loyal and would do anything for the people you love. You're confident within yourself, and you're not brash but almost reserved in the way you carry yourself. Is that enough?"

My cheeks heat at his words, and I've never been more grateful that my blush isn't visible to him. I didn't think he'd say something so... I don't know. I'm at a loss for words.

"Is it true?" I croak out.

"I wouldn't lie to you. You're an amazing woman, Alex."

For someone else.

He doesn't say it, but it hangs in the air between us.

In an effort to ease the tension inside myself, I blurt, "Why do you want this club?"

Out of the corner of my eye, I see him flick his gaze to me before returning it to the road.

"Not that it matters for our plan, but it would be the perfect location for what I have planned."

"I'd say it matters. You're asking me to lie for you."

He's quick with his reply when he states, "In exchange for me clearing your student loans."

When he says it like that it makes me feel dirty and like maybe this is a huge mistake.

"Is that the real reason? That it's the perfect location?"

He breathes out an exasperated sigh and I don't miss the way he squeezes the steering wheel. "Yes, Alex. That's the real reason."

I want to ask him more about what his plan is, but it's not really my place and I'm not sure he'd tell me.

We sit in silence for a while, the sound of the radio in the background the only noise. I'm thinking over his words as he concentrates on the road ahead.

A sense of longing is in my tone and I can't quite hide it when I say, "I don't have a ring."

He tips his head toward the glove compartment. "Check in there."

My brow pulls together. When did he have time to get a ring? Curiosity gets the better of me and I pop open the handle of the glove compartment to reveal a teal ring box from a famous Fifth Avenue jeweler sitting atop the car paperwork. My lips part slightly as my brow furrows deeper with a mix of confusion and curiosity.

"What did you do, Sebastian?"

"We need it to look real."

"Right, but we could have said it was getting resized or something. You didn't need to go and buy an actual ring. It's only for a week."

Ignoring me, he asks, "Are you going to take it out and look at it or just stare at the box?"

Tentatively, I pick up the ring box, closing the glove compartment before I sit back in my chair. A sense of nervousness takes over me as I contemplate whether or not I want to start whatever is about to happen.

I always thought the first ring that would go on my left ring finger would come with a proposal from the man I love. A real proposal. That he'd get down on one knee and tell me how much he loved me and that he couldn't wait to spend the rest of eternity with me.

Is it bad luck to put a ring on your finger if you aren't really engaged?

My chest tightens as my breaths come in short, sharp pants. Every inch of my skin prickles with a cold chill and this unexplainable sense of doom chokes me.

In a voice I don't recognize, I gasp out, "Stop the car!"

My eyes dart out of the passenger window as I look for something to focus on. But we're moving too fast, and the scenery flies by, adding to the dizziness now distorting my vision.

"Please, stop the car." Tears prick at the back of my eyes and I can't catch my breath.

Oh God, I'm going to cry.

I force in a deep breath, then count it out. One. Two. Three. Four.

"I'm going to find somewhere safe to stop. It's okay." Sebastian sounds far away, like he's a hundred feet away, not right next to me.

A hand gently rests on my jean clad thigh and he rubs his thumb back and forth, grounding me. I can't stop the tears as they flow or the way my body shakes. The urge to flee overwhelms me and as he pulls the car over to the side of the road, I grip the door handle, ready to bolt.

When the car comes to a stop, he unclips my seat belt before I can do it myself. I don't put up a fight when he drags me over the center console and into his arms. One hand rubs up and down my back as the other holds my head to his shoulder.

I drop the ring box I've been clutching as if it's on fire. It falls into the space between us. Freed from it, I clutch onto his black t-shirt and bury my face into the crook of his neck, inhaling his woodsy scent.

Minutes, maybe hours, pass as he holds me just as tightly as I cling to him. After a while, my body relaxes and my breathing finally finds a less frantic rhythm. I dry my face on his shoulder, but I don't sit back, not yet.

"You want to talk about what just happened?"

I shake my head and he squeezes me, then gently pushes me back to look at my face.

"I think maybe you should tell me why a ring box has you freaking out like that." His voice is soothing as he wipes away the tears on my cheeks.

"I'm fine. I don't exactly know why that just happened."

God, I thought I was done with these attacks. It's been years. I thought the therapy had worked and I had figured out ways to channel my anxiety. It's not like I'm still in law school, with all the stress and pressure that comes with that. The work I put in and the coping mechanisms I have all went out the window the moment I saw that ring box.

As my gaze roams his face, I make a mental note to call my old therapist when I get back to New York. I'm probably making a big deal out of nothing; it was just a ring.

It doesn't mean anything.

As I go to move back to my seat, he grips my hips keeping me in place. Looking at his hands, then back up to his face, I allow the question in my mind to coat my face.

"You forgot your ring."

I go to move again, replying with, "I don't need it."

His grip tightens on me. "I beg to differ."

"I have an aversion to rings," I lie.

He lifts a brow and pops open the box to reveal a

stunning cushion-cut yellow diamond halo engagement ring.

My jaw drops before I snap it shut and say, "What the actual fuck, Sebastian?"

A boyish charm about him, he asks, "You don't like it?"

"How much was it? Like twenty grand?" I'm mesmerized by it.

"I don't think you're supposed to ask your fiancé how much he spent on your engagement ring."

"Fake." My eyes are still on the ring nestled in the black velvet of the box.

"What?" he asks, confusion evident in his tone.

"Fake fiancé. You're my fake fiancé."

"Right, well, real or fake, I'm pretty sure you're not supposed to ask, but you don't need to worry, I haven't done the traditional two months salary thing. You'd end up with something akin to the Hope Diamond if I did"

"You should return it," I murmur, unconvincingly.

I want to try it on.

Not on my ring finger, of course.

I don't want or need any more bad luck when it comes to my love life.

"I'm not returning it."

I lift my gaze to his as I ask, "Why not?" I don't give him time to reply as I continue, "I guess you can keep it for your real fiancée. We'll just say that we're getting the ring resized."

Again, I try to climb back into my seat, but he grabs

my hand and slips the ring onto my finger. It fits perfectly, as if he'd had my measurements when he picked it out.

"Why did you do that?" I ask, my voice quiet, none of the annoyance I want to convey is in my tone as I fix my gaze on the ring.

"I'm not having people think I can't get my fiancée's ring size right the first time. Anyway, it's your ring. When all of this is over, you can keep it."

He's clearly lost it. Where am I going to wear a ring that probably cost more than all of my personal possessions?

With as much conviction as I can muster, I say, "I can't keep it, Bastian."

His voice drops when he says, "I like it when you call me that."

I lift my eyes to his and look into the depths of his blue-green eyes. I don't know what's happening. Who buys an expensive-ass ring for their fake fiancée? And then tells her she can keep it when their charade is over with?

"Get out of your head and don't overthink it, Alex."

Even as I move back to my seat, I'm still in a haze, my focus back on the ring that now sits proudly on my finger.

As I buckle myself in, my eyes are on the ring and my mind on the trouble I've got myself into with this man.

At this point, I'm not even sure having him pay off my student loans will be worth it.

THIRTEEN

Alex

It's past noon by the time we arrive in Lake Geneva, our pit stop for my breakdown, and an accident slowed us down. The radio has filled the intermittent quiet in the car. Sebastian focused on the drive and navigating traffic, whereas I stared at the ring on my finger as we discussed our backstory and I contemplated all my life choices that brought me to this predicament.

The navigation announces that we've arrived at our destination, and I look up from my lap to find a shiny black wrought-iron gate opening up in front of us. I gasp at the house I can see in the distance down the fir tree-lined driveway as Sebastian eases the car forward.

It's beautiful.

Thankfully, the coffee I brought along with us has perked me up enough that I don't feel like I could fall asleep anymore.

A tension has taken over me that I can only blame

on the ring on my finger. As we drive along the driveway, I feel some of it ease out of my body as I take in the
arca. A lot of land surrounds the house, and in the
distance, I see a person riding a horse along the
hedgerow that separates the garden from the beach of
the lake.

There's a sense of tranquility in the air. I look up at
the house and the front door opens. George and a lady
who I assume is his wife stand on the front steps. She's
dressed in a flowing mu-mu, with bangles climbing up
her forearm. Her gray hair is down, reaching her shoulders, with a head scarf wrapped around it. It's giving
hippie chick and I love it.

The house is a three story red brick home with a
porch wrapped around as far as I can see. Shrubbery and
flowers line the porch, giving the house a welcoming
feeling.

Sebastian pulls the car to a halt and I hang back as he
steps out. I need a moment to collect my thoughts. To get
into character. Two deep breaths in and out, and I reach
for the handle just as the door is pulled open.

"Come on, sweetheart. Let's go greet our hosts."

I love the way he says *sweetheart*. Like every letter is
pronounced and clear as it rolls off of his tongue. Sebastian holds out a hand for me, and as I place my own in
his, he drops a kiss to the back of it.

"It's so lovely to finally meet you both. George has
told me all about you. I'm Miriam, George's keeper,"
Miriam chuckles, pulling me into her arms.

"Oh, it's nice to meet you too, Miriam. I'm Alex, and this is Sebastian."

Miriam lets go of me and pulls Sebastian into her embrace before stepping away, saying, "Oh my. Aren't you delicious? If I wasn't already married and twice your age, I'd be trying to steal you from this beautiful woman."

Sebastian chokes at Miriam's words and squeezes the back of his neck, suddenly bashful.

"Stop embarrassing the kids and let's get them settled in." George smirks as he admonishes his wife.

Miriam loops her arm through mine as she turns towards the house, almost conspiratorially, she says, "He's such a spoilsport."

"I can hear you," George calls.

"I know," she sing-songs back, winking at me.

George chuckles at his wife's antics. "Our youngest is joining us later this evening as well. Jensen is an actor. He's based in LA, but his work has him traveling all over the world. I think you and him will get along great, Sebastian. Plus, you're all about the same age, so you won't need to hang out with us old farts all the time."

"Come, let's get you two settled in and then we can introduce you to our middle child, Daniel and his wife, Sophie," Miriam commands.

I can already tell this is going to be an eventful week.

We're led through the front door and into the hall-way, which has a vaulted ceiling that showcases a crystal chandelier. Ahead of us is a staircase that leads to the second level of the house. It sweeps up the center of the room, like a statement piece.

With her arm still linked with mine, Miriam leads us up the stairs. "We've put you in the guest bedroom. It has its own bathroom and is away from the other rooms, so you can be sure you have complete privacy."

Bedroom. As in we're sharing a room.

"I thought we would be staying in separate rooms," I murmur.

Miriam chuckles. "We aren't stuffy like that, dear. Honestly, you're young and in love. We wouldn't want you feeling like you have to sneak around. We're *very* open in this house."

Great.

Just what I need, to share a room with a man I have no self control around. I mean, this morning was a prime example of how easy I am around him.

We make our way to the guest room with Miriam and George chatting about the history of the house and telling stories of their children. It's obvious they love their family and that it's important to them. The whole time, Sebastian is in a weird funk, hardly saying a word to anyone. It worries me, but I'm too busy carrying the conversation to be able to ask him what's wrong.

When we arrive at the door, Miriam opens it with a flourish, her dress fluttering around her as she prances into the room.

Like the rest of the house, it's beautiful.

Heavy drapes hang around the window, a king size

bed sits against the back wall with pillows and a throw in fall colors spread over it. It looks so inviting. My eyes roam around the room in search of a couch, or something that I can sleep on, but I come up short.

Fuck.

Oblivious to my inner turmoil, Miriam points to the door next to the bed and whispers, "The bathroom is through there and it has a wonderful view of the lake from the tub, which can fit at least two people in. Also, don't worry about anyone peeping in. We have a privacy film on the window."

She hunches her shoulders in excitement before walking to the door with George, blowing us a kiss.

George looks at the watch on his wrist. "I'll come and collect you in two hours."

With the door closed behind them, neither Sebastian nor I say a word until we're convinced they've gone. I move toward the bed, flopping onto my back as I blow out a breath.

I think I'm in over my head here.

They're so nice and I feel so bad for lying to them.

Sebastian sits on the bed next to me. "You okay?"

"Not really. I feel bad."

He nods his head but doesn't say anything else. Instead, giving me the space to think over what we're doing. When I can't take the silence or closeness anymore, I climb from the bed, grabbing my bag on my way to the bathroom. I come to a stop in the doorway as I call over my shoulder, "I'll sleep on the floor. I don't think it's wise that we share a bed."

Closing the door behind me, I don't give him a chance to respond.

I come up short as I take in the bathroom. It's like something out of a home and country magazine, with its wooden floors and white furnishings. Along one wall is a white marble topped unit that houses the sinks, with the toilet next to it. Opposite to that is the walk-in shower, with a glass wall to close it off. Under the window that covers the whole of the back wall, floor to ceiling, is the bath. And what a bath it is. Through the window you can see the expanse of lawn that leads to the dark blue water of Lake Geneva.

With the clawfoot tub filling up, I stand in front of the window taking in the scenery. It's peaceful here. I can't wait to explore the area, anything to avoid having to lie to Miriam and George's faces anymore than necessary.

I undress before stepping into the deep tub. My body and mind are tired from the stress of being near Sebastian and the late night of partying. I'd gone out to avoid being in his space. Stupidly, I'd thought I could find someone to take over my body so that I could forget about him, instead I'd spent the night talking Winnie's ear off about the guy who makes me feel things I hadn't in a long time.

With my eyes closed, I lean back, luxuriating in the hot water. I'm physically and mentally exhausted. This is the first trip I've had in nearly three years. I've thrown myself into my work, wanting to climb the ranks and excel in my career. Relationships have gone on the back burner because one man has occupied my thoughts whenever I've tried to be intimate with someone.

I've compared *everyone* to him.

And yet he's been able to go about his life as if I meant nothing.

Because it did mean nothing.

Before I drift to sleep in the bath, I vow to myself that when I get back to New York, I'm going to make an effort to start dating again.

Two strong arms scoop me out of the bath and I snuggle into the wall of muscle as I'm held against a warm chest. My body shivers from the chill as the chest I'm pressed to grumbles.

"What were you thinking? Alex, wake up."

I don't want to wake up. I want to stay in the land of make believe where everything is perfect and I can be free from the man who has captivated my thoughts. Hold on. Remembering where we are and what I was doing, my eyes snap open as I realize I'm completely naked and Sebastian is carrying me out of the bathroom.

This is embarrassing.

"What are you doing?" I ask, ignoring his question.

He looks down at me and it's then I see his brow is wrinkled with concern. I run my fingers over the lines, in an attempt to smooth them out. In return, he clutches me closer.

"You could have drowned! Do you realize that?" he admonishes me as he comes to a stop next to the bed. He sets me down on it, taking a step back as he rubs his hand over the back of his neck while he turns away from me.

"I was fine. I wasn't anywhere near drowning."

"You don't know that. You were asleep for Christ's sake. If I'd have come in any later, you could have been under the water. You were shivering when I pulled you out, Alex." He starts pacing.

My eyes track his every movement, trying to understand why he's so concerned. "If I'd gone under the water, I'd have woken up Sebastian. You're overreacting."

I stand from the bed, conscious that I'm still naked and move to the bathroom to grab a towel. When I return, he's standing in front of the window.

"Have you calmed down now? You really don't need to worry about me. I'm an adult."

When he turns to face me, his eyes are cold and the concern that was in his voice is gone as he replies, "I wasn't really worried about you drowning, Alex. I was worried about the mess I'd have to clear up and how it would impact my deal with George if my fake fiancée drowned in his bathtub."

I flinch at his words as I bite my bottom lip to stop

myself from crying. Without saying a word, I walk back into the bathroom, locking the door behind me. I lean against it as a single tear tumbles down my cheek.

Wow, he can really be a cold hearted bastard.

To think that I thought he'd have cared even an iota about me. Him carrying me out of the bath was just because he wanted to protect his deal. His image.

Well, fuck you, Sebastian Worthington.

Securing my fluffy gray towel around my body, I empty the bath, grab my bag and walk out of the bathroom with my head held high. I feel his gaze on me as I cross the room and walk into the closet.

Dropping my bag on the bench in the middle of the room—Jesus this closet is as big as my bedroom—I walk back to the door and close it, shutting him out.

With my suitcase open, I start pulling out clothes and hanging them on the rails on one side of the room. Savannah did a good job when she repacked for me. *That feels like ages ago.* Instead of having outfits that would be more suited for the boardroom, I now have clothes a fake fiancée would wear. A mixture of dresses, jeans, and tops fill the space.

My shoes are unpacked last, and as I open the final pocket on my case, I'm greeted by a humongous dark purple cock. I snap my suitcase shut and look over my shoulder to the door, double checking he hasn't snuck in. Moving away from the offending bag, I grab my phone from the chest in the corner of the room and pull up the group chat.

ALEX

What the hell, Savannah?

MEGHAN

What's she done?

BEN

Oh, this is going to be good!

She doesn't respond for the longest time that I wonder if she's going to respond at all. Her name pops but as three little bubbles dance on the screen.

SAVANNAH

I take it you found them.

ALEX

THEM?!

I saw one thing and slammed the suitcase shut.

SAVANNAH

Oh.

ALEX

Oh? What were you thinking?

SAVANNAH

That you might have a little fun while you're away?

ALEX

I don't need to have that kind of fun on a work trip.

I decide not to tell them about how the trip has

progressed and is now as far from a business trip as it could get.

> **SAVANNAH**
> I mean, it wouldn't hurt.

> **MEGHAN**
> Is someone going to clue us into what is going on?

> **BEN**
> I think it might be sex related.

> **ALEX**
> I could have been stopped at the airport.

> **SAVANNAH**
> It's just some toys. I didn't think you were that much of a prude.

She's right. But I'll be damned if I tell her that.

I'm over reacting, and if it was me that had put sex toys in her friend's luggage, I would have been teasing them and laughing it off. That's what I should be doing.

I look down at my hand, grasping my phone. The light reflects off of the ring on my finger.

It's a beautiful ring.

I'm not going to keep it.

When this is done, I'll give it back.

> **ALEX**
> You're right, sorry, a lot has gone on in the last twenty four hours. Speak soon.

With that, I switch off my phone and slink down to

the floor. Doubt starts to creep in as a heaviness settles in the pit of my stomach. I hate lying to people, especially nice ones like Miriam and George. As I look around the closet, I wonder if I can hide out here for a week.

No, I can't do that. I have to remember what I'm doing this for.

Just before we left Chicago, Sebastian confirmed he'd paid off my student loans. A quick online check confirmed that was the case. Now I'm stuck in my own web of deceit.

When did everything get so out of hand?

FOURTEEN

Sebastian

I'd have to be blind to have missed the look of hurt that flashed across Alex's face before she turned away. A heaviness I've never felt settles on my chest, and I rub my fist across it in an attempt to relieve the ache.

She'd been in the bath for so long and I'd contemplated leaving her in there, but when I knocked on the door and she didn't answer, I knew something wasn't right. Seeing her so close to going under was... terrifying. Her chin was already under the water that had long since gone cold, and her lips were on the cusp of turning blue. I could feel the shivers wracking her body as I pulled her out.

A knock sounds at the door, pulling me from my thoughts. Reluctantly, with one last look at the closed closet door, I go to answer it. George greets me with a wide smile that I don't return.

"Sebastian, are you and Alex ready for lunch?"

"Alex is just getting ready. Give us five and we'll be right with you."

"Of course. I'll wait at the top of the stairs. Take your time. Jensen, our youngest, has arrived and is looking forward to meeting you both."

"Can't wait. We won't be long."

Closing the door on him, I turn to the closet door. Hesitation has me pausing before I suck in a breath and cross the room. My hand is on the door handle, ready to walk in, but I pause. She's already pissed at me, and I need her to at least pretend she likes me when we go downstairs. I rap my knuckles on the oak.

"Alex? George has come to collect us. Do you want me to tell him you're not fe—" the words die on my tongue as the door swings open and Alex emerges.

She looks fucking delectable. Her hair is tied in a low bun with two pieces left out to frame her face. She's wearing a white dress that hugs her at the waist but is puffy on the sleeves and hem. It comes to mid thigh, and she's paired it with a pair of green wedged heels.

What catches my eye is the deep v-neck on the dress. It's just the right amount of cleavage to make the dress sexy, yet still classy. She breezes past me and I get a whiff of her spicy lavender-amber perfume.

Fuck my life.

"Do you need to change?" she asks as she walks into the bathroom and applies a sweep of lipgloss to her full lips.

179

Her gaze connects with mine in the mirror and when she raises a brow at me, I spring into action, tugging my t-shirt over my head as I walk into the closet.

Business.

I'm here to do business, not get my dick wet. *Again.*

From my case, I put on a white tank before pulling a shirt from the hangers, glad I'd organized myself while Alex was in the bathroom. With a squirt of aftershave, I leave my black jeans on and slip my feet into a pair of black suede loafers, then walk out to meet her.

"Ready?" I ask.

She looks up from examining her nails, flicks her eyes over me, and then nods and walks toward the door. I follow behind her, admiring the long line of her legs.

True to his word, George is waiting for us at the top of the stairs and when he sees Alex, his eyes light up. "Don't you look like a vision. Come, a late lunch is ready, and the family is waiting to meet you."

He holds out his arm, and Alex links hers with his. My jaw clenches at the sight. She smiles at him as he leads the way.

The house is vast and once we reach the bottom of the stairs, it becomes clear just how large it is. George leads us down a long corridor toward the back of the house, pointing out the study, library, bathroom, *one* of the lounges and a large dining room.

He seems to have done well for himself, but I can't help but feel a sense of resentment toward him.

"The dining room is more for entertaining large

groups. When it's just the family, we like to use the kitchen. It feels less formal and has a more homely feel to it. I hope you don't mind if we eat there," George babbles, looking as if he would have all the meals we'll have held in there if Alex so desired.

A genuine laugh leaves Alex's mouth as she says, "Not at all, George. We want to feel part of your family, if that's okay?"

Maybe she does, but I have no such desire.

"That is fantastic, as that's what we want too."

All but ignoring me as we walk, it seems if I just keep my mouth shut, Alex will charm the pants off of George.

The kitchen is a hive of activity when we arrive. Miriam fusses around, plating up an assortment of delicious smelling dishes. One of their sons, that I can only assume is Daniel, is standing next to a stunning petite brunette woman, whispering who knows what in her ear. Whatever it is, she's barely able to contain the blush that steals across her cheeks as she swats at his chest.

"Get a room, will you?"

This must be Jensen, the movie star. I'm man enough to admit when a guy is attractive, and objectively speaking, he is. He's probably as tall as me, with striking blue eyes and almost jet black hair. He looks almost Mediterranean, but I'm guessing his tanned complexion doesn't come from a heritage, but more likely a sunbed.

George bellows to the room, turning all heads in our direction, "Everyone, this is Sebastian." He points behind him to me and I signal to the room with my hand as I curl my lip in what's supposed to be a smile. "And Alex, his fiancée."

"It's nice to meet you all," Alex mutters, a shyness taking over her.

Jensen stands from his seat at the kitchen island and stalks toward Alex. A cocky smirk lifts the corner of his mouth as he approaches.

Holding out his hand, he waits for her to take a hold of it. When she does, he brings it to his lips as he bends at the waist. "It's a pleasure to meet you, Alex."

I don't think anyone else sees it, but I see the moment her breath hitches and mouth falls open.

"You're Jensen Bennett," she mumbles, her voice all sultry and breathless.

Time to step in, because I'm not having my fiancée fall for another guy, no matter how fake our engagement is. I move behind Alex and slip my arm around her waist, thrusting my hand out to Jensen.

Not today, buddy.

"That I am, sweetheart." He takes a hold of my outstretched hand with a firm grip. "It's nice to meet you, man."

"Jensen, stop trying to flirt with Alex. She's an engaged woman," Miriam scolds.

Jensen throws a wink at Alex before turning around and walking back to his seat at the kitchen island.

"Come, take a seat at the table," George calls.

With my arm still around Alex's waist, I guide her to the seats at the oak table, far away from Jensen.

The kitchen is a modern space with a large island at the center of it. White cabinets fill one wall with the perfect view of Lake Geneva on display through the sliding doors on another. Pulling out a seat for Alex, I push her in once she's settled, taking the one next to her.

"I'm Sophie, and this is my husband, Daniel. It's nice to meet you both."

"It's nice to meet you, too," Alex and I say in unison, before we exchange a look of amusement at our synchronization.

Sophie takes the seat next to Alex with Daniel taking the one next to her. Jensen waltzes over and sits opposite Alex. His focus is on her, even when Daniel tries to draw him into a conversation.

What the fuck is wrong with this guy?

Clearing my throat doesn't break the *fucking* staring competition they're having.

Almost as if on instinct, I rest my hand on the back of Alex's neck, turning her head and capturing her lips with mine. She doesn't pull away, instead turning to rest her hands on my chest. *Like it's the most natural fucking thing in the world.*

I break the kiss and rest my forehead on hers, as I pick up her hand and play with the seventy thousand dollar engagement ring *I* put on her finger. Her gaze drops to it before lifting back to mine.

So nobody can hear I lean in and whisper in her ear, "Don't forget whose ring is sitting on your goddamn finger, Alex. I'm not beyond bending you over this table and fucking you so he gets the message."

Her breath hitches, and if I didn't know any better, I'd think my words had turned her on. Well, I do know she likes the risk that somebody could see, but we've never gone as far as having someone watch us. My hand itches to slip under her dress and find out if my 'fiancée' is as drenched for me as I think she is.

I turn back to the table and find George and Miriam smiling like two proud parents. At least they're buying our whole facade. The quicker they do, the quicker we can get out of here.

Lunch goes by without incident if you don't count Jensen, *'The Dickhead',* flirting outrageously with Alex. Instead of being my dutiful fiancée, she flirted right back.

Okay, so maybe it wasn't right back. Maybe she was just being her friendly, sweet self.

Or not. I don't really have a fucking clue.

She's been adamant to keep me at a distance ever since that night we first met, and it's worked well until I roped her into my scheme. Now I regret not getting to know her more, to find out if she's usually a flirty person or just like this with people she has an interest in.

Instead of allowing her the time to wrap her head around the rock I'd put on her finger, I should have demanded she tell me things about herself. Like the fact that she gives her smiles out freely. Or that she laughs loudly and without being self conscious of how she might sound when she finds something funny.

All day, I watch her draw the Bennett family under her spell. They hang on every word she says and delight in her company.

Right now, she's pulling Miriam in for a hug as she says goodnight.

"Thank you so much for today. I've had the best time. Coming here was just what I needed."

"You're both welcome here anytime," Miriam offers.

I wrap my arm around Alex's waist and tuck her under my arm before replying, "I have no doubt we'll be back. We'll see you in the morning for that trail walk."

"Goodnight, and thank you again."

I steer Alex toward the staircase as I ask, "Did you have a good day?"

She's all sleepy and instead of pulling away like I expect her to, she snuggles into my side as I drop a kiss on the top of her head. She's the perfect height that it isn't awkward when she's in this position.

"Such a good day. I was nervous about coming." She lifts her head to look me in the eye as we reach the top of the steps. "What with everything."

What do I say to that? I can't tell her I'm glad she came or that I couldn't imagine doing this with anyone else because that might give her the wrong impression. I don't want to ruin her day by reminding her of what is at stake.

Alex leads the way into the bedroom. I close the door as she walks into the closet. I suspect to change, until she walks out a moment later carrying a blanket, then snags a pillow from the bed.

"What are you doing?"

"I figured I'd need a blanket and a pillow for my bed," she shrugs as if it's no big deal, throwing the blanket out on the floor and plopping the pillow at one end.

I'm still by the door but take a few tentative steps further into the room. She's crazy if she thinks I'm letting her sleep on the floor.

"We can share the bed, Alex. It's big enough for us both."

"No offense, but I don't want to share a bed with you."

It's hard not to take offense to that, but I put on my big boy pants and walk to the closet, calling out to her over my shoulder, "Fine, if you insist on one of us sleeping on the floor, I will. You can take the bed."

"It's okay. I don't mind."

Fucking hell. Does she have to be so argumentative with everything?

She breezes past me as she walks to the bathroom and closes the door. The water starts running and my mind fills with images of Alex under the spray of the water. Naked and running her hands over her body.

Adjusting my now semi hard cock, I enter the closet and undress, urging myself to get my shit together.

I've never lived with a woman, but as I pull on my navy pinstripe pajama bottoms, I take in the half of the wardrobe now filled with Alex's clothes.

Sure, I've slept over at a woman's house, but I can't say I've ever gone on a tour of their closet space. Besides, this isn't any woman, this is Alex. This is Alex's clothes hanging up in the same space that my clothes are. I'm fully prepared for panic to overwhelm me, but seeing her clothes with mine feels... almost normal.

I walk back to the bedroom at the exact moment Alex exits the bathroom, dressed in the same t-shirt she wore back in Chicago. It still looks fucking sexy.

As she moves to the pillow and blanket on the floor I say, "I'll sleep on the floor. You take the bed."

"I don't mind, honestly. I—"

I cut her off with a growl. "Alex."

With silent acquiescence, she moves to the bed, pulling back the covers and climbing under. I don't miss the way her t-shirt rides up her thighs as she climbs onto the high bed. Or the way she avoids looking at me. I walk to the bathroom and she rolls away so her back is to me and I can't help but feel dismissed.

I can already tell this week is going be fan-*fucking*-tastic.

I'm starting to regret this whole asinine plan.

FIFTEEN

Alex

Sebastian blows out a heavy breath for the fifteenth time in as many minutes. I swear to God, if he keeps making noises, I'm going to grab my pillow and smother him to death.

And make it look like he died in his sleep.

The sound of something cracking fills the air and I sit up. In the darkness of the room, I can only make out the lightness of the blanket at the bottom of the bed.

"What was that?" I ask, although I'm fairly certain it was a joint popping.

"It was nothing. Just go to sleep, Alex."

"I would, but someone, aka you, keeps making noises. Can't you just be quiet?"

It's a stupid question really because I'm certain that I'd be making twice as much noise if I'd actually had to sleep on the floor. It's just a thin, scratchy looking rug separating him from the hardwood floor.

"I'm really trying, Alex."

He sounds frustrated and it makes me feel bad. I drag my bottom lip between my teeth as I consider if I'm really about to say the words that come tumbling out of my mouth. "You can share the bed with me."

The blanket shifts as I think he turns to face me. He stands from the floor and walks to the side of the bed as I roll over so my back is to him.

On an exasperated sigh, I say, "Just stay on your side and let me get some sleep."

"I promise not to touch you."

The bed dips as he climbs in and even though he's not touching me, I can feel the heat from his body behind me.

As silence surrounds us, my eyes grow heavy and I wiggle further under the covers. My mind replays the events of the day, from my moment in the car to the possessive words Sebastian spoke to me when Jensen was flirting.

I won't lie, I liked the attention from Jensen. But, and it annoys me, I liked the possessiveness from Sebastian more.

My last thought before I slip into sleep has a smile drifting over my lips.

Tomorrow, I'm going to be the best damn fiancée that anyone has ever had. Sebastian Worthington, the commitment-phobe, is going to wish he never forced me to go along with this whole charade.

The front of my body is ridiculously warm and something incredibly hard is poking into my stomach. Slowly, my eyes open, coming face to face with a bare chest as I lie wrapped in Sebastian's arms.

I blink the sleep away as my memory mocks me with replays of me telling Sebastian he could sleep in the bed. But I also remember telling him to stay on his own side.

I go to move away, but the arm that's curving around my back tightens, as does the one resting on my thigh that's casually thrown over his leg. When I look up, I find two beautiful bluey-green eyes peeping down at me from under thick, long lashes.

His voice is thick with sleep as he tells me, "Stay put, Alex."

Feebly, I reply, "You were supposed to stay on your own side."

With my hands on his chest, I push away again, but this time instead of tightening his grip he loosens it, using the space it affords him to roll on top of me as I turn onto my back. Resting on his elbows, he settles between my legs, his gaze intent on me.

"What are you doing, Bastian?" I whisper, my voice coming out quiet and almost timid.

With him this close to me, I slip into using the nickname I've given him, except this time I'm not trying to tease him, far from it. My mind is too focused on taking in every facet of his face, from the dark stubble covering his jaw to his straight nose, full lips, and eyes that I could get lost in. I don't think I've ever taken the time to step back and just look at his face.

Of their own volition, my legs spread wider, and he drops down further, his hard cock resting against the heat of my pantie clad pussy. His voice is hoarse as he growls my name when I roll my hips into him.

"Please, Bastian."

I could lie to myself and say I don't know what I'm asking for, but I do know. What I want is to forget that I'm living a lie and that I can't have him in the way we're pretending we have each other now.

Do I really want him like that?

I mean, I know I want him in a physical way, there's no denying that, but do I want him to be mine and only mine?

"Come back, Alex. Get out of that pretty little mind of yours."

His voice pulls me from my wandering thoughts. I know one thing for certain is that I'm helpless to resist my need for him.

"There's nothing little about my mind," I quip back.

He runs his thumb down the column of my throat, his eyes following its path. I swallow thickly at the feel of his skin on mine and the strength of the man above me.

"Don't I just know it, princess. God, you could bring a grown man to his knees."

"Have I brought *you* to your knees?"

A smirk lifts one corner of his mouth, popping out his dimple. "Not a chance, sweetheart."

"Oh, really?" I arch an eyebrow in disbelief.

"I've got thick skin. It would take more than your quick little mouth to hurt me."

He runs his thumb over my lips and when I part them, it drops in. Gripping it between my teeth, I nip at the padded flesh. There's a storm of chemistry fizzing between us and at this point, in this position, it's inevitable that something is going to happen.

One quick fuck and then I'll go back to keeping that barrier between us, I promise myself. My hands rub down the sides of his waist until I reach the waistband of his pajama bottoms.

"Are you sure?" He pulls his thumb from between my teeth.

I nod, pushing his pants down his legs. He pulls away from me and helps me sit up to remove my t-shirt before laying me back and slipping off my panties. As he crawls up my body, I go to reach for his cock but he takes my wrist in his hands and lifts it above my head.

"No touching," he commands.

A whimper leaves my mouth. Not one to be told what to do, I try to use my other hand, but he grabs that one too, and now I'm being held captive by him.

In a vain attempt, I try to get him to release his hold on me. "It's going to be no fun if you don't let me touch you."

There's an almost wicked gleam in his eyes as a mischievous smirk falls on his lips. "I think we can have plenty of fun without you being able to touch me."

He dips his head, dropping kisses along the exposed column of my throat. When he grazes his teeth over the sensitive skin, I tip my head to the side, giving him more access. My hips rock against his cock, but it's not enough. I need him inside of me.

I'm not in the mood to argue with him. We're both naked. We should be doing other things that involve less words.

"You know, if you ask nicely, I might just give you *exactly* what you want."

My head snaps back to him. *Does he expect me to beg?*

"Please, Bastian. I want to touch you and taste you."

He twists his lips to the side as if he wants to think over my words. "No, I don't think that's quite right."

If he didn't have me restrained with one of his big hands, I'd throw my own up in exasperation at this point. "What do I have to say?"

His face takes on a level of seriousness that wasn't there a moment ago. "Tell me you need me."

My brow pulls in at his words. Tell him that I need him? In what way?

Not wanting to think too much into it, because that would be dangerous, I say, "I need you."

A look I can't quite decipher flits across his face. "That's my girl."

His girl?

He drops his head to the gap between my neck and shoulder, licking up the column of my throat. Nipping at my ear, he whispers, "There will be plenty of time for you to touch and taste me later."

I want to tell him there won't be a later, that this is a one time thing to satisfy both of our needs, but something tells me that now isn't the right time to talk about that. Even if I wanted to, he distracts me as he captures my mouth with his own.

His lips part, causing mine to open, and he takes the opportunity to tangle his tongue with mine. He's distracted and so his grip has loosened on my wrists, the intensity of the kiss has increased and I take the opportunity to bring his body closer.

The heavy weight of his cock rests between us, and as he brings my thigh up to wrap around his waist, it settles into the slit of my pussy.

He pulls away. "You're so fucking wet for me, Alex."

I want him so bad. All the time.

I close my eyes, willing the thought to go away.

Sebastian moves down my body, dropping kisses, licks and nips as he goes until he reaches my breasts, taking them in his hands and massaging them. I look down and watch with fascination at how perfectly they fit into his large palms.

When he tweaks each nipple in turn, I can't help but arch my back and release the moan that's built up. Sebastian takes my right nipple into his mouth, dragging his teeth over it, soothing it with his tongue, then sucking on it hard. The pain and pleasure mix only increases the ache building inside of me.

I shift my hips, looking for some sort of relief. Sebastian laughs as he moves further down my body, his licks and kisses continuing.

He buries his nose into the skin just above my pussy, pulling in a deep breath through his nose before he blows it out through his mouth right onto my clit. The cool air has a shiver racing through me and I moan, rolling my hips, trying to find his mouth.

"Are you feeling a little needy, princess?" He chuckles.

"Bas—" the words die on my lips when he sucks on my clit. My back arches off of the bed and my hands grab at the sheets looking for some sort of anchor.

Shit, I'm already so close.

He slips a finger into my pussy, twisting and turning it before he adds another. The pace that he fucks me with his fingers is both agonizingly slow and too fast at the same time. Bringing me further and further to the edge. He keeps up working on my clit, sucking it, grazing it with his teeth and flicking it with his tongue.

The pressure is building inside of me and when I'm about to implode, he pulls away, crawling up my body. A whimper leaves me before the realization of what he's just done sinks in. My eyes seek him out, demanding to know why he stopped.

He captures my mouth, giving me a taste of myself. Lining himself up with my entrance, he doesn't give me any warning, he just enters me with one smooth thrust. His hand covers my mouth as I scream out my orgasm into his palm.

Sebastian's body is still above me, the grinding of his pelvis the only movement. As I come down from my high, I grip onto his hips and urge him to move. He drops down to his elbows, lifting one of my legs and wrapping it back around his waist.

Our eyes are locked and the moment takes on a more... intimate feeling. When he starts moving, I close my eyes, enjoying the feeling of him stretching me.

He drops his forehead to my own, whispering, "Eyes on me, princess."

I do as he commands, looking into the depths of his eyes. It's then that I notice his usually more blue than green eyes have darkened to a more forest green. There's an intensity to them that holds me captive. Even if I wanted to, I can't tear my gaze away from his.

This is so much more intense than anything I've ever experienced. Every cell in my body is aware. Of him. Of me. But most importantly, of the feelings building inside of me.

It's as if I'm on the edge of coming, with Sebastian hovering over me, as he looks deep into my soul, that it all hits me.

This is more than just sex.

The one thing I've been scared of happening—falling for the unattainable guy—is already happening.

I'm not on the precipice, I've fallen over the edge of the cliff.

I shutter my eyes to keep my newly discovered secret from him.

The realization I've just stumbled upon, coupled with my impending orgasmic bliss, is too much to bear. My body tenses as my mind goes blank. I call out his name as an orgasm stronger than any I've had before hits me. He follows shortly after, coming deep inside of me. His jerky thrusts stroke my walls and extend my own orgasm as I grab onto the sheets beneath me.

He drops down onto his elbows and brushes a strand of hair from my forehead. My body slowly comes back to earth. I feel loose and languid, a lazy smile spreading across my lips. It falls from my lips when he moves and an abnormal amount of wetness seems to drip out of me.

Shit.

My hands push at his shoulders, desperate for him to move. My high shattered at the realization that we didn't use a condom. I'm on the pill, but Meghan was too and she still got pregnant.

He slips out of me and I briefly take in the look of confusion marring his handsome face as he moves to my side, giving me space. Ignoring the questions I can see forming, I jump from the bed and run to the bathroom.

How could I be so fucking stupid?

I've never not used double protection. Yes, I could argue that it's on both of us, but we all know men—most of them anyway—think only with their dicks when in the moment.

Using some tissue, I clean myself up, pushing out his fluid, or at least as much as I can. My mind tries to do the math on where I am in my cycle but too many emotions are fighting for supremacy and I can't figure it out.

Breathe. It's going to be okay.

I can't bring myself to move. I'm completely naked with nothing but his diamond ring shining up at me.

It's taunting me.

I want to throw this stupid ring at his stupid head.

Today, I'm going to find a drugstore and pick up a Plan B, then I'm going to take some much needed time out.

Without this ring and Sebastian Worthington.

I slip the rock off of my finger and carefully place it on the bathroom counter, my gaze lingering on it for a moment.

With a plan in place, I flush the toilet and turn on the walk-in shower. Tying my hair up, I step under the spray. My eyes close as the hot water runs down my body, but when two strong arms wrap around me, I let out a yelp of surprise.

Sebastian dips his head to whisper in my ear, "Whatever you want, I'll do it."

I turn in his arms, my eyes searching his face for what he could mean because I'm certain he doesn't mean what I think he does. He smooths a loose strand of hair off of my forehead as he cups my head.

My voice is soft as I ask, "What do you mean?"

"Just that. If you want us to only be fucking each other, I'll do it. You want to have only you fucking other people." His jaw ticks as his arms tighten around me for a fraction of a second. "I'll fucking do it, Alex. I'll do anything you want if it means I can bury my cock in you like I did this morning."

He smooths his hands down my back and over the curve of my ass, lifting me into his arms.

"Say yes," he murmurs against my lips, the tip of his hardening cock at my entrance.

I'm so tempted to say yes, to set my demands and take what I want, but what happens when he's had enough and tosses me to the side? Or when he finds another woman he wants more?

Pulling my bottom lip between my teeth, all I can get out is, "I'll think about it."

He looks at me for a moment, quietly assessing me. With a nod, he captures my lips with his own. Reluctantly, he says, "Okay, I'll take it. I'll shower after you."

He sets me on my feet, walking from the shower and picking up a towel on his way back to the bedroom. He pauses at the door, his chest bare and still wet from the shower, as he turns to say, "And Alex, don't take that ring off again."

When he's gone from the room, I look down at my left hand to find my engagement ring glistening up at me.

When did he put that on?

But more importantly, he realizes this is fake, right?

My mind is reeling from his request as I wash my body. The plan I made before I fell asleep last night has well and truly gone out of the window because I'm in no position to try and make him regret this when he's just told me he wants only me.

Today, I need some space from him because never in a million years did I think that Sebastian Worthington would come to me with an offer like that.

SIXTEEN

Sebastian

After my proposition in the shower this morning, I've barely seen Alex. We went down to breakfast with the Bennetts, where Alex outrageously flirted with the movie star–*fucking Jensen*. I barely kept my shit together.

Miriam and the girls went into town to do a bit of window shopping. When Miriam brought it up, Alex practically jumped out of her seat. She's been gone all day, which is why when George suggested we go to his favorite local bar, I couldn't say no.

I didn't think we'd go out and get absolutely shit-faced, but George and his sons know how to drink. It was harder to keep my motives under wraps as the alcohol flowed. I never would have drank that much, but I felt like I had something to prove. Especially with *fucking Jensen*. To top it all off, I didn't learn anything useful that will help with my plan. The whole lot of them seem to be obsessed with family and legacies.

We stumbled in at around four in the morning, so I shouldn't really be surprised when I wake up to a cold, empty bed. With my arm stretched, I search Alex's side of the bed for her anyway. When I come up short, I turn my head on the pillow, peeking open one eye.

Fuck.

My head is killing me.

The bathroom door clicks open, and when Alex comes into view, I sit up in bed faster than I should. My hand goes to my head as I take her in, starting at her feet encased in a pair of sneakers and traveling up to her hair that's pulled back in a high ponytail.

"Going somewhere?" I ask, rubbing at my forehead.

"Just downstairs." She sits on the end of the bed and fiddles with the white sheet. It's a stark contrast to her bronzed skin tone.

As I look down at the ring sparkling on her finger, I wonder for a moment what she would look like in a white wedding dress.

I quickly shut that thought process down and send up a silent prayer of thanks as Alex speaks again.

She's not looking at me, instead smoothing out and then folding a corner of the material in her hand. "Where did you go last night?"

"We just went to a bar," I reply, not sure where she's going with this.

"Did you... you know, hook up with anyone?" There's

a hint of insecurity in her tone, which I'm surprised to hear.

I can't help the sharp intake of breath that comes at her words. "Jesus Christ, Alex. I went out with the guy I'm trying to convince I'm *engaged* to you."

I look away from her, strangely hurt that she'd think so little of me. It's then that I see the glass of water on my bedside table and two painkillers. Snatching them up, I pop the pills and gulp the water down.

"I'm sorry. I don't know why I thought you would." More nervous twiddling ensues and I cover her hand with mine, causing her to lift her focus to me. "My mind's been a bit confused since yesterday morning. What with your proposal and all. I just don't understand what's changed."

That makes two of us.

"Look, I won't make any promises to you other than I won't fall in love with you, Alex. If you don't want either of us to see anyone else, then we won't see anyone else. The minute that becomes a thought for me, I will tell you and we will call this off. I enjoy your company as much as I enjoy being inside of you."

"I'd want us to be exclusive." It's barely audible, but I hear it nonetheless, and if I wasn't so hungover, I'd fist pump the air, then fuck her senseless.

"Okay, but if we're doing this, you've got to quit flirting with dickhead Jensen."

A laugh erupts from her mouth before she throws a

hand over it. "Dickhead Jensen? Really, Sebastian? What are you in sixth grade?"

Sheepishly, I shrug my shoulders, grabbing onto her hand and pulling her into my side. She settles into it as if she fits perfectly. I kiss the top of her head, closing my eyes as I inhale the sweet scent of her shampoo. The combination of her in my arms and a smell that is becoming so familiar eases some of the tension and pounding behind my eyes.

She goes to move away, but I tighten my grip around her and eventually she relents, resting her hand on my stomach. She shifts slightly to kick off her sneakers before swinging a leg over my thigh.

"This is reminding me of yesterday morning," I mumble, my voice thick with sleep.

"Don't fuck it up, Sebastian," she whispers.

I barely hear her as I slip into sleep, and yet her words are replaying in my mind even as I drift deeper.

I'm really hoping I don't fuck it up either, Alex.

It's late when I wake up. Even before I open my eyes, I know Alex isn't lying next to me. On my back with my eyes still closed, I think over everything that's happened in the last few days. From dragging Alex into my hare-brained scheme, her going along with it, and then us agreeing to sleep with each other exclusively.

I can't help the grin that spreads over my face. I bet I look like a damn fool. This woman.

She's something special.

The unfiltered thought has the smile dropping from my face before I can stop it. I don't know where that came from, but what I do know is I can't be thinking shit like that about Alex.

About anyone.

I can't start confusing fucking and a fake fiancée as anything more.

Throwing the covers off, I climb from the bed and walk to the closet. A quick look at the analog clock on Alex's bedside table tells me it's nearly dinnertime. I haven't slept this long since I was in college. *Maybe I should lay off the alcohol.* A quick shower, some fresh clothes, and I'm certain the remnants of my hangover will be gone.

When my head is covered by the fabric of my t-shirt as I get dressed, I feel a hand skate down my chest and over my stomach. Based on the zap of electricity that heats my blood, I know exactly who it is.

"I came to get you for dinner. Do you think we have time?"

I pull my head through the hole of my t-shirt, coming face to face with Alex's heated gaze. Her plump bottom lip is between her straight white teeth, and her focus is on the hand that is playing with the buckle of my belt.

"As much as it pains me to say this, I don't think we

do." I cup her cheek, tipping her face up to mine. "For everything I'd want to do to you, I'd need more time."

She blinks slowly up at me, her eyes dropping to my mouth. Unable to resist, I bend to capture her mouth with my own.

Just one kiss, I promise myself.

Alex takes a step closer to me, her hands resting on my waist as I hold her face between my palms. Her lips part with my own, and I sweep my tongue into her mouth, luxuriating in the taste. It's a mix of red wine and a salty yet sweet taste.

She moans, and as I drop my hands to her waist, her arms lift to wrap around my shoulders. Her chest presses closer to my own, and I tighten my grip on her waist.

Of their own accord, my hands smooth down to the backs of Alex's thighs and I lift her so her legs are wrapped around my waist.

Our mouths are still connected, like we're two starving people trying to devour a meal. My feet move to the unit that sits on the back wall of the closet and I place Alex atop it. I break the kiss and rest my forehead on hers, trying to calm down my racing heart.

This damn woman.

Remembering where we are and what we're here to accomplish, I step back before things go any further. Clearing my throat, I say, "Sorry, I shouldn't have done that. Not when I can't finish what I started."

Her fingers run over her swollen mouth, and she

blinks up at me as if she's not sure what the hell just happened.

Before she can say anything more, I sweep my thumb across her bottom lip and say, "Mark my words, though, Alex. When we've done what we need to do downstairs, I'm going to bring you back up here and fuck you into oblivion. You'll still be able to feel me deep inside that pretty little cunt of yours for weeks to come."

I drop my hand and step back out of her reach, scrubbing my hand over my chin. My eyes roam over her from head to toe. She looks a little shell shocked and—if the way she's wriggling on the counter is any indication—a lot horny.

"You need a minute?" I ask, certain that she does based on the fact she hasn't said a word since she ran her hand down my chest.

She only nods her head, but that's not going to do. As if I'm a glutton for punishment, I step back between her legs, running my thumb back over her delectable mouth. My eyes intent on her lips.

"I need you to use your words, Alex." Even to my own ears my voice is thick with desire.

"Yes—" she croaks out before clearing her throat. "I'm going to need a minute."

I drop a kiss on the top of her head before I walk out of the bedroom and make my way downstairs. I adjust myself in my jeans and will the hard on I've had since she touched me to deflate. The last thing I need is to walk into this kitchen with a tent in my jeans.

Sucking in a deep breath, I push open the kitchen door and walk into the room. George has Miriam between his body and the kitchen counter. She's giggling at something he's said. I fight the scowl that's trying to break out onto my face.

Sophie is sitting in Daniel's lap at the kitchen table, engrossed in the newspaper laid out in front of them. Jensen is nowhere to be seen.

When neither couple acknowledges that I've walked into the room, I clear my throat, stuffing my hands into the pockets of my dark blue jeans. George pulls away from Miriam, turning to face me. A smile stretches across his face, and he genuinely looks pleased to see me.

"Come in, Sebastian. Take a seat and I'll grab you a drink. We've got beer, whiskey, water, soda, wine?"

"Water would be great."

George chuckles as he moves to the cabinet and pulls out a glass. "We don't normally drink that much, but it's good to see you could keep up."

"I'm not sure I'll be doing it again."

I take a seat at the kitchen table with Sophie and Daniel. Sophie gives me a soft smile, running her fingers through Daniel's hair. He nuzzles his nose into the column of her throat and I wonder if I've chosen the wrong seat and should have given them some space.

Alex walks into the room just as I'm considering moving to a stool at the kitchen island. She doesn't make eye contact and I see the blush that steals over her cheeks as she takes in the couples in the room. When she goes to walk past me, I snake my arm around her waist and tug her into my lap. She lands with a gasp, her eyes searching my own.

"Bastian?" she whispers so only I can hear her. There's a question in her tone.

I dip my head so it looks like I'm mimicking the position Daniel and Sophie were in moments ago.

My voice is low, and I don't miss the slight tremor that passes through her as I say, "What has got you blushing, princess?"

"I don't blush," she protests, dropping her chin to her chest as she tries to hide from me.

"I don't believe you, because I can see it... right here." I run my finger across the apple of her cheek where a soft blush glows.

"Are you still thinking about what's going to happen later, or did you slip your fingers into that tight little pussy to give yourself some relief before you came downstairs?"

I lift her hand to my mouth and smell her fingers as I kiss the back of each finger.

Holy shit.

I was only teasing her, but the distinct smell of her arousal fills my nostrils and tells me I hit the nail on the head. When my gaze meets hers, it takes all of my self control to not lift her from my lap and carry her back upstairs.

Like an addict, I take her index finger and pop it in

my mouth, trying to get my fix. The taste I get is faint and I'm certain she tried to wash away the evidence.

Alex shifts in my lap, rubbing on my hardening cock. I pull her finger from my mouth, resting my head on her shoulder as I try to get my shit together.

George chooses that moment to burst our bubble. His question is like a bucket of ice cold water bringing us back to reality.

"So, have you two set a date yet?"

SEVENTEEN

Alex

"So, have you two set a date yet?"

I pull away from Sebastian, the sexual fog lifting as George's question registers. My eyes go back to Sebastian, silently begging him to answer. One side of his mouth tips up as he pushes a loose strand of my hair behind my ear. He looks like he's enjoying this, which is crazy.

"Not yet, but we'll be tying the knot *very* soon," Sebastian replies, as calm as ever.

My eyes widen a fraction of a second before I drop my chin and fiddle with the hem of my sweater, hiding the emotions I'm sure are all over my face. Why does that feel so much more real than it is?

It's all pretend. It's all pretend.

"Oh, that's wonderful," Miriam says as she joins us all at the table.

"Isn't it just? Maybe we can sign the deeds over as a

wedding gift," George replies as he pulls Miriam into his side.

I feel Sebastian's grip tighten on my thigh at George's statement. Confident that the shutters are down, I turn to face Sebastian and cup his cheek as I say with a wide smile, "Wouldn't that be amazing, Bastian?"

His grip loosens as his mouth curves up into a smile that doesn't quite reach his eyes but still has his dimple peeking at me, "Yes it would, baby."

Sebastian is quiet for the remainder of the evening, barely interacting with conversation and even then it's only when he's asked direct questions that he responds.

After dessert, I excuse us, claiming to have a headache. With heavy footsteps, Sebastian follows behind me as I move into the bedroom. When the door is closed, I turn to face him from my position in the middle of the room.

"Are you okay?" he asks, moving toward me.

I frown before shaking my head, a small laugh escaping my lips. "Oh, I'm fine. You just didn't seem too... with it."

"I think we should do it."

Sebastian walks to the bed, sitting on the end of it, his hands clasped between his legs. Desperation is practically seeping out of his pores.

"I'm not following. What exactly should we do?"

He lifts his gaze to me, and for a moment I'm distracted by how incredibly handsome he is, that is until he says, "Get married."

I laugh. Hard. A snort erupts from me at the hilarity of his suggestion, and as I'm trying not to double over with laughter, my focus rests on him.

He's not laughing, and that image sobers me up, fast.

"You're joking, right?" I ask, wiping at the tears that have formed in my eyes.

"No, Alex, I'm not joking. I think we should do it."

"What, so you can get a fucking building? You can't be serious, Sebastian," I whisper-shout, my anger rising.

"I am serious. It's not a big deal. As soon as the papers are signed for the club, we can get an annulment."

There's a pounding in my ears as I try to reign in my temper. Is he really that arrogant? I band my arms around my waist as my body trembles. An innate need to protect myself from his blasé attitude and the hurt it's pouring down on me propels my body forward. I march into the bathroom and close the door behind me. My fingers grip onto the edge of the ceramic sink as I pull in deep, reassuring breaths.

Why doesn't he understand that he can't just take away all of my firsts and taint them with lies? First an engagement and now a marriage. I refuse to let this man have all of the firsts I have left when they mean nothing to him.

I'm going to tell him. It's not in my nature to cower away. Yanking the bathroom door open, it swings wide and Sebastian turns in my direction.

"It *is* a big deal, Sebastian. And the fact that you can't see that tells me all I need to know about you."

Deflated, I move about the room, picking up my t-shirt and removing items as I get ready for bed. That headache I'd feigned earlier seems to have come true.

"Can we at least talk about it?"

His words and the note of resignation in his tone have me stopping in my tracks.

I close my eyes and pinch the bridge of my nose. I swear it's like talking to a brick wall. "There's nothing to talk about. I'm doing you a favor already by pretending to be engaged to you. You're asking too much of me to tie myself to you in the eyes of the law."

"And there's nothing I can do to change your mind?"

"Not a thing. The only way I'd marry *you* is if I was partially blackout drunk, in Vegas, and I thought you were..." I wave my hand in the air, trying to think of a hot British guy. "Alex Pettyfer." I finish with a nod.

He stands from the bed and I wonder for a moment if I've hurt his feelings. One hand goes into his pocket as the other comes up and scrubs over his stubble covered jaw.

His gaze is assessing as it roams over me. He lifts his shoulder in a shrug and says, "Okay."

My eyes narrow, because he's accepted what I've said without the fight I was expecting. "That's it? Just okay?"

"I'm respecting your decision, so yes, that's it."

We stare at each other in the silence of the room. I wait for him to tell me that he's messing with me and that he'll have us in Vegas tomorrow because it's a 'solid plan', but nothing comes.

"I'm going to bed." I hesitate before I continue, unsure what his reaction will be. "I promised Jensen I'd go horseback riding with him in the morning."

A growl bursts from his lips as he looks away and I watch the ticking motion of his jaw. My head tips to the side as I examine him, almost fascinated by his reaction. If I didn't know better, which I do, I'd think Sebastian was jealous.

A sly smile I can't keep under wraps slips across my mouth. "You know, I was thinking of asking Jensen to show me how to mount the horse tomorrow. It's been a whi—"

Bastian's hands dive into my hair as he crashes his mouth down on mine. It's a punishing kiss. Meant to tell me who I belong to.

He pulls away, our labored breaths mingling in the small space between our mouths. His eyes are intent on me. "Finish that fucking sentence, princess. I dare you."

"What happens if I do?" I breathe.

His fingers tighten in my hair as he pulls it back exposing the column of my throat. He dips his head, his nose running along my sensitive skin.

"You don't want to know."

I pout, because I kind of want to. "I think I do."

He pulls away from me, his face coming into focus.

Running his thumb over the apple of my cheek, much like he did earlier in the night, he says, "You won't be horseback riding tomorrow. I'll spank your ass until it's red and then when you're dripping wet for me, because that *will* turn you on. I'll edge you until you're begging me to let you come. Except I won't. And I'll keep doing it for days if I need to, because his name does not belong on your tongue. Only mine does."

I want to tell him he's being possessive and that people who are just screwing don't get to say things like that, but my mind is blank and I'm so turned on that he could kiss me and I'll come.

My need for him is clear. I'm way past the point of trying to hold my desire for him back. I swallow thickly as I whisper, "You said that you'd make it so I could still feel you tomorrow."

His hands run down my body until they rest on the curve of my waist. "I believe I said I'd fuck you into oblivion, until you could feel me in your pussy for weeks."

My breath hitches at his words and a current of electricity zaps through me.

"Are you going to follow through?" I ask, a pleading note to my tone.

"Why wouldn't I?"

He doesn't wait for an answer, capturing my lips with his own. His hunger matches mine as he walks me to the bed, our clothes ripped from our bodies with desperation until I'm naked and he's only in his jeans.

When the backs of my legs hit the edge of the bed, he gently pushes me onto my back, climbing over me. His hand skates down my thigh, leaving a trail of goosebumps in his wake. When he switches thighs and comes up, closer to my core, my legs instinctively widen for him.

Instead of touching me where I need him most, he skirts up and rests his warm palm on the bottom of my stomach.

"I know yesterday was unplanned, and I promise I'm clean, but I don't have any condoms."

"I—" I move my eyes over his shoulder, looking for some courage, before returning to him. "I don't feel comfortable not using condoms. I took Plan B yesterday, just so you know."

"I wasn't implying we should go bare, and although I'm not opposed to filling you with my cum, there would always need to be a layer of protection there. I don't want children and I wouldn't want to put you in any positions you aren't comfortable with. Tonight is all about you. I can fill you in other ways."

The corner of his mouth lifts, causing his dimple to pop. At that moment, I consider telling him to fill me with his cock and take me because I'm *his*.

No, I'm not.

Making sure the words are vaulted away, I smile back and say, "Okay."

The fire in his eyes is unmistakable as he moves between my legs, his eyes on my pussy. "You're fucking stunning, Alex," he murmurs, running his tongue through my slit.

My back arches off of the bed at the first swipe, and a

low moan fills the room. He sucks at my clit as he eases a finger into my tight channel, twisting and turning it, stretching me out.

"Bastian," I practically purr.

Sebastian chuckles, and the cold air on my heated pussy is a mix of torture and pure pleasure. The hand that isn't inside me coasts up my stomach to pinch my left nipple. He rolls it between his thumb and forefinger before massaging my breast.

His mouth is still devouring me as he eases his finger in and out at an excruciatingly slow pace. I'm closer to the edge than I'd like to be at this point, and even though I'd taken care of myself earlier, I'm still needy for his touch.

Just being in the same vicinity as him has my panties wetter than they should be. I've dated good-looking guys before, but there's so much more to him than his looks— although that doesn't hurt. It's the strong eye contact, the dirty mouth and the almost primal need he brings out in me.

He turns onto his side, and as he pushes his jeans and boxers down over his hips with one hand, his cock bobs out, standing proud and angry. His fist grips his base and I see his knuckles tighten around himself.

Coming up onto my elbows, I try to get a better view of his cock, wishing I could feel him inside of me. Sebastian pulls away from my pussy and sits up onto his knees, a finger still inside me.

"What are you thinking, Alex?" he asks, lazily stroking his cock, adding another finger.

I close my eyes as I'm stretched by him, unable to form a coherent thought. The bastard stills and as he withdraws his fingers from me, I look up at him, my confusion no doubt evident.

"Do you remember our first day in the apartment?"

I nod my head, captivated by the stern look on his face. I'm not sure now is the time to start reminiscing over something that happened like four days ago.

"What did I say to you?"

"I-I... don't remember," I stutter like a fool, because who would remember something like that when they're in the throes of pleasure and he seems so serious.

"I told you when I ask you a question, you answer me."

He's still sitting there on his knees, stroking his magnificent cock as he looks down on me. I can just imagine the image I must paint. My legs spread for him, my drenched pussy on display as I try to wrap my head around what the hell is happening right now.

"I don't understand."

"I asked you what you were thinking. Your mind wasn't here."

"Oh," is all I can manage to say as a blush steels across my cheeks and I look down.

"Are you going to tell me, or am I going to dress you and go to sleep?"

Now that has my gaze snapping to him. "I was thinking, I want to suck your cock as you eat my pussy."

He huffs out a laugh as if what I've just said shocks him. Surely he can't think that I'd be thinking anything else when he's just pulled out his cock.

"Get on your side," he growls, moving to lie on his own.

Sebastian moves my thigh under his head, pulling my other leg up to rest under his arm, his face fully in pussy. Moving himself into position, he lifts his leg so his foot is flat on the bed. I rest my head on his other leg and we end up in a sideways sixty-nine position.

I'm spread out for him, giving him the perfect access to both my pussy and ass.

As soon as his thick, impossibly hard cock is in front of me, I wrap my hand around it, stroking him from tip to base. A grunt vibrates through Sebastian's chest as his hips buck forward into my hand. He buries his face between my legs and licks my pussy from my clit to the bottom of my slit.

God, it feels divine.

I take him into my mouth, flicking my tongue around the tip of his hard cock, greedy for his salty taste. Sebastian moans low in his throat and the vibrations cause a wave of pleasure to roll through me, my body quivering almost uncontrollably, as he continues to eat my pussy.

It's like a race for who can get who off first. On one hand, I want to win and taste him on my tongue, but on the other, I'm eager for my own release.

With a hand at the base of his shaft, I take as much of him into my mouth as I can fit without gagging. Slowly, moving my head back and forth, alternating between sucking him and lightly grazing my teeth over his shaft.

I hum around his cock as he glides one thick finger into my core. It's not enough.

I need more.

The pace of his finger matches that of my mouth on his cock, but it's near on excruciating. The control he has over my body and how he can have me so close to the edge so quickly, it's unreal.

Trying to concentrate on his cock, I slip him from my mouth with a pop. With my tongue out flat, I lick him from his balls to the tip of his head. Swirling my tongue around it, I use my hand and the salvia still on his length to stroke him.

Adding another finger, he stretches me further and although it feels glorious, it also still doesn't feel like enough. I'm so close to begging him to fill me with his cock. I'm certain it's the only thing that will tip me over the edge. That is until he adds a third finger.

God, I feel so deliciously full.

I'm so lost in the feelings he's building inside of me that I can't focus on my own task of bringing him with me over the cliff. My hips thrust on the hand that's buried inside of me and as he grabs a rough handful of my ass.

The mix of pleasure and pain brings me back to the moment, and I move my mouth and hand in tandem.

We're back to being in sync as we pleasure each other, and it isn't long before I feel the spasms take hold of me as my orgasm builds. My body tenses as a zap of electricity jolts down my spine. Tingles start to form in my legs, working their way up my body as I tumble over the edge into ecstasy. The vibrations of my moans have him bucking into my mouth, fucking my face with abandon.

"Alex, I'm going to come," he rasps, turning his forehead to rest it on my thigh.

I don't say a word, cupping his ass cheeks so he doesn't pull out, I continue to take him into my mouth and urge him to release.

"Baby, you need to stop if you don't want me to come in your mouth," he warns me.

One hand moves to cup his balls and as I tug and massage them gently, Sebastian releases a hiss of air at the sensation.

"Fuck," he roars, and with one final thrust his hot, salty cum fills my mouth.

I drink it down, savoring the taste. We collapse onto each other, too spent to move. The sound of our labored breathing filling the slice.

When I feel like I can move, I detangle myself from him and roll onto my back. My eyes are focused on the ceiling but I feel the bed move and Sebastian repositions himself on the bed beside me, resting his head on his palm as he looks down at me.

"You okay?" I ask, unsure what else to say.

Sebastian chuckles before saying, "I'm fantastic, princess. Are you?"

He smooths his hand down my stomach, resting it on my hip. All I can manage is a nod as my eyes grow heavy.

I make a note to ask Sebastian in the morning why he keeps calling me princess. It's another thing that's blurring the lines of our arrangement, and I need him to stop for my own sanity.

EIGHTEEN

Sebastian

lex isn't in bed when I wake. Her side of the bed is cold, and when I walk into the bathroom, the faint smell of her perfume still lingers in the air. A sense of disappointment that I can't have her before we face the day settles in my stomach.

An overwhelming urge to see her has me getting ready quicker than I would normally, but as I wash my body, I force myself to slow down. This is only supposed to be two people scratching an itch for each other.

Dressed in a pair of black jeans, a white t-shirt, and a pair of boots, I head to the kitchen for a cup of coffee. I come up short when I walk into the room and find it empty. Since we arrived, the kitchen has been a hub of activity every morning.

A pot of coffee is sitting in the coffeemaker on the counter and a clean cup sits on the draining board. I swipe it up and make myself a cup of the still hot nectar.

I lean against the island counter looking out the window into the backyard, my ankles crossed and my cup pressed to my lips when George comes through the back door.

"Good morning, Sebastian. Did you sleep well?"

"Morning, George. I did, thanks. You?"

"Always." He moves to the coffee pot and refills his mug.

"Where is everyone this morning?"

"Miriam and I are on the side porch." He pauses, turning to face me as he assesses me, "Daniel and Sophie popped into town, and Alex and Jensen are in the stables."

"Oh." I try to keep my features neutral.

Internally, I'm picturing all the ways I can punish Alex tonight because I can guarantee she's flirting up a storm with dickhead Jensen.

"Come, they should be heading out soon." George moves past me, but not before I catch the look of skepticism on his face.

Something tells me today isn't going to be the easy day I had planned. I move to refill my cup, then follow George out to the side porch. Miriam sits in a rocking chair, a colorful knitted blanket thrown over her legs. When George hands her the mug, he must say something to her because she peeks her head around him and gives me a warm smile.

"Good morning, sleepyhead."

I throw her a smirk that I know brings out my dimple. "Morning, Miriam."

She motions to a chair next to her and says, "Come sit, dear"

"I'm goo—"

My words are cut off as my gaze flies to the door of a large wooden stable as it opens. Alex comes out, her hair braided down her back, a tight fitting navy tweed jacket hugging her curves, and trousers like a second skin on her legs. Riding boots encase her feet, and under her right arm sits a black riding hat.

Even from here I can see the light glint off of the diamond sitting on her finger. *My diamond*. I can't help the smirk that sneaks across my lips.

Her left hand leads out a silky brown mare with a shiny long black mane. Both two creatures of beauty, but Alex is the one that holds my attention. I'm barely aware of Jensen as he follows her out; that is until he helps Alex settle onto the back of the horse. I watch his hands intently as he helps her up, looking for any excuse to lay him out.

She's mine.

It's my ring on her finger.

I'm the only one that gets to touch her and... taste her.

My grip tightens on my coffee mug. In an effort to not break it, I put it on the side table next to Miriam, my eyes still on Alex.

"She's on one of our tamest mares. Her name's Coco,"

Miriam tells me, her soft gaze finds mine as I look down at her before I turn back to the railing.

She's mistaken whatever she's seen in me as for concern over Alex hurting herself. She should be concerned about me hurting her son if he touches what's mine in the wrong way.

Alex moves the horse with ease, walking in circles as Jensen gets himself settled on his own. She moves to a trot, following behind Jensen as he takes a trail along the back of the property. As they move further along, Alex kicks the horse into a canter to match Jensen.

What happens next moves both in slow motion and at super speed. My stomach plummets at the same time as the carefree smile that was on her face turns to one of fear.

The horse rears up, and she slips in her seat.

Hold on, Alex.

When the horse rears up again, Alex slips further in her seat, unable to have righted herself from the first movement.

Her scream of terror will stay with me for eternity. It echoes around the field, across the lake and back up to the house.

I can only watch as she's thrown in the air and off of the horse. I don't even think about it; my feet are in motion, my gaze is locked on her even as I vault over the porch railing, running as fast as I can.

I'm coming, baby.

The moment she hits the ground, a guttural roar releases from me and I push myself harder. Further forward, across the space between us.

But it's still not enough.

"Alex," I scream.

My lungs burn and my voice is hoarse as I shout for her, praying she can at least still hear me.

She's not fucking moving. Why isn't she *fucking* moving?

Come on, baby, just get up.

Please, Princess.

"Call a fucking ambulance," I shout over my shoulder to the porch behind me. It's then I see George following behind me, his pace much slower, and Miriam nowhere to be seen.

"Miriam is calling them," George calls back, the worry clear in his voice.

It feels like a lifetime by the time I reach her. Falling to my knees next to her, I pick up her hand in mine, cradling her soft skin in my palm. Jensen is kneeling on her other side, his hands are on her wrist, searching for her heartbeat. I want to rip him off of her and ask him why the fuck he thought this was a good idea.

Deep breath in... one... two... three... and blow it out.

Her helmet has come off and is laying on the ground a foot away. I breathe as I look down on her, willing the beast inside of me to calm down. It'll do her no good if I burn this world to the ground like I want to.

She might not make it.

A small cut marks the smooth skin of her forehead, but aside from that, she physically looks okay. Her skin looks pale, and as I hold her hand in mine, I notice how cold it is. I bring her palm to my chest, desperate to have her close but knowing it's best not to move her.

Bending to her ear, my voice is thick as I murmur, "Princess, I need you to wake up. I can't lose you. Not when I've just found you."

I'm lost.

I don't know how to make this better.

My misty gaze finds Jensen's. I don't need to voice my question; it's clear in my eyes.

"She's got a heartbeat, and it's strong. I think she's just been knocked out by the fall." He doesn't say anything for a moment before continuing, "I'm so sorry, Sebastian."

"It won't fix what's happened. I just hope for your sake she pulls through."

I turn back to Alex, dismissing him. In the distance, I can hear the sound of the ambulance and am aware of the horses standing not too far from us.

"Sebastian?" George calls my name and pulls me from my focus on Alex. It's then that I notice Jensen and the horses have gone.

"Yes?"

"The EMTs are here."

George steps to the side, and I see two men running across the field from the house. It doesn't look as far away as it did moments ago. I guess that's the thing with perception when you want to get somewhere, but time slows down and it feels like you're trudging through mud.

I move aside as they approach, not wanting to get in the way of Alex getting the best possible medical care.

"Can you tell us a bit about what happened?" the older of the two paramedics asks.

I scrub my hand through my hair as I try to get my mind straight on what happened. I'm really fucking worried.

"She—Umm... she fell..."

My eyes well, and my throat clogs with tears. I haven't cried since I was kid. What has this woman done to me? Bending at the waist, I drag in a deep breath, blowing it out harshly.

Why hasn't she woken up yet?

I hear George talking, but can't hear exactly what he's saying. A million questions run through my mind, all them without answers.

Will she ever wake up? Is this it? Is this how I lose her?

FUCK!

A handkerchief is held under my nose and I stand to my full height and take the cotton square of material, only now registering the dampness on my cheeks.

"Bastian." It's barely audible, but I hear her as if she was shouting it from the top of her lungs.

I whip around and move toward her, picking up her hand. I drop a kiss across her knuckles, my voice filled with concern as I say, "Hey, baby. You had me so worried."

She's strapped to a gurney, her head secured in a brace, yet still her gaze fills with concern *for me*. "I'm okay, Bastian. I'm sorry I made you worry."

"Don't worry about me, princess," I mumble, and as if reassured, her eyes flutter closed.

The younger EMT interrupts, pulling my focus from Alex. "Are you coming with us, sir?"

"I am."

We move across the field to the house, her small delicate hand still grasped in my much larger one. She's always seemed so strong and like nothing could phase her, but seeing her unconscious on a gurney, she looks so fragile and delicate. My grip tightens on her hand. I won't let her go, not now.

Maybe ever.

Today has been the worst day of my life. Even with everything I went through as a child it's nothing in comparison to the feelings that stirred inside of me as I watched Alex plummet to the ground. As I waited for her to wake up, I've been worried out of my mind that she might not.

Thankfully, the ambulance ride is uneventful, and I'm reassured by the EMT that her vitals are good.

Alex hasn't woken back up since we left the house, and as we ride to the hospital, I take in every inch of her face as if for the first time. When we arrive, we're greeted by a doctor as we climb from the back of the ambulance.

Medical terms are exchanged and then Alex is wheeled to a room.

"Hi, I'm Doctor Turner and I'll be looking after Alex for her stay here. Who might you be?"

"Alex's fiancé." My tone is sure and leaves no room for doubt.

Doctor Turner is a woman in her mid-fifties, her red hair is pulled back into a tight bun at the nape of her neck, her face looks tired. A pair of reading glasses perch on the tip of her nose as she reads a chart.

"Can we get Alex moved to a private suite? Money is no object. I just want her to be comfortable."

"I can look into it, but we need to get her looked over and have some tests run first. Alex will need to be sent for an x-ray and a CT scan."

"Thank you." I move to Alex's bed and pick up her hand, my thumb moves back and forth in a soothing motion. I'm not sure who I'm trying to reassure more, me or Alex.

Shouldn't she be awake?

I don't know what I'll do if there's something wrong with her. I'll never forgive myself. It was my fault she was out on that horse in the first place. If she hadn't been pressured into coming with me, she'd never have been out there.

I'm such an idiot.

I should never have dragged her into this situation, and if something happens to her, I only have myself to blame. I want to scream at the top of my lungs, an ache I've never felt before sitting in the pit of my stomach.

I'm staring into nothingness when a nurse enters the room. She's dressed in a pair of lilac scrubs, her blonde hair pulled back into a ponytail. A small smile spreads across her mouth as she looks at me before going back to her task of checking the monitor hooked up to Alex and writing things on a chart. I follow her movements as she goes about her duties.

"I'm just checking her vitals, then we will take her for her scans. Everything is looking good so far," she reassures me, continuing as if I'm making her uneasy. "With head injuries we always start with a CT scan to make sure everything is okay then we will take her for an x-ray."

"Thank you," I mumble, my focus going back to Alex.

She looks so delicate. None of her feistiness is there, and I'd give anything for her to open her eyes and bring me back to earth with her words. *Fuck*. I'd give anything to hear her say my name again.

"We're ready to take her now. You can wait here. We shouldn't be too long. I'll give you this to keep safe." The nurse looks at me expectantly, and when I hold out my hand, as I'm sure is expected, she drops Alex's engagement ring into my hand.

Tears well in my eyes as I remember the conversation Alex and I had in the shower the other day. When I told her to never take my ring off of her finger again. I hadn't given her a chance to say anything, and now I wish I'd told her exactly how I feel and why I don't want her to take that ring off.

How do I feel?

Isn't that the million dollar question? I didn't say how I feel because I don't have a fucking clue. Yes, I have feelings for her and want to claim her as mine, but I think that's more of a caveman instinct than anything else. What am I supposed to do, bang on my chest, grunt and say 'mine' and hope that conveys how I feel?

No.

These *feelings* I'm feeling are just from the events of the day. Alex is a... friend, and because she's been hurt, I'm naturally worried about her.

It's nothing more.

It can't be. I'm not capable of loving someone, and I'm sure not worthy of someone else's love.

My mind is lost in a future I will never have when the door opens and Alex is wheeled back in. She's still asleep and I run my hand over my jaw as I stand, the tension leaving my body now she's back with me.

"Why isn't she awake?" I ask, my focus moving from Alex to Dr. Turner.

"It is a concern that she's not awake, but we will monitor her for the next twenty-four hours before we can determine if it's anything serious." Dr. Turner looks down at the chart in her hand, then flicks through the monitor next to Alex's bed.

"Her CT scan has come back normal, although she does have a broken arm, which we will need to put in plaster. I suspect she will have a concussion from hitting her head, so she will need some monitoring once she's awake. I'll send a nurse in to do her arm within the hour. There isn't much more that you can do, aside from keeping her company."

I don't put much thought into it when I say, "I'd like to stay with her tonight, in case she wakes up. I don't want her to be alone."

"Of course, I'll let the nurses know and they'll bring you a pillow and blanket. Once her arm is plastered, we can move her to the room you requested."

"Thank you."

Dr. Turner finishes writing something on the chart before leaving the room. The sound of machines whirling is the only sound filling the silence. Pulling my chair closer to the bed, I pick up Alex's hand. Her warmth seeps into me, reassuring me with just her touch.

Please let her be okay.

Even now, after the doctor has reassured me she has nothing but a broken arm and possible concussion, my concern isn't eased. It won't be until she's awake and I can see and hear for myself that she's okay.

I pull her ring from my pocket and slip it onto her finger. My lips touch her knuckle in the barest of kisses.

"Do you remember two days ago when I told you not to take this ring off? Well, I guess today would be an exception, but I like seeing it on your finger."

My guard is down, knowing she probably can't hear

me, and even if she can, she won't recall what I'm saying to her.

"I think we should go home. You can come and stay with me until you're better." I sit in silence for a moment before a burst of courage has me saying, "It was like the world stopped spinning and everything happened in slow motion when I saw you being thrown from that horse. When I finally reached you..." My voice breaks as I'm overcome with emotion. "It was like nothing was worth anything anymore if you weren't going to be okay. Fuck, Alex, I'm pulling the plug on the plan."

Seeing her lying in this bed, almost lifeless, tells me this is for the best.

It's not worth it.

The club, my revenge—the whole reason we were in this situation—is not fucking worth it.

I pull my wallet out of my pocket and unfold the photo that I've kept in there since it was given to me almost eighteen years ago. The familiar face of the woman I don't remember stares back up at me. A grin spread over her face and the arm of a faceless man casually swung round her shoulders. In the background is the neon sign that reads *Sanctuary*.

This is the only picture I have of my mother and father.

Of my mother and George Bennett.

Even though George is my father and abandoned my mother to come back to America, my priorities have changed. The plan was simple: take his club, tell him I know who he is and then walk out of his life and sell the club to the highest bidder.

Plans change.

My gaze lifts to look at Alex, before focusing back on the picture in my hand.

My mind is made up.

NINETEEN

Sebastian

Alex is finally awake. Her arm is wrapped in a pink cast and the color is back in her face. The anxiety that was sitting on my chest when she wasn't awake is gone and I can finally breathe with ease.

We were moved to a private room on the sixth floor of the hospital yesterday. A cot was set up in the corner for me, and the staff were more than happy for me to stay when I made a generous donation.

"Damn, my arm is so itchy. Can you find me something to scratch it with?" Alex asks.

I lean back in the chair, one hand resting on the arm and the other scrubbing over my jaw, the bristles from my stubble catching my palm.

"I didn't think it was supposed to be itchy until you had it on for weeks?"

Alex throws me a glare and I can't help the smirk that spreads across my mouth.

God, it's fucking fantastic to be able to tease her.

"It's not funny. It's itchy," she pouts.

The smile falls from my face as I stand, prowling toward her until I tower over her. Alex's gaze darkens as she looks up at me, her mouth parting and her tongue darting out to swipe across her plump lips.

Without a word, I swoop down and capture her mouth with my own. My tongue slips into her waiting mouth and tangles with hers. The fingers on her unbroken arm grab at the material of my t-shirt as the other one rests on my chest. My hands cup her cheeks, tipping her face to just the right angle. I want to savor her taste because when we go back to New York, I don't know what she's going to want to do.

When I pull away and rest my forehead on hers, we're both breathing heavily. Her eyes search my face, darting from my eyes to my mouth and back again, looking for answers I don't have.

"When they say you can leave, we're going home," I murmur in an effort to remind myself that this is short term.

Short term is all I want.

Isn't it?

"Back to the house?" she asks, her confusion evident.

"No, to New York."

"But what about the club?"

"I'm pulling the plug. You don't have to be my fiancée anymore."

A frown pulls at her brow as she looks up at me. I can practically see her mind whirling as she tries to figure this out.

"But you... I don't mind helping. I know I said—"

I cut her off as I say, "It's okay. This accident put everything in perspective. I don't need this club. There are more important things than making money."

You're more important than making money.

"What about George? Isn't he expecting us to go back to his home? To finish our visit?" There's a hint of desperation in her tone and the plea in her gaze tells me she's not ready to leave.

She's probably not ready to leave *Jensen*.

Fuck, I hate that guy.

"Given what's happened, he was more than understanding when I told him we would be going back to New York."

She blinks as she looks down at the ring sitting proudly on her finger. When she looks up, I don't miss the slight sheen in her eyes, but she holds her chin high and defiant.

There's my girl.

My eyes drop to the movement in her lap as she slips the ring from her finger. When she holds it up to me, I make no move to take it from her.

Why does this feel like a break up?

My body is heavy and an ache settles in my chest,

pressing onto my heart. Sadness hovers over me like a cloud, threatening to burst and shower me with regret and... heartbreak.

I shove my hands into the pockets of my jeans as I rock back on my heels. I need some distance from her. Everything has been too much for the past twenty-four hours. For something that was supposed to be fake and fun, it's been incredibly real.

George and Miriam visited last night, dropping off a change of clothes and some food. They were apologetic, despite my reassurances that it wasn't their fault. I'm the only one to blame for Alex being hurt because if she hadn't been roped into my deception, she would never have been on that horse.

The hours spent at the hospital did nothing but give me time to realize that this was all becoming too much. Too many feelings that I swore to never feel.

I promised her I'd never fall in love with her and I haven't, but it's beginning to feel a lot like that could become a possibility.

There's a war taking place inside of me. A primal need to see my ring on her finger fighting with the protective desire to be alone, not relying on anyone but myself.

A nurse I haven't met yet walks into the room and smiles at Alex and says, "It's good to see you awake, Miss Williams. I'm Jose, and I will be your nurse today. How are you feeling?"

Alex smiles back, but it doesn't reach her eyes. "I have a slight headache and feel a little tired."

Jose jots down some notes in the chart he pulls from the end of the bed, nodding his head as he looks over the monitors. Feeling awkward but not wanting to leave, I sit in the chair in the corner of the room.

"Okay, we can get you some painkillers for that headache and then you can head home and get some rest."

"Will she be okay to fly?"

"It's best to avoid it for at least ten days, but if she must there are precautions," Jose replies over his shoulder, he turns back to Alex before continuing, "Do you have far to travel?"

Alex clears her throat, replying, "To New York, it's just over two hours."

"Okay, well, if you must fly, you should stay hydrated and rest as much as possible. Try to avoid using a screen and use earplugs and sunglasses if you have some. Will you have someone to look after you when you get back?"

Alex looks over at the ring gleaming on the table before moving her gaze back to Jose.

"No, there's nobody."

Jose tsks, looking over his shoulder at me, then focusing back on Alex. "I'd prefer it if you would have someone to stay with you for the next forty-eight hours."

"I can call one of my friends. I just don't want to be a burden to them."

"She's staying with me." The words are out of my mouth before I can stop them.

"Perfect." Jose claps his hands together with glee. "I'll go and get the doctor to sign off on your discharge and then you'll be free to go."

When he's gone, silence settles back over the room. My command hovers around us. I hold my breath. There's no way she lets that slide.

Alex breaks the silence. "Do you have my phone?"

"Umm, I think it's back at the house." I dig my phone out of my pocket and carry it to her in the bed. "Here, you can use mine."

With a half-hearted chuckle, she says, "I-I don't actually know anyone's numbers by heart."

A blush steals across her cheeks as she looks down at the cotton blanket spread out over her legs.

"Who do you need to call?"

Her eyes lift to mine and with defiance filling her tone states, "I just wanted to call Savannah and ask her if she wouldn't mind getting me from the airport." She waves her hand through the air, leaning back in the bed, effectively dismissing me. "It can wait until I get my stuff."

"Did you not hear me when I said you're staying with me?" I ask incredulously.

"Did you not hear yourself? Our whole charade is over. You don't need to take care of me. And anyway, I'd rather stay at my place. It's right round the corner from work and... my bed is really comfy."

I can't stop my laugh or the smile that slips onto my lips. She's certainly something special.

"Fine, we will stay at your place. It really doesn't bother me."

Her focus shifts to me and her mouth forms the perfect 'O' of surprise. "I didn't mean for *us* to stay at my place. I feel like you aren't listening to me. I'll be fine, and I'm sure Savannah won't mind checking in on me..."

Her words trail off as I stalk towards her. When I'm towering over her at the side of the bed, my hands slide into her hair and I drop my forehead to hers. Our breaths mingle and I don't miss the barely audible hitch in hers.

"*I'm* going to look after you, Alex. It's my fault you've ended up here with a broken arm."

Her eyes move to my mouth as her tongue darts out, her voice breathy as she says, "It's not your fault. I shou—"

My mouth drops to hers, cutting off whatever it was she was planning on saying. It is my fault, despite what she might think. I'm just glad she's okay, or as okay as she can be, considering she was thrown from a horse.

Alex moans into my mouth. Her hands grasp onto the front of my t-shirt and at the insistence of my tongue, she opens her mouth. It's a kiss of desperation. Like she's reassuring me. Her tongue tangles with mine, matching my need, swipe for swipe.

We're lost in the moment when a cough sounds in the room. I step away and grab onto the back of my neck as I look around sheepishly. Jose is standing at the end of Alex's bed, a brow cocked and a smirk on his face.

"Sorry for interrupting, but I have your paperwork all signed, the painkillers as promised and so you're good to go. Do you have any questions?"

"No," Alex croaks. Clearing her throat, she continues, "No, thank you."

"Perfect. I'll go and get a wheelchair to take you out. You can get dressed and I'll be back in ten minutes."

"Thank you," Alex and I say in unison.

I move to the bag that Miriam and George brought, lifting it to the chair I was sitting in before unzipping it and removing Alex's clothes. Alex is perched on the edge of the bed, the hospital gown making her look fragile and in need of protection.

Miriam had packed Alex a pair of ripped jeans, a white short sleeve t-shirt and a clean set of underwear. I move so that I'm standing behind Alex. My hands find the string on the back of the hospital gown and I undo it, baring Alex's naked back to me.

She sucks in a breath as my fingers graze her smooth soft skin. "What are you doing, Bastian?"

With great effort, I resist the urge to dot kisses across the expanse of her back. Instead, I focus on the task at hand, getting her dressed so that I can take her home.

"I'm dressing you," I reply, as if it's obvious.

I pick up her bra and hold it up for her to slide her arms into it. She does so without question, and I can't help but be pleased that she's letting me do this. She's letting me take care of her. It's the least I can do.

It's on me that she's here.

"I can see that, but I'm capable of dressing myself."

I don't hold back from kissing her silky skin this time. My lips press onto her shoulder, and I move up the expanse of her neck. Alex tips her head to the side, giving me more access before dropping her head to my shoulder.

From my angle above her, I can see that her eyes are closed and her chest is heaving with labored breaths.

What a fucking vision she makes.

The hospital gown pooled around her hips and her chest heaving in her bra as she tries to restrain herself. The only thing that's missing is my *fucking* ring on her finger.

It's not real.

I dismiss the thought because for a moment, at least until we get back to New York, I can pretend she's mine.

My lips brush over the shell of her ear as I say, "I know, but I want to do this."

A whimper escapes her lips and as I move back from her, picking up the t-shirt, I can't help the smirk that graces my lips.

When she's dressed, my eyes land on the ring, resting on the table where she abandoned it earlier. I pick it up, staring down at it for a moment, the weight heavy yet light in my hand. Stepping between Alex's legs, I pick up her left hand and slide the ring onto her finger. She swallows thickly, her gaze intent on the action.

"You'll need to keep this on for a little bit longer," I mumble.

Her voice is scratchy as she replies, "Okay."

Despite what may come next when we get back to New York, I know that Alex still wants me, just like I want her.

This isn't the end of us.

TWENTY

Alex

I don't even know where to start with analyzing everything that has happened in the last forty-eight hours. After being released from the hospital, we went back to the Bennett's and packed up our things. Everyone was so apologetic for what had happened, despite me reassuring them that it wasn't their fault.

It wasn't anybody's fault.

Things like this just happen, but no matter how much he tries to hide it from me, Sebastian is blaming himself. I've tried to tell him it's not his fault, but he won't have it.

Before we left, I went and said goodbye to Coco. I know something spooked her. Something I couldn't see or hear, but something nonetheless. She nuzzled into my neck as if trying to apologize. It might have been my imagination, but her big, beautiful eyes seemed glassy and filled with concern. I tried to reassure her, too, that it wasn't her fault.

She seemed to accept it more than Sebastian.

Sebastian and I arrived back in New York late last night, after staying for dinner with the Bennett's. Bastian hired a private jet to bring us home and it was like nothing I have ever experienced before.

When I got back to my apartment, I was exhausted. Too exhausted to argue with Sebastian when he insisted on sleeping on my couch, refusing to leave despite me telling him Savannah could come over if I needed anything.

My phone pings with an incoming text and I pick it up, expecting it to be the group chat. I sent a message when we boarded the flight, explaining we were on our way back and there had been a small accident. When I switched my phone back on, I was bombarded with twenty missed calls and what felt like hundreds of messages asking what had happened and was I okay.

It's not the group chat.

SEBASTIAN

I'm just heading back, do you need anything from the store? Painkillers? A drink? Food?

ALEX

You don't have to come back, I'm fine.

SEBASTIAN

I'll pick up a couple of things. Shouldn't be more than twenty minutes.

There's no point in replying, because he'll just ignore me again. Instead, I flop back onto my bed, throwing my arms above my head. The impact of my broken arm hitting the bed has me wincing. I've never broken anything before and I certainly didn't think I'd be breaking bones in my thirties.

As it often does, my mind goes back to Bastian. I don't understand what he's hoping to achieve by being so attentive. He told me the plan was off, so why is he being so insistent about looking after me? He's so confusing.

I'm still staring up at the ceiling when a knock sounds on my front door. Climbing from the bed, I walk to the hallway and swing the door open. Sebastian stands in the corridor, a back duffel bag slung over his shoulder and four—that I can count—tote bags from the local supermarket in his hands.

A grin breaks out on my face. I step back from the door as I say, "You need a hand?"

"Nope, I've got it."

"Good, because I've only got one," I chuckle as I hold up my broken arm.

With a shake of his head and a small smirk, he walks to my kitchen, making the space look smaller than it already is. As he lifts the bags onto the counter, I can't help but be mesmerized by the flex of his biceps.

He doesn't look up, instead pulling things out of the bags, asking, "Are you going to shut the door or keep standing there staring?"

My cheeks heat as I spring into action and close the front door. I move into the kitchen and peek around him to look at what he's brought.

"Grab a glass."

On autopilot, I walk to the cabinet next to the sink and pull out a glass. For a second, I hesitate before pulling down a second and walking back to him. He picks up the carton of fresh orange juice and pours two glasses. Holding one out to me, I grasp it from his hand and bring the glass to my lips.

His eyes are on me, watching my mouth as I drink down the cold liquid. "I got the Calcium fortified one. Vitamin C. It's..." He scrubs his hand over the back of his neck. "Good for bone healing."

He's taking care of me.

My eyes burn with tears that are threatening to spill. I turn away, sliding the glass onto the counter. It's a sense of guilt that has him looking after me, and I'm not going to allow him to put what happened onto his shoulders.

"You should go," I murmur, my chin held high with certainty.

"I'm not going to leave you alone. You need someone to stay with you for the next twenty-four hours at least."

"Savannah is just down the hall. If I need someone, I can call her, but I'm telling you, I'm fine."

His eyes bore into me, and unable to take the weight of his gaze, I look down at my hands that rest on the counter. It's then that I realize the engagement ring is still sitting proudly on my finger. In the short space of time that I've had it, I've become attached to it. I'll be sad to see it gone.

Briefly, I wonder if my future husband will give me a ring as nice as this one. With a huff of a laugh at the ridiculous thought—because whoever I marry won't be a billionaire, that's for sure. I slip the ring off.

Turning to find Sebastian still staring at me, an unidentifiable look in his blue-green gaze, I hold my arm out for him. "You should take this back."

When he makes no move to take it, I pick up his hand and place the ring into his palm, closing his fingers around it.

Taking a step back, I drop his hand and move to lean back against the counter. He follows and crowds me, his arms caging me in.

Running his nose up the expanse of my neck, I can't help but tip my head back. It's instinctive. He exhales, and it's as if the weight of the world is resting on his shoulders. I want to pull him closer, to tell him if he needs me that I'm right here, but that isn't my place so I keep my hands where they are, resting on the edge of the counter.

He pulls back, his eyes searching mine as he says, "Are you sure?"

"Yes," I breathe. I need the space from him. Everything has become so confusing since we got back.

"I don't like it but I'll respect your choice. If you need me, you call me, okay?"

I can only nod, even though I won't, because we need to go back to normal. I need us to not make this any more than it's already become. I'm on the edge of a cliff, about to fall over the edge and free fall into love with this man, but there isn't any guarantee that he will be the safety net I need to catch me.

Sebastian brushes his lips over mine in the faintest of kisses before stepping back. He grabs his bag and moves to the front door. On autopilot, my fingers brush over my lips as if trying to touch the ghost of his kiss.

"Alex?"

I turn at the sound of my name and the question in his tone, looking at him through the doorway.

"That ring." He inclines his head to my hand. "Doesn't get taken off. It belongs to you, and I meant it when I told you not to take that ring off again."

He's gone before my mind can catch up with my mouth and ask him how he managed to get it back on my finger and why he's being so insistent about me wearing it.

What the hell is happening?

Our arrangement is over, right? I mean, I know it is. We don't need to pretend, which means I don't need this—I look down at the ring he slipped back onto my finger—anymore. For a moment I hesitate, before shaking my head and snickering at my foolishness, pulling the ring off my finger.

This means nothing to Sebastian. Well, I *think* it means nothing to him. The fact he's being so pushy about me wearing a fake engagement ring is messing with my head. I walk to my bedroom and put it on the top of my dresser.

I'm sitting on the back of Coco as we gallop through a field of wildflowers. Hills roll around us and in the distance, I see a house. I can barely make out a man standing on the porch but with his broad shoulders, tapered waist and height, I know it's Sebastian.

He waves out over the field at me, and a smile breaks out on my face. My hair whips behind me as I kick at Coco with my heels urging her to go faster. I need to get to my man. I dig down as she picks up speed.

I've never ridden a horse this fast before.

It's exhilarating.

That is until something scares Coco and the house seems to get further away as she rears back. I can't hold on. I want to, but I can't. My palms are slick with sweat and I'm sliding from the saddle, my feet leaving the stirrups.

I brace myself, waiting to hit the ground, but it doesn't come, instead it's like I'm falling from the sky. My stomach somersaults. My arms are flailing around, looking for some-thing to land on.

"Bastian," I scream.

It's my own screams that wake me. I'm tangled in my sheets, my body slick with sweat as tears run down my cheeks. On autopilot I reach for my phone, which is charging on the nightstand and dial his number.

He answers on the third ring, the worry evident in his tone. "Alex, are you okay?"

My shoulders sag with relief at hearing his voice.

I can't mask the sob that breaks free as I cry, "Bastian."

"It's okay, baby. I'm coming."

I hear him on the other end talking to someone and it's only then, as I pull in deep calming breaths, that the faint sound of music registers. He must have gone to the club. My eyes snag on the clock on my bedside table and it's then that I realize it's two am.

"Bastian," I murmur into the phone, suddenly feeling shy.

"Yes, princess?"

"It's okay. If you're at work, you should stay there. I'm going to try and go back to sleep."

"I'm on my way."

TWENTY-ONE

Sebastian

I'm sitting in a meeting with my club manager, Sam, when my phone dances across the table. Normally I'd ignore it, but as my eyes catch Alex's name on the screen, my hand reflexively reaches out to grab it.

"Alex, are you okay?" I ask, trying to keep the concern building inside of me at bay.

It's two in the morning. She should be sleeping, not calling me.

The line is quiet, and I wonder if she's accidentally called me. That is until the sound she makes has my heart dropping to my feet. When she calls me by the nickname only she uses, I know I need to get to her.

I'm already grabbing up my wallet and keys from my desk when I say, "It's okay, baby. I'm coming."

I'm vaguely aware of Sam throwing me a questioning

look as I move to my office door—because I've never taken a personal call in a meeting with him or called anyone *baby*. I can hear Alex on the other end of the phone breathing.

In.

Out.

In.

Out.

It calms my own heart as I subconsciously mimic her breathing pattern.

I turn to Sam. "Something's come up. I've got to go. We can finish this meeting tomorrow."

"Of course. I'll pop you over an email and we can pick it up tomorrow."

"Thanks, Sam."

"Bastian," Alex calls, pulling my attention back to her.

Fuck, I love it when she calls me that.

"Yes, princess?" I ask, a smile on my lips now that she doesn't sound as panicked.

"It's okay. If you're at work. You should stay there. I'm going to try and go back to sleep."

I'm not going to leave her alone tonight, not after she called me when she needed me, so with as much authority as I can inject into my voice, I say, "I'm on my way."

Pulling the phone away from my ear, I drop a quick text to my driver, asking him to meet me out back. His response is to tell me he's already there and I thank fuck for the fact that I was getting ready to leave before she called.

I walk out of my office and down the stairs into the club. The bass from the music drowns out any conversation I might have with Alex.

When I step into the corridor that leads to the back exit of the club, the music is muted as the door closes behind me.

She doesn't speak, content to listen to the sounds on my end of the phone. If it wasn't for the sound of her breathing, I'd think the call had disconnected.

Duncan, my driver, has the door open and ready for me when I walk into the alleyway.

When I'm settled into the back of the car, I ask her, "What did you do today, after I left?"

She needs a distraction from whatever had her picking up the phone and calling me, that much I know.

"Umm... I took a shower," she hiccups as she drags in a breath. "Then I watched a film. I didn't do much."

"What film did you watch?"

"You'll laugh at me."

I chuckle, saying, "I would never."

"Promise?"

"Cross my heart."

"I watched *The Lion King*."

"Did you cry?"

"No," she says, and I can just picture her now sitting among the sheets on her bed as she bites on her plump bottom lip.

"Honestly?" I ask, teasing her.

"Fine. I'm not dead inside, of course I cried. Who doesn't cry at *The Lion King*?"

"Hey," I hold a hand up even though she can't see me, "I was only going to say you were a monster if you didn't."

I keep her distracted for the rest of the ride to her place, right up until I knock on her door and take her into my arms.

She sobs into my chest, her delicate hands grabbing onto the front of my t-shirt. "I'm sorry. I didn't know who else to call," she hiccups.

I lean away from her, my hands rub up her arms as I look at her face. "What are you sorry for?"

"For disturbing you at work when all I've had is a bad dream."

My thumb wipes at her wet cheeks before I tuck her under my arm and walk us into her apartment.

"Don't ever apologize for calling me, princess. Come on..." I step away from her, shrugging out of my jacket, my body sluggish with fatigue. "Let's go and get into bed. I'm tired."

I grab her hand and lead her down the hallway to her bedroom. The room is lit with a soft glow from the bedside lamp she has on. Pulling back the sheet, I guide her into the bed, brushing back a strand of hair as I stand over her.

Emotions course through me and for the first time in

a long time I'm not afraid of them. I just don't know what they mean or how to channel them.

Her gaze follows me as I move to the armchair in the corner of the room and sit down to pull off my shoes. Next go my black jeans, then white t-shirt, until finally I'm standing in just my black boxer briefs.

When I stand to walk to the bed, I don't miss the very obvious appraisal of my body that Alex does. I fight the urge to flex for her.

When I move past the dresser, I pause as my gaze lands on the ring I told her not to take off. It doesn't seem like she listened to me. Swiping it up as covertly as I can, I turn to walk back to the bed and climb under the cover with her.

I pull her into my arms, my lips finding her hair, as I band one of my arms around her waist, anchoring her to me. Being wrapped around her feels like a warm blanket on a cold winter's day. It just feels right. She's starting to mean more to me than a friend or a casual hookup.

Alex's head rests on my shoulder as I hold her in my arms. Picking up her left hand with my free hand, I rub my finger over the bare skin before I slip the ring back where it belongs.

On her finger.

My ring.

Lifting her hand, the ring glints in the dim light of the room.

"You're testing me, princess. I'll have to think of a

punishment if you take this ring off again," I whisper, my lips brushing the shell of her ear.

I can see all the questions in her eyes as she looks up at me. They're questions I don't have the answers to because I'm asking them of myself.

Why am I so adamant about her wearing the ring?

What is this? We don't have to pretend for anyone anymore and yet I want to make her happy, to comfort her when she needs it.

"Get some sleep, princess."

I breathe in her scent; all the tension that was holding my body taunt since I left her earlier, easing out.

"Why do you keep calling me princess?" she asks, her voice laden with sleep.

I'm not sure she meant to ask me, but the answer that comes to my mind is damn near instant. When her breathing is steady and labored, I check to make sure she's asleep, calling out her name.

It's only when I'm certain she's asleep that I say why. My voice a hushed whisper, "I call you princess because you're like royalty and too damn good for me."

TWENTY-TWO

Sebastian

I wake up to the smell of coffee and a cold, empty bed. It took me over an hour to fall asleep, my mind replaying the question she asked me over and over again.

Climbing from the bed, I pull on my clothes from last night, cursing myself for not leaving the duffel I'd brought over yesterday. Fully dressed, because I don't want her to think I have expectations, my nose follows the smell of coffee as I walk to the kitchen.

She's standing in front of the coffee machine, pouring a cup, her long legs on display as the oversized t-shirt she's wearing sits mid thigh.

Standing behind her, I band one arm around her waist as the hand of the other lands on her thigh, smoothing up under the t-shirt. My nose finds her neck as I drop a kiss on her bare shoulder.

"Good morning," I hear the smile in her voice.

"Morning. How are you feeling?"

"Much better." She tips her head back onto my shoulder as her eyes seek out mine. "I'm sorry I called you away from work. I'd had a bad dream and it kind of feels silly in the cold light of day."

"I'm glad you called me." I don't say any more than that because how do I explain that I want to be someone she can rely on when she's made it clear being casually exclusive—or whatever this is—it's not enough for her?

I don't even know what I want us to be.

Her eyes drop to the mug in her hand and then to the ring on her finger, before she asks, "Why do you want me to keep this ring?"

That's a good question and one I do have an answer for. If she'd asked me why I want her to keep it on her *finger*, I'm not sure what reason I'd give or if I'd even have one.

"Because it's yours. I got it for you."

"But ou—"

Her words are silenced as my fingers slip under the hem of her shirt and into her panties, where I'm met with her already wet core. I suck on the sensitive skin on the base of her neck as I rub over her clit.

Her voice is breathy and filled with desire as she says, "Bastian."

Yes, I'm playing dirty. Distracting her from asking questions I don't have answers to, but I don't want to analyze this when we could be doing things that are *much* more fun.

"Tell me what you want," I groan.

"You," she rasps, her hips grinding into my crotch.

If my dick wasn't already rock hard, it would be now.

"No, tell me *exactly* what you want me to do."

"Fill me," she moans as I dip two fingers into her drenched core.

"Like this?" I ask, knowing full well she wants my cock.

"No, it's not enough."

My thumb swipes over her clit as I finger-fuck her tight pussy. God, I want to bury myself deep inside her as I feel her contract around me. I move the hand that was around her waist up her body, tweaking a nipple as I go until I reach her throat. Keeping the grip on the smooth column light, I urge her to turn her head to me.

"Words, princess. I need you to use your words and tell me exactly what you want."

Her eyes are heavy as her tongue darts out to swipe across her lips, pulling my focus to them.

Not yet.

As soon as I get a taste of her I'm not going to stop and I want to please her. To do what she wants me to do to get her off.

"I want—" I feel the movement of her throat under my palm as she swallows before continuing, "I want to taste you. I want to choke on your cock."

Fuck.

Never in my wildest dreams did I think she would say *that*. Taking a step back, I release her from my hold, moving to the living room. Her eyes follow me as I walk around her apartment. I drop a cushion onto the floor, inclining my head to it in silent instruction.

Pulling her t-shirt over her head, she moves from the kitchen into the living room in only her G-string. I watch the gentle sway of her hips as she walks. Coming to a stop in front of me, she drops to her knees and looks up at me with wide eyes.

I smooth the backs of my fingers down her cheeks, then hold my hands behind my back. "If you want this, you need to be the one taking action, princess."

Her delicate fingers lift to the buckle of my belt. Undoing it, she pulls the leather through the loops, dropping it to the floor. She moves onto the buttons, popping each one, her focus on the task at hand.

When my jeans are undone, Alex pushes them down my legs, helping me to step out before she discards them to the side. Pausing on the hem of my boxers, she looks up at me, demanding when she says, "Take your top off, Bastian."

Her voice is husky with desire and when I whip my t-shirt over my head, she runs a hand over my abs, her nails gently grazing the skin. There's a beautiful contrast between her skin and mine, and I'll never tire of seeing it.

"Alex," I groan when she runs a single finger over my cock, making it jerk inside my boxers.

"I know, Bastian. Believe me, I know."

She's gentle when she releases me from the confines of my boxers. My cock bobs next to her head as she helps me step from my underwear. Her fingers wrap around me and I hiss at the contact, wanting more but also needing less.

The warmth of her mouth is almost too much to bear as she sucks me down, then pulls back. This might have been a bad idea. Her tongue flicks around the head of my cock and she hums at the salty taste of my pre-cum.

Breathe.

I drag in a deep breath, willing myself to not explode.

"You taste so good, Bastian." She looks up at me, a teasing glint in her eyes as if she knows exactly what she's doing to me.

Moving my hands from behind my back, I cup her face and rub my thumb over her bottom lip, opening her mouth for me. My hips buck forward and my cock slips into her waiting mouth.

Alex sits there, her hands on my thighs, her mouth open and wet, allowing me to slowly ease my cock into her hot little throat. I'm teetering on the edge and it takes every ounce of control I have to not fuck her face forcibly.

"You look so good like this. In front of me, swallowing my cock into your pretty little mouth."

At my words, her eyes flutter closed, and she moans around me, the vibrations hitting me right in the balls. Too close to the edge, I withdraw from her mouth. Her brow furrows momentarily in confusion but the motion of my thumb swiping over the apple of her cheek wipes it away.

I ease back in, some semblance of control back in place. I'm going slowly, being gentle, not because I'm afraid of hurting her but because I don't want this to be over so soon.

Popping off of my cock, she says, "Bastian," before she moves her hand to the base of my cock. "I can't choke on you when you're being so gentle."

Fuck, if she isn't right.

I rack my brain, trying to think of something to get my mind off of coming too soon. *Puppies*, yes, that will do. Some of the tension eases in my lower back as I feel myself come back from the edge.

Alex smooths her hand up and down my cock, both of us mesmerized at the sight. Her mouth envelopes me again and as the head of my cock hits the back of her throat, my hips buck.

"God, Alex, your mouth feels so good wrapped around my cock."

We've found a rhythm now; every time she takes me to the back of her throat I push a little further. Saliva is running down her chin unchecked, and I only let her up for air every so often. She's a fucking vision like this.

"You're such a good girl, taking my cock like it's what you were made to do. I don't know what I prefer more, seeing your mouth or pussy filled with my cock. Are you wet for me, princess?"

She hums in confirmation, the vibrations on my sensitive flesh another push toward euphoria.

I want to see how ready she is for me. "Show me," I growl, so close to coming in her mouth.

Alex dips her fingers into her panties, her whimpers fill the quiet. When she pulls them out they glisten back at me, covered in her arousal. *Fuck me.*

"Play with your pussy and get yourself off."

When she pops off of my cock, she's panting for breath. "I'm already so close though, Bastian."

"Good, I want you to come on your fingers as I fill your mouth with my cum until you're choking on it." I smirk down at her.

Without hesitation, she does as I demand, taking me into her mouth as her fingers dip back into her panties. Her hand is moving between her legs in sync with her mouth on my cock. The visual of her on her knees, with her legs spread and her fingers moving over her clit, is almost too much for me to take.

My balls draw up as I get closer to coming. When her mouth sucks me in harder, I feel the first squirt of my cum shooting to the back of her throat. Gripping her hair I grunt as my hips buck into her mouth. The stream of cum is never ending as it spills out of her mouth and onto her chin.

Her eyes are glassy as she stares up at me, moaning around my cock as she reaches her own orgasm. I withdraw from her mouth, my cock still semi hard, as I use my thumb to swipe the cum on her chin up.

"Show me," I command, and she knows exactly what I'm asking of her.

Alex opens her mouth. My cum is nowhere to be seen, at least until I put my thumb in her mouth and she licks it clean.

"You're such a good girl, aren't you, princess?"

I brush a strand of hair away from her face, bending and capturing her lips with my own. She moans into my mouth and I can taste the saltiness of my release on her tongue and I'll be damned if I don't get hard just kissing her.

"Please tell me you have condoms?" I rasp against her lips.

"Bedroom," she mumbles, throwing her arms around my neck as I carry her there.

I stop in the middle of the room, her arms and legs wrapped around me as I devour her mouth. I can't get enough of her. My hands are full of her ass cheeks, but I inch my fingers toward her core, needing to feel her. *She's fucking soaking wet for me.*

My cock bobs against my abs and as tempting as it is to slip inside her heat, I can't get the look on her face out of my head when she told me she wouldn't be comfortable.

I rip my mouth away from her as I carry her to the bed and rasp, "I need you now, hard and fast."

"Yes. Bedside table." She points to the table furthest from me and I make quick work of pulling out the packet of condoms.

I rip one off and throw the strip on the bed next to

her. Tearing open the wrapper, I roll the condom on, briefly wondering how long ago she used them.

My eyes close as I will my heart rate to slow down.

"Aside from you, it's been a while since I... you know," she gestures to me, reassuring me as if she can sense where my mind had gone.

She's wrong, if she thought I was taking a moment because it had gone there, but the relief I feel at what she's just said is like nothing I've ever felt before.

"Move into the middle of the bed, princess."

Her movements are hasty as she shuffles into the middle of the bed. *She wants this as much as I do.* I stalk toward her, climbing onto the mattress as I cover her with my body.

Settled between her legs, I smooth her hair back, looking into her eyes I ask, "How long?"

A frown pulls at her brow before she blinks, and what I'm asking registers for her. She looks into my eyes, her gaze searching. For what, I'm not sure.

"Nearly three years," she whispers and if I wasn't so close to her I might not have heard.

"You haven't had sex with anyone else since we hooked up nearly three years ago?"

I can barely believe it. She's fucking stunning and I know for a fact—because I've kept tabs on her—that she's dated people.

She shoves at my shoulder and if my cock wasn't nestled between her legs, I'd move away, but I'm desperate to be inside of her.

"You don't need to make a big deal about it. These things happen." She holds my gaze, as if defying me to tell her any different.

She's lying. Not about the three years thing, but the 'things happen' thing. She's not ready to tell me the real reason, and I'm not going to push her to give me an answer, but I know there is one.

A real answer that is.

Instead, I move her head to face me and capture her lips with mine.

Alexandra Williams is going to be the end of me whether that's from trying to work out all the intricacies that make her, her, or from the way I can't get enough of her.

TWENTY-THREE
Alex

I'm curled up on the couch watching reruns of *Friends*, munching on a bowl of popcorn when I'm hit with an overwhelming need to itch my scalp. Wiping my hand on the cotton of my leggings, I tentatively scrape my nails over the offending spot.

My focus goes back to the scene playing out in front of me, with Ross telling Rachel they were on a break. Without even thinking about it and almost too aggressively I scratch at my scalp again. A moan of appreciation leaves my lips as I relieve the sensation that's taunting me. I think I need to admit that it's been about a week too long since I last washed my hair.

I'm lucky that I only need to wash it once a week, but it's been over two since we came back from Chicago. Which means it's been at least three since I last washed it.

My phone is in my hands as I contemplate who to

call. Or more importantly, who I don't mind seeing me naked. My mom is on the other side of the country, so she's out of the running.

Meghan is a billion years pregnant, and it's not fair to drag her into the city to wash my hair. That leaves Savannah... and Sebastian.

Dialing Savannah, I bring the phone to my ear and wait for her to answer.

"Hey, darlin', you okay?"

It's noisy in the background and that's when I remember that Savannah is away with her job this week. *Fuck.*

"Sorry, I forgot you were away. I just need someone to help me wash my hair," I whine.

Savannah chuckles and the line goes quieter as I imagine her moving away from the crowd. "Can't your boyfriend do it for you?"

My brow furrows. "My boyfriend?"

I can hear the smile in Savannah's voice as she says, "Yeah, Sebastian."

"He's not my boyfriend."

"Whatever you need to tell yourself, sweetheart, but you've been with him constantly for the last few weeks," Savannah chuckles.

I'm distracted when I reply, absentmindedly scratching my scalp. "I've got to go call Se—" I stop myself before I say his name. She doesn't need any more fuel for her stories.

Savannah doesn't hold back when she laughs this

time, and I can just picture the looks she must be getting. "Let me know how it goes."

With a murmured goodbye, I hang up the phone and look down at his name on the screen. Instead of calling him, I pull up the trail of messages.

ALEX

I need your help.

I'm typing out a second message when my phone rings. His name displayed on the screen as my familiar ringtone plays out. I hesitate to answer, unsure why because I do need his help and it's not like he can wash my hair through a text message.

Savannah's words replay through my mind and I run my sweaty palm over my thigh, suddenly feeling hot.

On the last ring, I connect the call.

"Hello." My voice is uncertain, like I don't know who's on the other end. Clearing my throat, I sit up straight as I say, "Hello, Sebastian."

"What's wrong? What do you need my help with?" Worry is evident in his tone, and immediately, I want to put him at ease.

I run my fingers through my hair, stopping at the back of my head to scratch an unbearable itch.

"I was just wondering if you wouldn't mind... I mean, it's a bit of a strange request, but with my arm in a cast, I kind of can't wash my hair. Would you mind—"

He cuts me off, breathing a sigh of relief. "Jesus, princess. I thought something was wrong. I'll send a car to get you and meet you at my place. If you're there before me, fill the bath up."

Wow, I didn't think he'd say yes. Hold up... he wants me to go to his apartment? In the whole time I've known him, I've never been to his apartment.

"I don't have a key to your place."

"The concierge will let you in. Get ready, the car will be there in fifteen." He's quiet for a moment, as if he's considering his next words carefully. "Pack some clothes for tomorrow. We might as well stay at my place tonight. I'll see you soon, princess."

What the hell is happening?

I'm distracted when I say, "See you soon."

I disconnect the call and race to my bathroom, gathering up the products I need and swiping my bathrobe off of the back of the door. Throwing everything onto the bed, I rummage through my closet for a duffel bag. Some pajamas, clean underwear and a change of clothes for tomorrow go into the bag with my toiletries.

Suddenly overcome with nervousness, I sit on the end of my bed as nausea rolls through me. My stomach rolls and I swallow down the panic that threatens to overwhelm me.

SEBASTIAN

Take a breath, get out of your head and go downstairs. The cars waiting.

How did he know?

As if on autopilot, I stand from my bed, swiping up

my duffel bag as I move through my apartment. Downstairs, the driver has the backdoor of the town car open and his hand outstretched to take my bag.

"Miss Williams." He tips his head in greeting as I hand over my bag.

"Thank you."

I climb into the car, Sebastian's familiar woodsy scent enveloping me. He's sitting on the opposite side of the car, papers in his hand and his reading glasses perched on his nose, as he reads over them.

"I thought I was meeting you at your place."

The corner of his mouth lifts, and the faint indent of his dimple appears. "I thought I'd pick you up on the way there."

I try to keep my face neutral as what he's just shared sinks in. Surely the club is closer to his place than it is to mine. *I'll know soon enough.*

On the drive to his apartment, I ask Bastian questions about the club, trying to distract myself from scratching at my scalp. The drive passes by in a blur and he seems more than happy to talk, the papers long forgotten.

When the car pulls up outside, I look up at the gleaming building in front of me. It's got to be at least forty stories tall. The late October sun glints off of the mirrored windows. Sebastian holds the door open for me, his hand ready to help me from the car.

As I move onto the sidewalk, my steps are sure as I walk toward the revolving door. As if it's the most natural thing to do, his hand finds the small of my back as he falls into step beside me. The warmth of his palm, the reassurance I didn't even know I needed.

The lobby is clean and *very* empty. My sneakers squeak as we move across the lobby to the elevator. Sebastian presses the button and the doors swish open. He directs me in, following closely behind. It's then that I notice he has my bag. I was obviously too distracted to have remembered that.

When he steps back from pressing the button for the Penthouse, I ask, pointing to the bag in his hand, "Do you want me to take that?"

He turns his body toward me, a small smile on his lips as he picks up my hand and kisses the back of my fingers. "I've got it, princess."

I swallow thickly, my gaze locked on his as I stand mesmerized by him in the confines of the elevator. As the doors open, he gently tugs me forward by the hand he still has a hold on.

There's only one door on this floor. White waist-high wainscoting runs around the lobby, with the upper walls painted a dark blue. Sebastian unlocks the front door and holds it open as I step in. His apartment kind of reminds me of the place we stayed in, in Chicago.

I stand by the front door, unsure what to do. It's so clean and sterile, I'm almost afraid to mess it up.

"Why don't you go and run the bath and we'll get your hair washed? I can give you a tour later."

"Okay." I go to move before realizing I don't know where I'm going.

Sebastian chuckles, his straight white teeth sparking in the daylight coming through the glass walls. "It's just upstairs, second door on the left."

"Right." I move in the direction of the wide staircase.

It's a modern apartment, but it feels bare. The walls are stark white and the mahogany furniture looks, for the most part, unused.

His bathroom, on the other hand, is magnificent. White marble countertops line one wall, with his and hers sinks. One has men's toiletries scattered around it— a razor, toothbrush, shaving cream etc. The other is bare.

A large walk in shower is on the opposite side of the room. In the middle of the room, with a perfect view of Manhattan, is a deep, white, double ended, free-standing bath and brushed brass faucet. I waste no time in going to the bath and running the water.

When the bath is nearly three quarters of the way full, I turn off the faucet and test the temperature of the water before I undress. Wrapping my arm in a plastic bag I brought with me, I ease myself into the piping hot water. Careful not to submerge my arm, I relax back. It feels *so* good. The stress that seems to have hounded me these last few weeks, seeps out of me with every minute that passes.

"You look like you're enjoying that." His voice is like honey running over me.

When I look over at him, I find him leaning against

the doorjamb, the sleeves of his shirt rolled up. His arms are folded over his broad chest, and I've never wanted him more.

A smirk graces his lips as he pushes away from the frame and practically stalks towards me. If I didn't need my hair washing so badly, I'd stand up and beg him to carry me to his bed.

"Don't look at me like that, princess."

Slowly, I blink up at him as he stands tall above me. *God, he's handsome.* We maintain eye contact as he undoes each button on his shirt, shrugging out of it when it falls open. When his hands drop to the buckle of his jeans, so do my eyes. I watch in rapt fascination as he strips from his jeans too.

In just his boxers, he stands next to the tub expectantly. "I'm going to need you to move so I can sit on the edge." There's a gruffness to his voice, as if he's fighting his desire for me, just like I am with mine for him.

I do as he asks and move for him to step into the water. He sits on the edge and directs me to sit between his legs. My shampoo and conditioner are already lined up on the edge. He lifts the shower head from its cradle and turns on the faucet, testing the water before he runs it over my hair.

When he starts to shampoo my hair, I can't help the little whimpers that slip from my lips as he massages my scalp.

"You're so good at this." I moan.

He chuckles, the water sloshing in the tub slightly. "Am I?"

"Yes. Have you had a lot of practice? Did you do this for your mom?"

As soon as the words leave my lips, I realize I don't really know anything about his childhood. *Like he doesn't really know everything about me.*

He doesn't say a thing for the longest time. His fingers pausing for a fraction of a second is the only sign that something I've said has disrupted him.

His voice is the quietest I've ever heard it when he finally speaks. "I didn't know my mum. I grew up in foster care."

It's my turn to freeze, staying as still as a statue, afraid that if I move, he might stop talking. Instead, I watch him in the reflection of the window, his focus on washing my hair.

"There wasn't really anyone around who took care of me. Nobody wanted to have a three-year-old that's constantly acting out." He smirks at the memory. "I don't know anything about my family because nobody else did. I had to look after myself. You're the first person I've ever taken care of."

Bastian rinses out the shampoo, the sound of running water the only noise in the room.

TWENTY-FOUR

Sebastian

Releasing the breath I've been holding since I stopped talking, I turn off the faucet, shrouding the room in silence. I'm not quite sure what possessed me to open up to her like this. Even my closest friends don't know the intricacies of my childhood. Maybe it's the last three weeks that we've spent together and the fact that I've spent nearly every night with her, but the words just came out before I could stop them.

My eyes connect with Alex's in the reflection of the window. She turns to face me, her good hand resting on my knee, the diamond glistening under the lights, as she looks up into my eyes.

"Thank you for sharing that with me. I can't even begin to imagine what you must have gone through, and I really appreciate you doing this for me."

There's no pity on her face, like I was expecting. Instead, there's only empathy coating her words.

Of its own accord, my hand rises and pushes away a wet strand of her hair before cupping her cheek. Alex tips her head into my palm, wrapping her fingers around my wrist.

"My parents divorced when I was eleven. We were living out in Sacramento at the time, and my mom had cheated on my dad. I remember nights full of screaming matches between them, and how they tried to hide the ugliness from me. It's hard to do that when you have an inquisitive child."

I don't say a word as I direct her to turn around and finish telling her story. She hands me the shampoo bottle again, her fingers lingering.

"Eventually, they decided to divorce, but it took them five years of fighting to get to that point. My dad told me later that he didn't want me to have to choose between them for who I wanted to live with, but I think it did more damage than good. I know it's a good childhood in comparison, but I just wanted to share something about me with you."

"I appreciate you telling me." I pause before speaking again. "I'm sorry that you had to go through that, because although you had your parents with you as you grew up, they weren't there how they should have been. You're an amazing woman, Alex. I hope you know that."

"Hmm," she murmurs.

"You really are."

"Just like you're an amazing man? You've really gone above and beyond for me these past few weeks, Bastian."

"It was my fault you were on that horse, Alex. It's the least I could do."

She turns to face me, the water sloshing up the sides with the fast movement. "Do you really believe that? That it was your fault?"

"If I hadn't forced your hand with my plan, you never would have been on that horse."

Her hands cup my cheeks, her eyes intent on mine. "God, Bastian. It wasn't your fault. Something spooked the horse. It could have happened to anyone."

"But it happened to *you.*"

"And all I got was a broken arm." She searches my gaze. "Promise me you'll stop blaming yourself."

I don't know if I can. The guilt weighs on me every time I see her, and none of what I've done these past few weeks will ever make up for it.

"Promise me, Bastian."

"I promise, I'll try."

Fuck, I'd promise her anything she asked of me.

She turns back to face the window, and I rinse her hair. We fall quiet again, and as my hands massage the conditioner, I wonder if maybe I can have it all. The girl. The relationship I've always closed myself off from. The *family*.

Once the conditioner has been rinsed out, Alex stands, my attention on her instead of the fantasies flitting through my mind. She's naked, her body glistening in the light of the bathroom, New York City lit up behind her. My eyes roam over her.

"Eyes up here, big boy."

My smirk matches her own as I stand up, towering over her. Now we're both standing in the bath as the water drains out.

I step from the slippery tub, my arm going round her waist as I tug her to me. She's over my shoulder before she can protest, my hand landing with a crack on her now damp ass cheek. I grab a towel and carry her out of the bathroom.

"I'll look over *my girl* any way I please."

"I think you need to get your head checked, Mr. Worthington."

Another crack on her ass.

"I thought we were past that, princess."

Alex catches me by surprise when she smacks her hand across my ass. She giggles, and fuck if it doesn't make me feel light as a feather.

"You'll pay for that, princess."

When we reach my bedroom, I put her on her feet at the end of the bed, handing her the towel. She wraps it around her body as an almost overwhelming urge to rip it from her has my hands fisting at my side.

"How, exactly will I pay for it?"

I can't help the huff of a laugh that leaves me. "Not in any way you'd like."

She folds her arms over her chest, pouting up at me.

"Come on, let's get your hair dry and get into bed."

Her eyes drop to my arms as she says, "I hope you didn't do an arm workout today."

My brow furrows as I look at my arms, flexing my biceps. "Why?"

She moves to her bag that sits on the bench at the end of the bed. Unzipping it, she pulls out her hairdryer and some hair products before handing them to me.

She smirks up at me. "You'll find out."

It takes us nearly two hours to dry and style her hair. And although it gave me a workout I wasn't expecting, it was two hours of laughter, stolen kisses, and heated looks filled with promises of what was to come.

It's going to take time for me to open up to her fully, but even sharing what I did today is more than I've shared with anyone before. I'm starting to realize that Alex is really someone special that I could build a life with.

TWENTY-FIVE

Alex

Over the last five weeks, Sebastian and I have fallen into a routine. He's been attentive and going above and beyond what I ever would have expected from him. It's the best relationship I've ever been in. Because that's what this is; a relationship. No matter how much I try to fight against falling more in love with him everyday, I have failed. Miserably.

He even has a key now. I mean, it made sense at the time, and so I went out the day after he'd suggested it. Now he just lets himself into my apartment when he comes over after work. He stays here nearly every night. When he's done with work, he lets himself in and climbs into bed. He pulls me into his arms and tells me how much he's missed me. At least that's what he's done the handful of times I've pretended to be asleep when he comes in. That's the other thing. Sometimes, I can't sleep without him.

He gets mad when I take off his ring, and on more than one occasion he's bent me over the back of the couch and spanked me. It was thrilling, and after the first time, I started to do it on purpose because it always leads to explosive, can't get enough of him, sex. I don't think he minds.

It's Saturday morning and we're lounging on the couch, my head resting on Sebastian's thigh as I read a book, when his phone rings, breaking through the silence. He pulls off his reading glasses, as he puts down the documents he's been working on. I sit up, ready to give him some privacy.

He picks up his phone from the console table next to the couch.

"It's George Bennett," he murmurs, before swiping to answer the call and putting it on loudspeaker.

"George, it's good to hear from you, how is the family?"

My head tips to the side at the way he's just said that. It was… fake. I've been around Sebastian when he's made a lot of calls and none of them have had him using this almost too nice tone of voice. I study him as the call continues.

"Hi Sebastian, the family is doing well, thank you." A note of concern enters George's voice as he says, "I haven't heard from you in a while. How are you and Alex?"

My brows lift. He hasn't heard from Sebastian in a while?

His gaze flicks over to me, and he rests his hand on my thigh before he continues, "I'm great, thanks. Alex is doing much better than the last time you saw her. The cast was taken off the other day and she's been back at work for a few weeks now."

"Oh that's fantastic to hear." George pauses for a moment and I imagine him and Miriam exchanging glances as he continues.

"Miriam and I are going to be visiting the city soon. We would really like to take you and Alex out for dinner, as an apology of sorts, but also to discuss Sanctuary. I know we said we could look at transferring ownership after your wedding, but as you don't know when that's going to happen, especially after the accident, let's talk about it when we come. I'm rambling now, but let's talk when we visit in a couple of weeks."

Sebastian looks over at me, then down at his phone. I know what he's about to do. Even if he didn't have the look of resignation that's currently on his handsome face, I'd know.

"Look, George, there's something I have to tell you." He leans back, resting his head on the back of the couch.

I watch as his chest rises and falls, as if he's trying to find the courage to come clean.

The words form on my tongue before my mind has time to catch up. "We actually already got married, George," I blurt out, a flush of adrenaline tingling through my body as I realize I can't take that back.

Sebastian's gone above and beyond, looking after me

when he doesn't have to. I want to see him happy. I'd do anything to make that happen. Even going so far as to bring our lie up a notch.

Sebastian's eyes widen as he mouths 'what the fuck, Alex?'.

I sit taller, facing him as my shoulder lifts in a shrug, trying to play it off as nothing.

George cuts through the silence as he gleefully says, "Wow, that is wonderful. When did that happen?"

Neither of us says anything, too caught up in a silent argument. Me trying to defend my actions and him promising I'm going to pay. Sebastian rests a hand on my thigh, closing his eyes and pulling in a deep breath, as if to ground himself.

An internal war wages inside of me as I try for the thousandth time in a matter of weeks to tell myself that what we have isn't that serious. That I'm not falling for him, I can't.

"Hello? I think I've lost them, Miriam. Hello?"

Sebastian drags his eyes away from mine, clearing his throat before replying to George, "Sorry, the signal must have gone. We eloped. It was... Uh, a very spur of the moment thing. The accident put everything into perspective."

Sebastian's hand squeezes my thigh at the mention of the accident. I know he's still struggling with what happened—even though it's not his fault. I lay my hand over his trying to offer some sort of comfort.

"Of course." George's tone is somber as he speaks, as

if he feels guilty too. "We can't wait to see all the pictures and to hear all about your special day. I'll get in touch in a couple of days to confirm the details of our trip and we can plan a dinner. It looks like it'll be the fifteenth. Speak soon."

"Take care."

The fifteenth is in two week's time and we have to somehow get pictures of a wedding that hasn't happened.

"I think I messed up," I whisper.

"You think?" Sebastian asks, as cool as ever.

My hand reaches out and slaps across his bicep. "You don't need to be a dick about it."

I stand from the couch and start pacing in the small space between the coffee table and the television, my nerves getting the best of me. Sebastian sits forward, his elbows resting on his knees as he looks at me in amusement.

"This isn't funny, Bastian."

"No? Because from where I'm sitting, it looks like my fiancée is having a meltdown over having told someone we already got married."

His fiancée.

"Come here, Alex," he demands, leaning back on the sofa and opening his arms for me.

There's no hesitation as I walk to him and climb into his lap. *My safe space.* The sound of his heart beating at a steady rhythm under my palm calms me. I close my eyes and pull in a deep breath as his strong arms envelop me.

"It's okay, princess. We can figure this out."

His hand smooths up and down my back, but it's doing nothing for me. My mind is whirling with thoughts on how I can get us out of this. How we can come clean without fucking it up for Bastian?

"The way I see it, we have two options. I come clean to George about everything or we stage a fake wedding."

I lift my head to look at him so I can search his eyes for some sort of answer. What does a fake wedding even entail?

My voice is barely above a whisper as I ask, "A fake wedding? How would we do that?"

Because Bastian coming clean isn't an option. He might have put us in this position by lying about me being his fiancée, but I don't want him to tarnish his reputation to—what—make me feel better?

"We'd get some friends together and take some pictures to make it look like we had a wedding. We can hire a professional photographer and a venue, so it looks real. Take my black Amex and get whatever you want."

"I don't need to spend your money," I murmur.

Staging a fake wedding sounds a lot more doable than legally tying myself to Bastian. Especially when he's promised he won't fall in love with me.

I sit back and observe his weirdly calm demeanor. It seems to be in stark contrast to my internal freak out.

My heart races. This is a lot to process. I detangle myself from Bastian and walk to my bedroom. Climbing under the covers, I pull the duvet over my head and try to calm my breathing. I hold up my hand and look at the diamond as it shines, even under the darkness of the covers. It calms me. I need to call my therapist.

When this charade with George is over, we don't have to end. Right?

He has me in an emotional chokehold, and I'm not sure how to get out of it. Or if I even want to.

The covers are pulled off and I look up to find Bastian standing next to the bed looking down at me. Concern is etched across his face when he sees me curled into the fetal position in the middle of the bed.

Instead of laughing at me or telling me to get over myself, he climbs in next to me and pulls me into his chest. I shouldn't take this much comfort from him. I've already taken so much.

"What's wrong, princess?" he asks, his arms tightening around me momentarily as I burrow into his t-shirt.

"Nothing," I whisper.

"It's not nothing, baby, especially if you ran out like you did. Come on, talk to me."

"I..." I close my eyes, my heart racing as I dig deep and look for the courage to ask him what I've wanted to know for weeks because I can't keep wondering. "What happens when you get the club? Do we just forget everything we've been doing as if it never happened?"

He's quiet for so long I'm not sure if he's going to answer me but I don't miss the way his arms seem to loosen around me or how he exhales a heavier breath. The words are too much for him to speak.

"I care about you, Alex." He pauses, trying to find the right words. "When I promised you that I wouldn't fall in love with you, I meant it. I've enjoyed the time we've spent together for the last month and when this is over, I don't think I'll be ready to walk away. We don't need to put a label on this. We can just take it one day at a time."

A frown graces my brow, and I pull away from him, needing to look into his eyes. I search his gaze for answers but come up short. There's nothing but an unreadable expression reflected back at me.

"Don't think too much into it, princess."

He's right. What we've had this last month has been nothing short of amazing. He's mine in every sense of the word, just like I'm his. We don't need labels to define us.

"Okay."

His lips brush over my hair as he pulls me closer.

"I need to go to work soon. I've got a conference call with London, but I'm going to leave my card and I want you to get whatever we need for next weekend."

When he's gone, I climb out of my bed and find my phone, shooting off a text to Meghan and Savannah, asking if they can come over. Within seconds my phone rings.

TWENTY-SIX

Alex

W hen I got off of the call with Meghan, I called Savannah. They both dropped what they were doing and came to my place. With drinks in hand, we're sitting in my living room and I'm updating them on everything that's happened since Sebastian and I got back from Chicago.

"So, let me get this right… You told the old guy, that Sebastian wants to buy the club from, that you already married him and now you have to stage a fake wedding? And your fake fiancé left you his credit card to spend *whatever* you want on a wedding that isn't real?" Savannah asks.

Even though her face is free of judgment, I can't help but smirk at the insane situation I've landed myself in.

"That's pretty much it."

My eyes flick between Meghan and Savannah as

silence fills the room. I collapse against the back of the couch as a lump forms in my throat.

"What's wrong with that?" Meghan asks as she leans forward.

I don't recognize my own voice when I reply to her, "I might, possibly, have feelings for him that are more than I bargained for."

Meghan's voice is filled with concern as she asks, "You know you don't have to do any of this, right?"

"I know," I whisper.

"But you want to... for him?" Savannah says, her face filled with a knowing look.

I don't need to think about it, my response is immediate. "Yes."

Meghan stands from her seat, smoothing a hand over her growing bump as she moves to grab her bag by the front door. "Come on, let's go get you a dress and organize your dream wedding. We have money to spend!"

"I don't need a dress. I can wear som—"

"No," Meghan interrupts. "I'm not letting you wear an already worn dress for your staged wedding. One day, you'll look back at these pictures and be mad that you didn't make the effort."

"You do know this is a *fake* wedding, not a real one, right?"

Savannah waves off my mild protest. "I agree with Meghan. What woman turns down an unlimited budget when shopping? Plus, when we've found you the perfect dress, then we can go and get drunk."

Getting drunk sounds great right about now because this is either the best idea I've ever had, or the worst. Only time will tell. As I move around in my bedroom, I hear Meghan and Savannah conspiring in the other room.

"Which card did he leave you?" Meghan calls.

Not wanting to shout through to her, I walk into the living room as I pull on my coat. "Yes, he left me a card, but I don't plan on using it." I move a piece of mail to cover the black card he left on the table by the door before she sees it. "This isn't real, so we really don't need to make a big deal out of it. We can go to the courthouse, get some photos on the front steps, and then go to the park or something for some more."

"Yeah, that's not happening. The least he can do, after dragging you into his mess, is pay for us all to have a nice dinner and get us all a new dress each," Savannah argues, a smirk falling across her face.

"I agree. This could be your only wedding, you have to do it right," Meghan chimes in.

Has she not been listening to anything I've said today?

"This is a *staged* wedding. There will be no vows, no party, no declarations. This isn't some fairytale where we'll live happily ever after."

"You don't know that," Meghan says with a grin. I think she's turned delusional since Cooper and her got together. She's intent on everyone having a happily ever after, and, for some reason, she thinks Sebastian is the one to give me mine.

Skirting around me, Meghan goes right for the mail I moved. She uncovers the card and her face lights up. "Ooh. A *black* Amex?"

I try to grab it back from her, but she tucks it into her purse and beelines it to the door. For a pregnant woman she's fast. Savannah and I follow her out, exchanging a look of amusement. It's useless arguing with Meghan when she's this determined.

Meghan and Savannah chatter amongst themselves as we ride in the back of a cab to one of my favorite department stores on Fifth Avenue. Sometimes, if I'm treating myself after handling a tricky case, I like to pick up something to make my day brighter.

Today feels like one of those days.

Despite what my friends think, I'm not a shopaholic. Sometimes I come and just browse the racks of expensive clothes and try on some pretty dresses, leaving without buying a thing.

As soon as we walk into the store, Meghan and Savannah make a beeline for a rack of royal blue evening dresses. They really are taking this way too far, but I guess it can't hurt to have a look. I move away from them to a rack of white dresses further back on the floor.

My hand lands on a white dress with big, long puffy sleeves. From how it hangs, I can tell it's off the shoulder and that it would cinch me in at the waist. It's simple yet classy.

I stare at the dress, lost in thought, when from behind me there's a gasp and a squeal. *Oh, please tell me they didn't see this.* I stuff the dress back on the rack as quickly as I can, because it's perfect. *Too perfect.*

I don't want this to be a memorable moment. Certainly not when no matter how good Bastian and I are together, our story won't end with me wearing a white dress like this for real. No, whatever dress I choose, I won't be keeping it.

"Oh, my God, that one is perfect. You have to try it on, Alex," Savannah demands, reaching around me to pull the dress from the rack again. "Meghan, get your butt over here. Is this not the most perfect dress?"

Meghan scurries over, her face filled with delight. "Oh, my God! Yes, it's perfect."

Before I know what's happening, I'm ushered into the fitting room and the dress is hung on the hook next to the mirror.

"The quicker you try it on, the quicker we can leave." Meghan winks at me, closing the door and leaving me in peace.

Is this how Meghan felt all those years ago when I shoved her into her bathroom to put the dress on that I'd bought her?

No, she at least had tequila to get her through it.

Heaving out a heavy sigh, I sit on the bench that runs along the back of the changing room and slip out of my brown ankle boots. Next goes my jacket, then my jeans and finally my t-shirt, until I'm in nothing but my strapless bra and G-string.

When I step into the dress, I know it's the one. At

least for the purpose I'd be buying it for. It's short, sitting just above mid-thigh but it fits me perfectly. Showing just enough cleavage that I feel sexy. It cinches me in at the waist, like I knew it would.

Briefly I wonder what dress I would have chosen if this was a real wedding. A sense of longing washes over me at the thought followed by a wave of nausea.

Will I ever get over him?

I'm scared that he'll walk away with ease as I fight to forget him.

But I can't think like that. He wants to see where this goes, which is more than I ever thought I'd get from him, so maybe my daydreams aren't so far-fetched. The obsessive way he is over the ring on my finger certainly speaks volumes, even if his tongue hasn't caught up yet.

I'm caught up in my own head when a gentle knock sounds on the door followed by Meghan's soft voice, "Alex? Are you okay in there?"

Probably not.

"I'm fine. Just coming out now," I say, as I pull the door open.

A collective gasp sounds as I strut into the seating area, my thoughts from earlier buried deep inside.

"I knew it was the one for you as soon as I saw it on the hanger." Meghan beams, a smug smile on her face as she follows behind me.

Savannah rolls her eyes before walking to me with a beautiful pair of royal blue shoes in her hand. They have a big bow on the back and add the perfect amount of statement to the minimalist look.

"We couldn't have you not wear something blue, like that old rhyme." Her smile is almost sly as she bends to help me slip on the heels.

"I'm only putting them on because they're beautiful. I don't need to follow some stupid tradition for a fake wedding photoshoot. In fact, you guys really need to think of it like that. It's a photoshoot, nothing more."

I move to the mirror and turn from side to side as I look at the dress. Truthfully, it's probably more something I'd wear for a night out than my wedding. I know Sebastian said to make it my dream wedding, but I do still have some hopes that one day I'll get married.

One can only hope it's to him.

TWENTY-SEVEN

Alex

The bass pounds in Passion and I scream-sing along to *Break My Soul* by Beyoncé. When we got to my place, Ben was waiting for us, and we hit the town as a foursome. Meghan and Savannah have disappeared someplace, and Ben, well, Ben found a guy hours ago and hasn't been seen since.

I've been content to just dance by myself. The alcohol still flows through me, and any anxiety I've had over this fake wedding thing is long forgotten. When the track changes over, my hips swing to the beat as I close my eyes and block out everything but the music.

Dancing is my therapy. No matter what's going on, if I can dance, I'm happy. I can get lost in the music, moving my body to the rhythm of whatever's playing.

My eyes look up to the privacy glass of his office, and even though I can't see him, I feel his eyes on me. Ever since I walked in, I've felt him.

Before I know what I'm doing, my feet carry me through the club and up the stairs to his office. Nobody stops me.

Not bothering to knock, I walk into his office to find him leaning against the glass, his hands stuffed in his pockets and the sleeves of his sweater pushed up his forearms.

When he approaches me, I look up into his bluey-green gaze, getting lost in their depths. In my tipsy state, I can't help but mess with him. "Hello, husband."

I expect him to shut me out, but his nostrils flare, and not in anger. No. I think my soon-to-be fake husband likes the title.

That's interesting.

Bastian wraps an arm around my waist and pulls me into his chest, a hand possessively resting just above the curve of my ass. I clutch onto the soft fabric of his sweater as I breathe in a breath of his woodsy cologne.

God, I've missed him.

"Princess, did you miss me?" he whispers against the shell of my ear.

I turn my head, my lips less than an inch away from his. Did he read my mind or have I lost my ability to hide my thoughts around him? My eyes flick between his heated gaze and parted lips.

"Always, husband."

He growls, capturing my lips in a punishing kiss. His tongue demands entry into my mouth and I give it willingly, my tongue tangling with his.

He breaks the kiss, resting his forehead on mine as he rasps out, "I need you, now."

A whimper of need slips past my lips and that's all the confirmation he needs as he bends to lift me up and into his arms. Bastian walks to the couch, taking a seat, making sure to keep me in his lap.

When he captures my lips again, it's nothing like the kiss only moments ago. This one is like he's savoring me. Like he's committing my lips to memory.

The thought is wiped from my mind when his hands slide under the hem of my dress, almost painfully grabbing onto my ass.

His labored breathing matches mine as he rests his forehead against mine, breaking the kiss. "Let's go back to my place. I don't have any condoms here."

"You know, for a man who was having a lot of sex, you sure are ill-prepared whenever we're out."

He chuckles and I think it's the best sound I've ever heard. "I really am. I'll do better, I promise, princess."

Bastian runs his thumb down the column of my throat. Such a simple touch and yet it has me shifting my hips and I try to ease the ache between my legs.

Neither of us speaks. The only sound filling the room comes from the music seeping through the walls.

His brow quirks when I don't make a move, and I find myself uttering, "I don't want anything between us anymore."

He looks into my eyes, not saying a word until I can't take the intensity of his stare anymore and look away.

"Are you sure?"

With a nod of my head as I turn to face him again, I say, "I'm sure."

"I should ask you this when we're both sober. In fact, we should go back to my place and get a good night's sleep then discuss this in the morning."

"I need you now, too. Make me feel good..." I run a hand down the front of his sweater, over the hard ridges of his abs until I reach the buckle of his belt. "Please."

He studies me for a moment and I can see the war taking place inside of himself as he contemplates if it's the right thing.

"Or are you..." My gaze drops to the obviously hard bulge in his hands before lifting to him again. "You know, broken?" I ask.

He bucks his hips up, and I moan at the contact. "Does it fucking feel broken, princess?"

God, no, it doesn't feel fucking broken.

Composing myself, I shift in his lap again, leaning forward to whisper in his ear. "Then use it, Bastian."

He lifts a hand and pushes a strand of hair away from my face as I lean back. "I just don't want you to regret this."

I see the hesitation in his eyes, as if he's afraid of what it means for me to do this with him, but my response is almost immediate because I wouldn't ever regret him. "I won't, I promise."

We both move at the same time, grappling onto one another, our mouths fused as if we've been starved. I shouldn't be feeling like this about him, but he means something to me.

That's the truth.

I feel grounded when I'm in his arms. When he's devouring me like he needs me to breathe.

I unzip his jeans, pulling his hard cock free from its confines. He hisses against my lips as I stroke his length.

"Princess, if you want me to last you're going to have to stop that."

Unable to resist his warm, solid length, I stroke him one final time, moving my hands to rest on his stomach. He pushes the hem of my dress to my waist before he rips my G-string from me. I hiss at the sting but his fingers rubbing over my sensitive clit, dipping into my dripping pussy, soon has me forgetting the pain. My moans are loud as he sinks his thick finger into me.

"Show me your ring."

What?

Wait, I need to use my words. "What?"

"Show me your ring."

My brows pull together as I try to comprehend what he's asking me. In my defense, my focus is on the sensations he's igniting inside of me, not on having a damn conversation.

The engagement ring.

I hold up my hand and show him the ring on my finger as I grind my hips onto his hand. He doesn't let me get the release I need, instead, he removes his finger from me, licking it clean before grabbing a handful of my ass, squeezing it almost painfully again. "Good girl, I was worried I was going to have to punish you."

He lifts my hips, lining himself up with me as he slides into my slick core, filling me completely. It feels like he was made for me. A perfect fit.

"Bastian, you feel so good," I gasp.

With a hand around my waist and his cock buried deep inside, he flips me onto my back on the couch. Hovering above me, he still doesn't move like I expect him to. Instead, he drops his forehead to my shoulder.

"Fuck, baby, you feel so fucking good. With your hot little cunt wrapped around me, strangling my cock. I'm going to fill you with my cum and then when you think you can't take anymore, I'm going to fill you up again."

"Bastian, please, just fucking move," I plead, rocking my hips to create some friction.

He has the audacity to fucking chuckle at me and if I wasn't feeling so needy, I'd get up and leave him with a piece of my mind and a set of blue balls.

His first few thrusts are tentative, almost as if he wants to make sure he doesn't finish too soon. As my moans grow with each thrust, they become more and more powerful. We move in sync as his cock strokes my walls, bringing me closer and closer to the precipice.

"Princess, you need to be quiet if you don't want to draw a crowd."

My eyes go to his, silently telling him that right now I don't care. I'm too far gone to be bothered that anybody could discover us.

Bastian chuckles darkly. "Oh, you don't care. Shall I take you out there now? Like this, impaled on my cock, with that wanton look in your eyes."

I tip my head back, unable to deal with everything he's throwing at me. The way his cock is stoking the fire inside of me, how he can read me like nobody ever has before, or the way he describes putting me on display for people I don't know and how it gets me wetter than I've ever been.

He latches onto the exposed column of my throat, sucking on the sensitive skin.

His breathing is ragged as he makes his way to my ear and murmurs, "No. I don't think I will. All of you is only for me to see from now on."

"I didn't say I—" I pant, unable to get the words out as he increases his pace.

Fuck.

It's too soon. I try my hardest to hold off, but he doesn't give me a chance to come back from the edge, he just keeps pushing me closer and closer until I fall over.

My cry of release is cut off as he captures my mouth, his tongue demanding entry. I give it to him without question, just as I have with my heart.

When he pulls away this time, he says, "That's it baby, cover my cock in your cum." He drops his eyes to where we're joined, a look of fascination on his face. "God, you look so good taking my cock in your hot little pussy, princess."

He reaches his hand between us, swiping his thumb

over my clit, building a fire inside of me again. I whimper at the contact, still sensitive from my orgasm.

"Bastian, I can't, not again."

"You can. Just one more, princess."

"I can't—" I cry out as my body is wracked with spasms.

Bastian follows behind me, grunting out his own orgasm. Our breathing is the only sound filling the room. The bass from the club shaking the glass, a reminder of where we are.

He still fills me.

Keeping his cum inside of me.

When he does finally pull out, I can feel his release sliding down my leg, but I make no move to stop it. My eyes follow him as he stands, tucking himself back in and moving to the bathroom. I'm vaguely aware that my lower half is still exposed and somewhere on the floor is my ruined underwear.

After a few moments, Bastian walks back into the room with a cloth in his hand. I can't take my eyes off of him as he walks toward me. His eyes roam over my body, heated with his need for me.

He stands tall above me, and I hold my hand out for the cloth.

"Move to the edge of the couch and spread your legs," he commands.

I consider for a fraction of a second arguing with him, but I decide against it as I maneuver myself to the edge. My knees meet, not quite ready to bare myself to him fully when he's still dripping from me. He takes a knee in front of me, pushing my legs apart, before lifting one and placing it on his thigh.

"I think this might be my favorite thing. You look so perfect like this."

His touch is gentle as he cleans me up. It shouldn't be sexual, but it turns me on, seeing this larger than life man on his knees in front of me, cleaning our mixed arousal from my thighs.

When he's done, he discards the cloth on the coffee table. He takes a seat on the couch next to me, maneuvering my legs onto his lap. Over the last six weeks, we've been in this exact position hundreds of times and it's been relaxing, but right now it's anything but. All I can think about is how this seems to have become so complicated over the last few months.

Sometimes I wish I could go back to the days when I hated him, because then I wouldn't want the things I do now. It was so much easier then. When I was certain of my feelings for him and his for me.

"I can practically hear the cogs turning. What are you thinking?" His hand smooths up and down my bare legs.

"I'm just wondering why George said he hadn't heard from you in a while," I lie. I have been wondering but it definitely wasn't what I was just thinking about.

His chest jumps as he chuckles, "That's what you're thinking about right after I just made you orgasm twice? Damn, I need to work on my game."

"I don't think you need your ego inflating any bigger than it already is, so answer the question, Bastian."

He holds his hands up, as if to ward me off. "Okay, princess. He said he hadn't heard from me in a while because he hadn't."

Oh, my God, why does he have to be so difficult?

I can't contain the eye roll that unleashes, sending my eyes to the back of my head. "But why? It's been six weeks since we came back."

"I think maybe I need to take your mind off of George Bennett. I can't have him occupying my girl's thoughts so soon after I've filled her pussy with my cum. It's unconscionable."

My girl.

For a moment, I'm distracted by the fact he's called me his. As I feel his hand skate higher up my thigh, I slam back into the present.

"Bastian, stop avoiding the question and answer it," I demand, my voice filled with authority.

He heaves out a heavy breath as he relaxes back into the couch. "I didn't reach out to him after we came back because your accident put things into perspective. I don't need that specific club, and I sure as hell don't need to jump through hoops to please him. Does that answer the question?"

I nod my head as a million questions fight for supremacy in my mind. If he doesn't want the club any more then why are we doing the staged wedding? He could have come clean to George even after I said we were married.

There was a hint of venom in his tone, which I know wasn't directed at me. So, does he not like George? Is that what all of this is about?

My eyes get heavy from the emotional rollercoaster of the day. With his hand smoothing up and down my leg, I succumb to the sleep that's dragging me under. All the questions I'm yet to have answers to, swirling around in my mind.

TWENTY-EIGHT

Sebastian

As soon as I have my revenge, I'll talk to Alex and convince her that what we have is enough. She'll see that how it's been with us these last few weeks is good. In fact, it's more than good. We have a connection. She's been consuming my thoughts, and I'm not entirely mad about it.

My mind goes to the events of last Saturday. I wasn't expecting her to come to Passion that night but, as with every time she comes to the club, I knew the second she walked in.

When she stepped into my office, it was like everything that was wrong, righted itself. I need her like I need air to breathe.

Fuck, I'm getting in so deep with her.

Holding her in my arms felt right, and having her in my lap, telling me she didn't want anything between us, it fucking blew my mind. That this woman, *Alex*, wanted me in that way. *Bare*. With nothing between us. She put her trust in *me*.

She fell asleep on my couch and when the club closed I woke her up and took her home. I haven't seen her since. I think maybe she's pushing me away again and I don't know why, but it could also be that she's been busy. The whole thing is messing with my head, how she can run hot and cold like this, because I never know what I'm going to get.

"Are you sure this is a good idea?" Cooper asks, dragging me back into the present.

He's been eyeing me skeptically since he arrived and this is about the hundredth time he's asked this question.

"For the *fifth* time, yes."

"Because Alex isn't the type of person that can just marry someone without feelings involved. She's not clinical like that."

"And I am?" I scoff, my brows reaching for my hairline at his comment. "Also, I don't know how many times I have to tell you this, but we aren't *really* getting married."

Cooper scrubs a hand over his jaw, leaning forward to rest his elbows on his thighs, "That's not what I meant and you know it. You don't do things like this. In all the years I've known you, you've never had anything as serious as this."

I see he's just going to ignore what I've said about this not being real.

"This is just for show. The wedding photos and stuff, that is. It's just so I can get the club. I've already told you all of this."

"I really don't think this is a good idea. Why do you want this club anyway? You could have any location in any city. Why *this* one?"

I'm not ready to share with anyone why I want this particular club. Or the fact that I was ready to give it up for her. If I tell anyone, it will be Alex.

I'm saved by the bell, so to speak, when Alex swings open the front. She's dressed in a pair of black jeans, a white t-shirt and a zip-up hoodie. Behind her trails, Meghan, Savannah, Ben and another guy that looks vaguely familiar.

My eyes meet Alex's, but all I get from her is a tilt of her head as she goes in the direction of the kitchen. It's been almost a week since I've seen her, and I can't wait a second longer to kiss her again. I'm on my feet and striding towards her when a hand on my arm stops me mid stride.

"I hope you don't mind that we brought the others," Meghan says, drawing my attention to her.

"I don't mind if that's what Alex wants."

"Not really, but we didn't give her a choice." I look down at Meghan, sympathy is etched across her face. "Just leave her be for now. She's... just leave her for now."

Confused, I don't say a word as I sit back in my seat, lost in my own thoughts, as the others fill the silence.

My eyes don't leave the entrance of the hallway that leads to the kitchen. I wait to catch a glimpse of her, wondering what she's up to in there.

What was Meghan going to say before she stopped herself?

Is everything okay with her?

It's like a weight has been lifted from my chest when she walks into the room with Savannah, an easy smile on her lips. She takes a seat and the girls and Ben huddle around her. My eyes don't leave her. I drink her in, tracing over the features of her face.

She's okay.

We settle into an easy conversation about the day, Alex running through the itinerary, letting us know where we need to be and what to expect.

Less than thirty minutes goes by when Alex ushers the men, minus Ben, out of my apartment. A look passes between us as she goes to close the door. It says so much but so little at the same time. I capture her hand, pulling her to me as the doors to the elevator close on Noah and Cooper, leaving me alone in the corridor with Alex.

"What are you doing?"

My eyes rest on her bare fingers, and as I capture her hand in mine, I say, "Where's your ring, princess?"

"Sebastian," she admonishes, as if now isn't the time.

I beg to differ. My ring should be on her finger at all times.

"It's Bastian, princess."

She breathes out a sigh as if it's all too much and, without thinking, I tug her into me, my arms enveloping her. *God, I've missed just holding her.* A sense of peace blankets me as I revel in the feel of her for the first time in nearly a week. The depth of my feelings for her terrifies me. I've never experienced anything like it before.

As I drink in her features, my mind replays the last time I saw her and how good everything has been between us. I don't understand why she's being so cagey now. Something must have freaked her out.

"Where's your ring, Alex?"

My eyes explore hers as she looks up at me. If she tells me she took it off and left it at home, I'll have her back in my apartment and bent over my knee faster than she can blink.

One of her fingers goes to the chain around her neck, and I breathe a sigh of relief as she pulls it free of her t-shirt to show me her ring.

"I told you not to take it off."

"Technically I didn't." She smirks.

I arch a brow as I ask, "Finding loopholes, princess?"

"It's kind of my job," she replies.

Fuck, I've missed her.

I bend and lift her up, forcing her legs to wrap around me. In three steps I have her pressed against the wall next to the elevator.

"I still think I should punish you," I breathe against her lips.

She captures my lips with hers, closing the distance between us. She tastes like tequila and just one lick of it makes me pull away. A frown tugs on my brow—it's only just gone midday.

"You been drinking, baby?"

Alex drags her full bottom lip into her mouth, nodding in confirmation.

"Why?" I ask, genuinely curious as I set her down on her feet.

Alex dips her head, before lifting her chin and saying, "I needed the courage to do this."

"Christ, Alex." It's my turn to look away from her now. I'm ashamed that she'd need to have alcohol to go through with this *stupid* plan. "Why didn't you call me? I'm sorry. I'm sorry that you felt you needed to do that. You don't need to do this. Just say the word and we can call it off."

"No," she says, almost instantly. "If we do that then it's all been for nothing. Just kiss me, Bastian."

My eyes roam over her face, searching for something, anything but I come up short. She's still got her guard up.

Just one kiss.

This kiss is different, I only meant to reassure her, but it turns into something much more. It's slow and sensual and has the power to undo me. Her full lips part, allowing my tongue to dive in and explore her. The pace is slow and steady. Neither of us are in a rush, content to take what the other is willing to give.

"Bastian," she moans.

The sound of a door opening pulls my attention away and over to Savannah who is standing in the doorway, a hand over her eyes.

"If you guys are doing stuff, you need to stop." Two of her fingers spread and she peeks through at us as I press Alex against the wall. "Urgh, you could have at least been doing more PG13 stuff. Jeez, guys, come on." With that she turns on her heel and walks back into my apartment.

I can't help the laugh that breaks free at Savannah's ridiculousness. As I step back, Alex lets go of the lapels of my jacket, smoothing her fingers down as she does.

"Go on, princess. Go get ready and I'll see you at the courthouse."

She turns away from me and walks to my apartment, stopping to look at me over her shoulder before she walks in and closes the door.

I don't move right away, instead I savor the taste of her on my tongue. And how we can't seem to keep our hands off of each other, because I know for certain if Savannah hadn't come out, I wouldn't have stopped at just one kiss.

When I arrive in the lobby of my apartment building, I find Cooper and Noah talking by the door.

"What took you so long?" Cooper asks as I approach them.

"I was just talking to Alex. Come on, let's go."

A knowing look creeps onto Cooper's face before he turns to leave the building.

Noah and I follow behind him as he climbs into the SUV that's parked out front. An easy chatter fills the car as we cruise through the streets of New York to the hotel that overlooks Central Park, which we've rented a room in.

"How long have you and Savannah been together?" I ask, looking for a distraction.

Noah chokes on the water he's just taken a sip of and I look at him with concern, patting him on the back.

"No, man, she's my best friend's little sister. Completely off limits. And anyway, I've just broken up with my long-term girlfriend."

I never would have guessed that, given how he looks at Savannah. The way his eyes tracked her in my apartment, much like mine did with Alex.

"She lives with you. Are you saying you haven't done anything?" Cooper asks.

"Not a thing."

"But you want to, right?" I ask, my gaze is assessing. "You're among friends here. We won't tell anyone, and the likelihood of us meeting her brother is slim to none."

"Fuck," he breathes, and with that single word, I have my answer.

Cooper and I glance at each other. Neither of us can stop the conspiratorial smiles that mirror on our faces.

"Whatever those looks are for, wipe them off your faces now. Nothing is going to happen. I promised her brother I wouldn't ever go near her."

"Rules are meant to be broken, my friend. Trust me. I broke the rules I made with Meghan—well, not all of them but most—and Sebastian here." Cooper slaps me on the shoulder before continuing, "Is well on his way to breaking the one he made with Alex."

I shove his hand off my shoulder, annoyed that he would say something like that, because I'm *not* falling in love with her.

"No, mate, I'm not."

Cooper just chuckles as he says, "Whatever you need to tell yourself."

Not wanting to dwell on the matter—because I'm not about to speak to the guys about how conflicted I am with my feelings—I change the subject. "How's Lizzie doing?"

A sure fire way to distract Cooper is to talk about his daughter.

"Oh, man, she's growing so big. She can't wait to be a big sister and keeps walking around with her belly pushed out, telling Meghan she's going to be a big sister soon too." He chuckles.

Cooper happily talks about Lizzie the rest of the drive to the hotel while Noah and I sit in silence, both lost in our own thoughts. Him, I'm sure, about Savannah and his feelings toward her, and me, about Cooper's accusation that I'm falling for Alex.

I should just ignore his comment, but when it's reflective of my own thoughts this past week, it's hard to.

TWENTY-NINE

Alex

"**A**re you sure you want to do this?" Meghan asks as she hands me a bouquet of pink peonies we picked up on the way to the courthouse.

"It's only some photos. It's not like I'm really marrying the guy. And, I gave my word."

She doesn't know that he's paid off my student loans in exchange for me going along with his plan. None of my friends know. And I plan on keeping it that way. Only Bastian and I know what we agreed he'd do in exchange for my help. Truthfully, I don't care about our deal. I just want Bastian to be happy and get what he wants.

"Personally, I think you're crazy for even—Ouch," Savannah cries as Meghan slaps her on the shoulder. If looks could kill, Savannah would be on the ground with the look Meghan gives her.

"Personally," Ben emphasizes while giving Savannah

a side-eye. "I think you're pretty damn smart. I mean, all you've got to do is take some pictures and you get to wear a gorgeous diamond. It helps that he's hella hot and makes you orgasm. It's a no brainer really."

My cheeks heat at Ben's words as I reply with a chuckle, "I wish I'd never told you that."

Ben smirks, stepping in front of me, blocking my view of the courthouse, as he fixes the short veil we picked up in a bridal store during our shopping trip last weekend. God, I love my friends. I shouldn't be nervous. After all, it's just a bunch of photos, but I am. I'm glad they've all come to support me on my fake wedding day.

Meghan grabs my hand and directs me away from the others to stand next to a pillar as we wait for the photographer to arrive. Concern coats her face.

"Just say the word and I'll have you in a cab away from here, *Sex and the City* style."

I pick up her hand and hold it in mine, a smirk gracing my lips. "Thank you, but it really isn't necessary. It's not like this is a real wedding..."

"I know, I know. It's just some photos." She rolls her eyes at me. "I know you have feelings for him, Alex. I've known you since we were five-years-old. I know when you're in love. I just don't want you to do something that could break you. Even something as simple as taking some fake wedding photos."

I should have known I couldn't hide *everything* from her. She's been with me through all stages of my life.

My eyes drop to the soft petals of the bouquet in my

hand, searching for the right words to admit out loud for the first time, just what I've gotten myself into. The more time I spent with him, the less I seemed to dislike him, until somehow I needed him like water to survive. My eyes sting with the burn of tears, because no matter how good it's been, it *will* end someday. He's not a forever kind of person, no matter how much his actions keep proving otherwise.

"You're right." My voice cracks and I clear my throat as I lift my chin. "I have fallen for him."

"What do you want to do?"

What I *need* to do and what I *want* to do are two very different things. I need to go through with this because I gave my word. He paid off my student loans, and Sebastian has a lot riding on us pulling this off. What I want to do is call this all off and ask him to make *me* his exception. To give us a chance at being *real*.

The lines have blurred too much and I don't know what's real and what's fake anymore. I don't want *any* of it to be fake.

"Megs, I'd do anything for him. Just like you would for Cooper. When you love someone, you'd help them bury the body. This is basically like that. Just without the body. I'm going to do it. When it's over I'll walk away, because he's been nothing but clear with me about his view on us being more. It'll hurt like hell but I'll do it. I'll walk away."

This is the only choice I have, unless I want to burn

everything he's worked so hard for down to the ground. Having him hate me for doing that would be unbearable.

"Damn straight you will. And you'll have the three of us right there for you to lean on."

Meghan pulls me in for a hug as Savannah and Ben join us.

Right on cue, Sebastian, Cooper, and Noah arrive from arranging things at the next venue.

It's showtime.

Savannah pulls me in for a hug, whispering in my ear as she kisses my cheek, "When all of this is over, we are going to find you a man that has twenty-twenty vision and can see the amazing woman that's right under his fucking nose."

I can't help the laugh that falls from my lips.

Similar words come from both Meghan and Ben, and for a moment I let myself believe in happily ever after without Sebastian.

Sebastian hangs back as our friends disperse, leaving the two of us to talk. I watch Meghan and Cooper for a moment as Cooper strokes his hand over her round stomach, dropping a kiss on her forehead as he tucks her under his arm. One day I *will* have that. I'd want nothing more than to have it with the man standing next to me but I have to be realistic. A heavy sigh leaves me as I look away from them.

"You look beautiful, princess," Sebastian murmurs as he dips his head to kiss my cheek, before pulling away.

I drag my teeth over my bottom lip, as with a wink I say, "Don't worry, you can mess me up later."

He huffs out a laugh as if my words are unexpected. "Fuck, princess. I can't fucking wait."

Sebastian is wearing a royal blue three piece suit with a matching bow tie. The color matches my shoes and the dresses Meghan and Savannah are wearing. If this was an actual wedding, it would be *very* coordinated.

"Did you know we were going to match?" I ask, running my hand over the lapel of his jacket.

Sebastian chuckles as he snakes his arm around my waist and tugs me into his side. "I didn't. Does that mean it's meant to be?"

Seeing that the photographer, Lucy, has arrived, I take a step away from him, breaking the hold he has on me. With a roll of my eyes, I state, "Not at all. You, my dear *fake* husband, could only ever wish to land a hottie like me." I tap a finger into the center of his chest as I spin away from him, a mischievous smirk on my lips. "Shall we get this over with?"

I don't bother waiting for his answer as I walk over to Lucy, his chuckle following me as I go. "Hi, Lucy. Thank you so much for doing this on such short notice. Where would you like us first?"

"Hi, Alex. Anything for a friend of Savannah's. We'll start with you on the steps, the bride and groom first, then we can call the others in."

When Savannah made the booking, she assured me that she hadn't told Lucy about the intricacies of our photoshoot. It was easier that way. Although, now I'm wishing that she had explained. I'm not sure I can go the majority of the day being called the 'bride'.

Lucy directs us effortlessly, pausing occasionally to show us the pictures she's taken. I make a mental note to keep in touch with her for any other events I might need a photographer for. She's made everyone feel at ease, drawing smiles and laughs out of us like a pro.

"Can I get a kiss for the bride, Mr. Worthington?" Lucy asks, pulling me from my thoughts.

Sebastian pulls me into his chest, his head lowering to capture my mouth. It's a chaste kiss. Nothing like any of the kisses we've shared before, but it still heats my blood. He could lick my face and I'm pretty sure I'd be turned on by it.

Cheers erupt around us from our friends, but I don't pay them any attention. Instead, my focus is on *him*.

Sebastian moves his mouth to my ear, his lips brushing the shell as he says, "Thank you, my queen."

Queen.

My eyes go wide and my jaw slackens before I catch myself. I turn to my friends, a fake smile on my lips, as Lucy snaps more pictures.

"Okay, now Mrs. Worthington, why don't we have you facing me, with Mr. Worthington facing the court-house behind you."

My stomach flips, and for a second I allow myself to luxuriate in the feeling of being referred to with his last name.

"Oh, I'm not Mrs. Worthington. I'm keeping my last name."

Sebastian's grip tightens on my hip, his fingers digging in through the fabric of my dress.

"The fuck you're not."

I turn to face him, ready for a fight, because who does he think he is to tell me in our fake marriage that I'll be taking his surname. "Excuse me?"

"You heard me, *Mrs. Worthington*."

"Yes, I did, but I also know you wouldn't be that fucking crazy to try and tell me what to do."

"I would."

Jutting a hip out, I fold my arms over my chest as I stare at him and he stares right back.

"If you can just give them a second, Lucy," Savannah rushes. I can just imagine what a spectacle this must be.

"Look—"

Sebastian grabs my arm and drags me up the stairs of the courthouse, hiding us behind one of the large pillars. His body crowds me in, forcing my chin to lift as I hold his gaze. "You will take my name. I'm not beyond bending you over right now and fucking it into you, got it?"

I'm feeling bratty and this is fake anyway. "No."

He growls, his hand wrapping around my throat, moving up to lift my chin even higher. His head drops, bringing his lips inches away from mine. "Do you want me?"

My brow tugs together at his abrupt change in

conversation as I search his gaze. "Always," I murmur, my gaze flitting between his mouth and eyes.

"Then take my last name."

"Okay," I breathe, because in this moment I'd agree to anything to feel his lips on mine.

His hand drops, releasing my throat as he takes a step back, his body no longer touching mine. The corner of his mouth tips up and his dimple pops. "Good, now let's finish taking these photos so I can take you home and punish you for being so difficult."

Sebastian walks away, leaving me in a confused and tumultuous state. What the fuck just happened? Did he use my attraction to him to get me to agree to take his surname in our fake marriage?

The rest of the day passes in a blur and by the time we get home, I'm both physically and emotionally exhausted.

THIRTY

Sebastian

I t's been a week since we had our fake wedding shoot. Alex moved in with me. Well, not technically, but enough to make it look like she lives here should George decide to go rummaging around my apartment.

I've never lived with a woman before, but having her in my space doesn't freak me out nearly as much as I thought it would. I'm starting to realize with Alex, there are a lot of things I've not done before that I find myself compelled to do. She consumes me in every way, and I don't exactly hate it.

We're headed out for dinner with the Bennetts. The cab we're in cruises down Eighth Avenue to the restaurant George picked. My hand rests on Alex's thigh as she scrolls through her phone, checking her emails and social media. It's a comfortable silence. In the short time we've been living together, we seem to have grown accustomed to each other.

I hope that tonight is the night George is going to agree to sell me the club. If it wasn't for Alex saying we were already married, I would have walked away by now. I've jumped through every hoop he's asked me to, despite my personal feelings toward him.

When it's all over and done with, I can see where this thing with Alex and I leads.

What if she wants out?

I'm not even going to think of that because when this is all over and we don't have the club hanging over us, I want us to be... something. *We* don't end when *this* ends.

My mind is going over a different conversation I'm hoping to have tonight when the cab pulls up outside of the restaurant. The valet opens the door and I step out, holding my hand out for Alex. Expensive cars line the street, restaurants with valets littered along the block. It's a nice neighborhood, clean and bustling with people heading to restaurants as the sun sets and darkness coats the city.

My focus goes back to Alex as she slips her hand into mine. Her skin is warm on my palm and it grounds me as I prepare for an evening of playing pretend. Of acting like I don't despise the man I'm trying to buy Sanctuary from.

Alex leans into me, one hand clasped in mine and the other wrapped around my bicep, as we walk across the sidewalk to the restaurant entrance. It feels like the most natural thing in the world for me to dip my head and kiss the top of hers.

Her voice is quiet on the bustling street, but I hear it nonetheless when she asks, "Are you ready for this?"

I want to tell her that with her by my side, I could conquer the world. But instead of saying that, I simply hum in confirmation.

The doorman holds the door open, and I nod my head in greeting as we pass through. I want nothing more than to turn around, take Alex home, and have *her* for dinner instead. To get lost in her. But needs must and all that. I want the cloud hanging over us, that is my revenge, to be gone.

Alex does the talking when we reach the hostess and I take the time to look around the restaurant.

I've never been here before as I'm usually at the club in the evenings and frequent diners and pubs during the day if I meet up with a friend. It's busy, which isn't surprising, seeing as it's a Saturday night in New York City. With high arched ceilings and dark furniture, the room exudes old-school New York.

The hostess moves to show us to the table and as Alex steps in front of me, my hand finds the small of her back to guide her. She's dressed in a silky black dress and looks fucking edible. I watch as the eyes of all the men and some women follow her through the restaurant. Subconsciously, I move closer toward her, needing them to know that she's *mine*.

I'm the lucky bastard that gets her.

George and Miriam are already seated when we arrive.

Standing, George holds his hand out for me. "It's so good to see you both."

With a smile that pains me to plaster on, I take a hold of his hand, giving it a firm shake. "It's good to see you both, too."

Turning to Miriam, I kiss her on both cheeks before taking a seat at the table.

With a look of sympathy mixed with guilt, George asks, "How are you doing, Alex? Miriam and I have been so worried about you."

Alex's hand reaches out to grasp mine across the table, resting her chin on her free hand as she replies, "I'm doing well, George. You didn't need to be worried about me. Bastian took good care of me." Her eyes flick to me and I see a storm of emotion in them.

God, Alex, please don't let that mean what I think it means. My chest tightens as my breath accelerates and my stomach churns all at once.

I don't deserve that look.

I'm not good enough.

Removing my hand from Alex's grasp, I pick up my glass of water, praying my hand doesn't shake and give away the spiral I'm falling into. The icy water does nothing to calm my racing heart. Thankfully, the waiter arrives to take our orders.

Once they're placed, with a measured tone, I stand and say, "Excuse me, for a moment."

Alex's eyes fill with questions as she looks up at me. As I move past her, I squeeze her shoulder. "I'm just going to the bathroom, queen." My thumb spins the cold band of my unfamiliar wedding band.

I weave my way through the restaurant, my focus on not falling down as I become lightheaded with the feelings coursing through me. As I crash through the bathroom door, I stumble to the sink, dropping my head to my chin as I pull in deep breath after deep breath.

What the fuck is happening?

I can't surely believe that Alex's eyes shone with... affection.

No, that's not possible.

Lust, always. Annoyance, I've seen that a lot. But pure, unadulterated affection, and dare I assume, lo—

No. That's insane.

I lift my head and my eyes catch my reflection in the mirror. I don't recognize the man staring back at me. My confident facade has crumbled, and the usual sun-kissed glow I pride myself on is pale and almost sickly. I need to pull myself together.

I'm overthinking this. *Yes.* That's what's happening. I'm overthinking a *fucking* look.

Get it together.

I turn on the tap and splash the cool liquid on my face. Grabbing a paper towel, I dry my face, taking one last look at my reflection as I blow out a breath and force my shoulders to relax. I need to end this whole charade.

It's overtaking me and I'm done with living a lie. As I walk back to the table, I resolve to do just that.

I want this dinner over with so I can sign the papers and *finally* confront George.

Dinner dragged on longer than I would have liked, but it did give me plenty of time to decide how I'm going to approach this. Or at least I thought it did. As George and I sit in my home office, I'm lost for words.

Instead of confronting him, I allow George to wander around, looking over the books of classic literature—which I haven't had time to read since I moved in—that take up space on the bookshelves on one wall.

"You know, I didn't think you'd actually do it." George picks up, and then puts down, a picture of Cooper and I that's sat on the mahogany credenza to the left of my desk.

My eyes follow George in the dimly lit room as he moves to the chair opposite my desk and takes a seat. Resting his elbows on the padded armrests of the chair, he steeples his fingers as he returns my stare.

"Excuse me?"

"I said, I didn't think you'd actually do it. Marry Alex, that is."

At the look of confusion on my face he continues, "I knew the second you introduced her as your fiancée that you were lying. She couldn't hide the shock from her face. I'm guessing she didn't know either." He cocks a brow in question.

"You've got it wrong," I argue, even though my heart isn't really in it.

George chuckles. Taking a sip of his gin and tonic, he levels me with a stare as he says, "Don't try and play me for a fool, Sebastian. I've seen a lot in my life, but I've never seen a man go to the lengths you have to get your hands on my club. I can see the girl has feelings for you. The question is, do you have feelings for her?"

"No, she doesn't. You don't know what you're talking about George, and you sure as shit don't know me," I roar as I stand from my desk, towering over him.

Turning my back to him, I look out over Midtown Manhattan. The lights glisten, and down below I can see the tiny specks of people and cabs navigating the city. I paid good money for this view, so the heavy curtains are always open.

I've had enough of playing pretend, of being nice to this man who doesn't deserve to even breathe the same air as me.

"You're a blind fool if you can't see it." George sits in his chair, unaffected as I try to control the need to grab him and demand answers from him. "Tell me why you went to these lengths?"

Fuck. He knows and that means that all of this has been for nothing. *God, it's all been for fucking nothing.* My lips press together and I lower my head, trying to sort through the jumble of thoughts in my mind.

Releasing a heavy sigh, my shoulders slump as I take a seat and down the remainder of my drink, leveling my gaze at George.

Why isn't he angry? I deceived him. He should be furious.

"You want to know why I pretended?" I sneer.

It's time.

Time for me to find out why my own father abandoned me.

Why I wasn't enough for him to stick around.

Reaching across my desk, I pick up my wallet and pull out the picture I've kept hold of for this exact moment. I take a beat to examine it again, to look at the young smiling faces of my mother and father. Of the people who abandoned me.

I hate that they look so happy.

Throwing it on the desk between us, George's eyes land on the faded picture. The corner of his mouth tips up and my nails dig into the leather on the arm of my chair in an attempt to keep myself anchored. Now isn't the time to launch myself at him. I need answers.

"Where did you get this?" he asks. His eyes flick to me before returning to the photo.

"It's the only possession of my mother's that I have."

My statement permeates the air and yet he still doesn't look up at me, too lost in the picture. *In the past.* He's probably remembering how he abandoned us when he came swanning back to America. I'm over here hanging on by a thread, and he's having fun going down memory *fucking* lane.

George's voice breaks through the silence, filled with amusement as he says, "You know, you and he are very alike. William always did have a way with women, but when Eliza came into the picture, that was it for him."

William?

My brow pulls together in confusion as I try to comprehend what he's saying. My middle name is William. Who is he talking about?

He lifts his eyes to mine. "Where did you get this picture?"

Although his focus is no longer on the picture, I don't miss the way his thumb strokes over it almost lovingly.

I clear my throat as I say, "It was in my belongings when I went into care in England. It's of my mother and father. Of *you* and my mother."

He's silent for a moment as if he's trying to put together the puzzle pieces. His eyes search mine, looking to see if what I'm saying is the truth.

George lets out a low chuckle as he shakes his head. "Oh this isn't me, son." His voice grows somber as he continues, "This is my brother, William. He died in a car accident with his wife, Eliza, back in England, nearly thirty years ago."

He has to be lying. I know that's him. Every bit of research I've done over the last fifteen years has told me that it's him. There's been no mention of a brother, or him dying in a car accident. Surely there would have been *something*. I don't understand. If what George says is true, then everything I've believed for most of my life is a lie. Did they die? They didn't just abandon me? They didn't throw me away like last week's rubbish? My mind races with questions I can't form on my tongue. Was I in that car? Did they *love* me?

My chest constricts with the weight of this revelation. The room spins and I grip the armrests on my chair, needing it to steady myself.

No! He can't be right.

I *know* that what he's saying is not right.

"I... Wh..." I clear my throat in the hopes that it will help me get the words out. "What do you mean they died in a car accident?"

With one last look, George puts the photo back on my desk, leaning back as he rests his arms on the chair.

George's gaze searches over my features as if seeing me for the first time. It almost looks like he's struggling as much as I am with this information.

Softly, he says, "We didn't know he'd had a child." His eyes glass over as he turns his head away to look over the credenza. "I'm ashamed to say we'd lost touch over the years." His tone holds all the memories I'm certain that he's reliving. "A silly fight and someone's left holding a grudge." His shoulders droop and I watch as the man in front of me is overcome with remorse.

"Miriam and I went to the funeral, but nobody ever reached out to say there was a child. That *you* needed us.

I'm so sorry, Sebastian. Sorry that you were left behind, that we didn't know about you."

"Why didn't you know about me? Surely the police or social services could have gotten in contact with you when you went to the funeral?"

George scrubs his hand over his face, his features downturned. It's like he doesn't want to share what he's going to. "We saw Eliza's brother at the funeral. The rest of her family was long gone, so he was all she had. He seemed shifty. His pupils were dilated and he didn't seem to be taking care of himself. I told Miriam my suspicions about him, but I convinced myself that it was down to having lost his sister."

"What do you mean, you had suspicions about him?" I lean forward, needing to know.

I didn't even know I had an uncle, let alone two.

"I thought he was drunk at the funeral. That's how some people deal with their emotions. We asked if he wanted any help sorting through their belongings, but he said no, so we left."

I stand and pace behind my desk, his words slowly sinking in as I try to interpret each word. Was I left with my uncle? Or was he not capable of taking me in and that's why they didn't know about me? Is my uncle still alive? Could things have turned out differently if I had been raised by George and Miriam?

As if he needs to fill the silence, George continues, "Eliza's parents had died when she was twenty-one, and it wasn't long after that, that she met William. They were both backpacking through Europe." There's a sense of longing in his voice, as if he wishes he could go back to those times. "I remember when William called me to tell me about her. He was so excited to tell his older brother that he'd finally met the woman he was going to ma—"

"I need you to leave." This is all too much. I've been so wrong about it all.

I'm done with listening to him remember people I never got to meet.

My legs carry me to the minibar in the corner of the room. I need something strong to numb the ache building in my chest.

George is still in his seat when I turn around. He waits for me to take a seat before he says, "I don't think that would be a good idea."

"Well, I didn't ask you if you did." My anger rises. "I need you to leave. *Now*," I bellow.

We stare at each other, both refusing to back down. I knock back my drink, turning to refill my glass again. As I face him, a look of sympathy flits across his face and he breathes out a heavy sigh, standing from his seat.

He studies me for the longest time, then reaches into his suit jacket pocket and pulls out a bundle of papers, dropping them onto the desk. "I think, more than ever, that you're the right person to take over Sanctuary. Please, call me when you've taken the time to wrap your head around this. It's a lot for me to process, so I can only imagine what you must be feeling right now." He pauses. "Especially if you thought *I* was your father. God, Sebastian, I wish I was. He would be so proud of you and all you've achieved. They both would."

With one last look and a rap of his knuckles on the mahogany of the desk, he walks out my office door. My nostrils flare as I empty the contents of my glass, throwing it at the wall.

It's the only way I can vent the anger that's built up inside of me over everything I thought I knew being a lie. The very foundation of who I am, is a *lie*.

I need to get out of here. Pulling my jacket off of the back of my chair, I swing open the door to my office. It bounces back on the wall with the force.

My stride falters when I reach the entryway. Alex is standing next to the couch, a frown tugging on her brow.

"George and Miriam left abruptly. Is everything okay?"

"Just go home, Alex. I don't know why you're still here."

She steps back as though I've slapped her. "What's happened?"

I ignore her because if I stay, I might say something I'll regret, and I already hate myself for pulling her into this farce. She calls out my name, hurt and desperation coating her words.

I don't stop. I can't.

She's too good for me. She always has been.

THIRTY-ONE

Alex

I've slept alone, in my own bed, the last five nights. Each night I've spent more time awake, wondering what Sebastian was doing, than I have been sleeping.

My mind replays the way George came out of Bastian's office, a look of worry on his face that he couldn't hide quick enough. He took Miriam's coat and ushered her through the door before I could ask if everything was okay.

Sebastian left that night, and I haven't seen him since. That was five days ago and the reason I'm sitting in the back of an Uber on my way to Passion.

Something isn't right, and I'm going to get to the bottom of it. I've given him enough time to figure out what the hell is happening and come home. *Back to me.* It's time we talked about everything that went down and where we go from here.

The car pulls up outside, and in hindsight I probably should have come in the daytime. The music pounds out onto the sidewalk as I walk up to the entrance. Nerves dance in my stomach as I get closer.

"Hey, Alex. You on your own tonight?" Matt, the bouncer, asks as I approach him.

"Just here to see the boss."

Matt is one of three bouncers. He's my favorite, but mostly because he's a giant teddy bear, quite literally. He stands at an imposing six foot six and has tattoo's covering his arms and snaking up his neck. Although he looks like he could snap your neck with one hand, he has the biggest heart.

The corner of his mouth lifts as he moves the rope, dipping his head to me as he says, "See if you can cheer him up."

"I'll try."

Whatever it is that made him walk out on me, it's still affecting him.

I make my way through the Friday night crowd as I walk to his office. A remixed version of *Bad Memories* by MEDUZA blasts through the speakers and I wonder if it's an omen for how my night is going to go.

Standing outside of Sebastian's office door, I briefly consider barging in before remembering the time I did that, and found him with another woman. I have no desire to repeat that. Not now when my heart is on the line.

I rap my knuckles against the dark wood of his door

and pray that he's alone. That everything we've been through together means *something* to him.

"Come in," his gruff voice calls through the door.

My hand finds the doorknob and I suck in a breath, exhaling it slowly as I turn the handle and push through the door. He sits behind his desk, his reading glasses perched on his nose, and thankfully alone. His face doesn't register any surprise as he looks up at me. It's almost like he's been expecting me.

"What do you want, Alex?"

Not queen or princess. Just Alex.

I feel needy as I take him in, sitting behind his desk. I want nothing more than to climb into his lap and just breathe in his scent. Instead, I close the door and move to stand awkwardly in front of his desk.

"I came to see you and find out what's going on. It's been nearly a week since I last saw you. What happened with you and George?"

"He signed over the club," Sebastian says, matter of factly. His gaze drops back to the screen of his laptop.

Nausea bubbles in the pit of my stomach. His whole demeanor is dismissive, as if I've served my purpose and he wants me gone. I know right then that the Bastian who looked after me for all those weeks is gone. And I don't know if it's for good or just for now.

I close my eyes. I thought I knew what would come after, that all of the intimacy we've shared would lead to more, or at the very least continue. He said it would. But as I stand in front of him now, I know the answer to the question that falls from my lips. "So, where do we go from here?"

A heavy sigh leaves him as he takes off his glasses and leans back in his chair. His eyes meet mine, but unlike any previous time that he's looked at me, I see nothing reflected in his gaze. There's no care, adoration, or even desire. We've always had the heat, even when we hated each other. We always had that. A chill runs down my spine as he looks right through me.

"Listen, Alex," he starts, but I hold up my hand, cutting him off.

The first crack appears in my heart but I hold my chin high, refusing to let him see me break. I can't hear him say it. I refuse to.

"Don't you dare tell me that we should go our separate ways. After everything we've been through the last two months, you can't seriously be ready to walk away? I know I'm not." There's a note of desperation in my tone that I wish wasn't there.

He ignores my declaration, and I think that's what hurts the most. That he can dismiss my feelings so easily.

His thumb and forefinger pinch at the bridge of his nose, as if I'm testing his last nerve, before he says, "I've been nothing but honest with you, Alex. I got the club so our arrangement is over and you can walk away, like we agreed."

He stands from his desk, moving to the door. My eyes fall to the engagement ring on my finger. It's a symbol of the lies we've told and the love that I allowed to grow.

Mocking me as it sparkles up at me. I don't understand how he can act like we were nothing. Like *I* meant *nothing* to him.

"Does how I feel mean nothing? Are you really that cold-hearted that you can just walk away, after everything? This isn't you. It's not the Sebastian I fell in love with."

"You don't know me, Alex." He holds his arms wide, his anger mounting but I'm not afraid. "This. This is the real me."

"No, it isn't."

A look I've never seen before fills his gaze. "It is. I was using you. It could have been any woman, it just so happened to be you."

I reel back, his words like a slap to the face. Shaking my head, I whisper, "You don't mean that." My eyes burn with unshed tears.

It's like he's coated everything we had in darkness, a poison seeping through into it. Ruining the happiness we had built. He's broken it and it won't ever be fixed.

"I do. You don't love me, Alex. You're in love with the idea of being loved, nothing more." He sounds frustrated, like how I feel is of no consequence for him. That my love is absurd to him.

Maybe we were never on the same wavelength with our feelings. Maybe the care he showed for me was all some sort of sick performance? Was all of this just a game to him? I don't know what was real and what was part of his master plan. It's like I never even knew him.

I slip the rings off of my finger and with an odd sense of calm I place them on his desk.

My chin is high as I walk away from him. There's no outward sign that the man I love with all of my heart has just dug a dagger deep into my heart and twisted it for maximum effect.

I promise myself I won't break until I get home.

The cab ride is thankfully quick, and I fumble with the lock as I let myself into my apartment. Tears blur my vision as I stumble through the space but the gut wrenching sobs don't come until I'm buried under the covers of my bed, still fully clothed.

Curled up in the fetal position, I hold onto my body, sobs wracking through me as I cry myself to sleep. Telling myself that Sebastian Worthington can't hurt me any more than he already has.

THIRTY-TWO

Sebastian

I think I fucked up.

When I'm certain she's gone, I sit down behind my desk, her ring's glinting under the overhead light. Taunting me. Instinctively, I reach out and pick up the engagement ring. It's heavy in my palm, the weight of my mistake in this single piece of jewelry.

Fuck. There's no use in denying it, I *know* I fucked up.

The worst thing is that I don't think she'll forgive me for the way I treated her and the things I said. I wouldn't fucking blame her.

Shaking my head, I put my glasses back on, and shuffle through the papers I was working through before she came in. I spend the next thirty minutes trying to get the look of disbelief mixed that marred her beautiful face, out of my mind. It doesn't work, the conversation just plays on repeat in my mind.

I slam my laptop closed, pushing away from my desk,

swiping up my phone, wallet and keys. When I reach the door, I glance over my shoulder, taking one last look at the room. I need to get out of here. Too many things have happened with her here.

My driver meets me out back and sensing my mood, keeps himself near invisible to me. I use the drive to make arrangements for a last minute trip. Every aspect of the city reminds me of her. From the partygoers, down to the lights that shine just like her.

I'm too wired by the time I get back to my place and although it's late I shoot a text off to Cooper.

SEBASTIAN

Can you get Meghan to check in with Alex?

I expect him to pick up the text in the morning seeing as it's gone midnight, but my phone buzzes in my hand, signaling a new text.

COOPER

What happened?

How do I answer that? I don't reply, instead I switch off my phone, leaning back on the couch as I stare at the view of Midtown Manhattan. In the hours when the night turns to day, I come to the realization that she's better off without me.

Although I knew that already, didn't I?

I'm a broken man that can't love her the way she

deserves to be loved, not when I've never experienced it myself.

Like a coward, I leave for Chicago that morning.

I left New York four days ago. I've not heard anything from Alex since she left my office. Not that I expected to, especially after the words I'd said to her. I've reflected on everything that has happened, not just in the last few months, but the last time I saw her.

The need to make things right with her has consumed me.

Stepping onto the sidewalk outside of Sanctuary after finishing up a meeting with the architect I'm hiring, my feet stall as I see George waiting. He seems unsure when I step out onto the sidewalk.

I watch him as he finds the courage to approach me, and he straightens his spine as he steps forward. His voice is clear and sure when he says, "I heard you were in town. I hope you don't mind that I showed up, but I didn't like how we'd left things. Do you have time to talk?"

Reminding myself that everything I thought about this man isn't true. I'm man enough to admit that I'd jumped to conclusions and ended up being wrong. *Am I man enough to admit I was wrong with Alex?* I push the thought away.

The least I can do is hear George out.

"Sure. Did you drive?"

"I have a driver. You can ride with me or I can follow you." He points over his shoulder to a black town car pulled up at the curb.

"I'll ride with you. I got a cab here."

We move to the car that's idling and climb inside. The silence is awkward as it hangs in the air between us.

Unable to take it anymore, I say, "I'm sorry I asked you to leave." I've had a lot of time to think since he left New York nearly two weeks ago.

"Oh, you have no need to apologize. I can understand that it must have come as quite a shock to you. I wanted to let you know that I've hired an investigator to find out what happened with you back in England, but I suspect your mom's brother put you into foster care." George picks at a piece of lint on his pant leg, unable to look me in the eye.

His shoulders are hunched, making my brow bunch together.

"I should have done more. I shouldn't have walked away from the life my brother built so easily. You were just a baby, Sebastian, and you needed your family. We all let you down."

A lump forms in my throat at his words. At the best of times, I struggle with showing my emotions, and this is no exception. I hate that I'm vulnerable because he's right; as a child, I was let down.

My voice is hoarse as I say, "But you didn't know. And

I know that if you had, you would have done something about it."

"In a heartbeat," he mumbles.

None of it fixes what happened or changes the man I have become, but at least there's some closure on that part of my life now. For so long I've carried a resentment toward my parents. I thought they'd abandoned me, that I wasn't enough for them to stick around and so they'd left. The reality couldn't have been any different.

George breaks through the quiet of the car as it cruises through the streets of Chicago. "We'd like to work on having a relationship with you. Miriam and I that is. If that is something you would like. It might not feel like it to you right now, but you are our family."

My head tips back to rest against the headrest. The abandoned child inside of me, the one that never had a family, who was shipped from home to home, rejoices. But the man I am now, the one who worked every hour under the sun and made sure never to rely on another person, wants to tell him it's too late.

"I don't know if I can do that." I lift my head to look at him before continuing, "Not right away, anyway. There's a lot to wrap my head around."

Hurt flashes across his face as he looks away and says, "Of course. The door will always be open for you, Sebastian. I'm just glad I got to meet you."

The car pulls up outside of my hotel. *When did I tell him where I was staying?*

"I know a lot of people in Chicago, and just wanted to

know where to reach you. Take your time, Sebastian, but reach out when you're ready. Give Alex my best."

With a muttered goodbye, I climb from the car, my mind a mess of jumbled thoughts. His reminder of Alex brings her back to the forefront of my mind, not that she'd gone far. My thumb mindlessly spins the ring on my finger.

I need to conclude my meetings in Chicago, go back to New York, and figure out a way to try and fix things with Alex.

THIRTY-THREE

Alex

The bass from the music vibrates through me as I grind into the warm, solid body behind me. Strong, thick fingers grip my hips, flexing against the bare skin of my right hip.

I'm about two margaritas past my limit, but I couldn't care less. I'm happy. I love to dance, I love the crush of bodies and the way they move as one to the rhythm on the dance floor.

It's probably how I've ended up in Passion. Savannah came out with me tonight, although she left about two hours ago. It's okay though, my new friend, Bjorn... or Brian, or whatever it is, wanted to come to the best club in town.

His club.

How could I say no?

The simple answer is, I didn't want to. My need to prove to myself that it meant nothing—that *he* meant nothing—seems to have taken control of me. I'm fine without him. He was just a blip on my radar.

Liar.

That's what I've been telling myself since I stepped foot in here. It didn't work, so I got too drunk to care. And now I'm on the dance floor of *his* club with another man's hands on my body.

With each hour that's ticked by, I've become more and more certain that I'm going home with Bjorn, even if it's just to prove that point to myself.

How long should you give yourself to get over a break up from a man you were only fake dating? Sorry, fake engaged to. Married to? Whatever the hell it was.

I'm certain that he's already moved on. Hell, he told me himself it was all a lie.

Bjorn dips his head, and the warmth of his breath skating over the shell of my ear does absolutely nothing for me. In theory, I should be excited to go home with this six foot three mountain of a man, but it couldn't be further from the truth.

Before Sebastian, I would have had no issues with this blonde haired, blue-eyed beauty taking me home. That thought is what drives me to nod when he asks me if I'm ready to leave.

I'm not.

Not with him.

I'm desperately trying to prove to myself that Sebastian hasn't ruined me for another man. That I'm strong enough to move on. The alcohol coursing through my blood helps me do just that.

We move through the crowd, my hand clasped in Bjorn's as he leads the way. My hips sway to the beat of *How Deep is Your Love* by Calvin Harris.

A hand lands on my waist, just below my ribcage, and I'm pulled into the side of another warm solid body, my hand slipping from Bjorn's. A thrill runs through my body that he's finally come for me, that's until I look up and see Matt's face pulled into a hard scowl as he talks to Bjorn.

I watch their exchange with rapt drunken fascination, but it soon dispels when Bjorn turns on his heel and walks through the crowd.

"Hey." I wriggle out of Matt's hold and move through the crowd, calling out, "Bjorn!"

He doesn't turn around, even though I'm certain he can hear me.

Maybe his name isn't Bjorn. Shit, I should have paid more attention.

When I turn back to face Matt, I find him hovering behind me with a look of uncertainty on his face.

"What the hell was that about?" I poke him in the chest and he takes a step back.

His eyes dart to the glass that hides Sebastian's office and almost instinctively I hold up my middle finger in a salute to the glass, because I know he's watching. I've felt him all night. Like I always do, and it infuriates me.

I step up to Matt, and he dips his head so I can say, "Tell him to fuck off and leave me the hell alone."

My stride is purposeful as I go to step around Matt, back to the center of the crowd, more determined than ever to find someone to go home with. I'm stopped mid-stride as Matt's large hand wraps around my bicep.

"I wouldn't do that if I was you."

I round on him, furious that he thinks he can tell me what to do. That Sebastian thinks he has any say in what I do. "Don't you dare tell me what I can and can't do. You don't have a clue what he's put me through. If I want to go and dance, then I can, and *he* isn't going to stop me."

Matt holds up his hands, a knowing smirk on his lips. "Hey, I was just saying, you don't want to piss him off any more than he already is."

"Piss *him* off? That's laughable. He'd have to feel something in order for me to do that."

Done with the conversation and wanting to find somewhere else to end my night, I turn around to walk to the exit. I come up short though when I see him and it's like I've been hit by a truck. *Is he real?* I hate that he looks so fucking good, like the time apart has been good for him. All of the air leaves me, the front I've put on crumbling to the floor. Tears form in my eyes and I pray to God they don't fall.

Fuck the alcohol leaving me with no control over my emotions.

I *want* to leave but I'm frozen like a statue, terrified to move in case I break. In case I show him how much he's hurt me. My eyes drink him in, like I've been stranded in a desert and he's an oasis. He's dressed casually in black jeans and a white shirt—my favorite of his outfits—on his feet are a pair of biker boots.

He looks good and I hate it.

Breathe.

My focus shifts to breathing as he moves toward me.

I don't want him near me but I can't fucking move.

He lifts his hand and moves a strand of hair from my face. It takes everything inside of me not to tip my cheek into his palm, to take the comfort I so desperately crave from him.

"Baby, what are you doing?"

Baby.

I scrunch my eyes closed in an attempt to stop the endearment from stabbing me in the heart. I can't do this, not right now.

My hand lifts and I watch, in an almost out of body experience, as it swings toward his face, connecting with his cheek. His face turns with the force of the slap. He turns to face me, his cheek red, but instead of the anger I expect, all I see is understanding.

No. He doesn't get to be understanding.

Without a word, I brush past him and stumble my way to the exit, my vision blurred with the tears that coat my lashes.

The cold, late November air hits me as I step outside. It's refreshing and the perfect thing to get my brain functioning enough to get home. My hands dive into my hair as I pace on the sidewalk.

People mill about, waiting for cabs or smoking, but it's not early enough for the club to be clearing out so it's not overly busy.

Get home, that's what I need to do. I march down the sidewalk, no more than five steps away when I come to a halt.

"You're going to need this," Sebastian says, his deep voice like a thrill down my spine.

He's holding out my clutch bag and I wonder for a moment if I can leave it with him and just hitchhike home.

That's probably not the best idea.

I snatch the bag from his hand, clutching it to my chest. "Thank you."

"I'll take you home."

I almost laugh at him, but when I see the look on his face I realize he isn't joking.

"No, thank you." I turn, intent on finding a cab.

His hand on my elbow stops me. "Alex, I'll take you home. Please. Let me do this."

"I don't need you." *Shit, that's not what I meant.* Well I did mean that, but that's more something I should say to myself. "I don't need you to take me home."

His jaw ticks, as if what I've just said has hurt his feelings. Good.

"My car is over there." He points over his shoulder

with his thumb. "Please, I just want to make sure you get home safely."

Folding my arms over my chest, I cock my hip as I say, "Who said I was going home?"

"I'm not above throwing you over my shoulder, Alex."

If he'd said that to me before, I would have gotten a thrill out of it but I'm scared that if he touches me I'll do something stupid like beg him to love me.

"Your options are, you get in the car, or I throw you over my shoulder and carry you to the car."

"If you lay a hand on me, I'll scream."

"Please, Alex. It's getting cold, you're wearing next to nothing and I just don't want you to get sick."

"What if I want to get sick?" Okay, that makes no sense. I need to go home.

He scrubs a hand over his mouth, hiding the smirk I know my words have caused.

"I'm going to get a cab."

"Meghan would never forgive me if I let you get a cab home." Oh, he's tried to pull out the big guns.

"I'm a big girl. I can look after myself. Now you're just wasting my time, so goodbye."

"Don't say I didn't warn you." He bends his knees, crowding into my personal space and before I know it, he's straightening up with me over his shoulder.

What the fuck.

"Put me down," I demand.

He ignores me, even as I smack at his back. When he

reaches the town car, I hear the door open and then I'm lowered inside. I fold my arms over my chest, huffing out a breath of annoyance.

Neither of us speaks as the car navigates the streets of New York, and when we pull up outside of my building, I'm surprised as he follows me out of the car.

"What are you doing?" I ask, stopping in the middle of the sidewalk.

He shrugs a shoulder before he says, "Just making sure you get home safe."

He is unbelievable.

"Well, as you can see, I'm home. Goodbye, Sebastian."

I cross my arms over my chest, stopping on the sidewalk as I wait for him to leave. We're at a standstill, neither of us budging. He puts his hands into his jeans pockets as if he has all the time in the world. He might but I don't and it's cold, so when he shows no sign of moving on, I stomp my foot and march into my building.

Sebastian chuckles as he follows closely behind. He walks into the elevator with me, then to my front door. I push my front door open, walking into the living room, fully expecting the door to close behind me but when I turn around, I find him standing there. His hands in his pockets again.

My arms spread wide as I say, "As you can see, I'm home safe and sound. You can leave now."

He doesn't say anything, he just stares at me, a look I can't quite decipher on his face.

God, I hate him.

No I don't.

Yes. I. Do!

Self-destructive mode kicks in, spinning me back to the front door, done with him and whatever game he's trying to play with me.

"When you leave, can you make sure you lock up? Oh, and slide your key under the door. Not like you need it anymore," I call over my shoulder.

I have the door open an inch when his palm slaps against the wood, forcing it shut. My eyes latch onto the platinum band on his ring finger. *Why does he still have that on?* His body cages me in, as his arm snakes around my waist and he pulls me into his body, burying his nose in my hair. "Don't fucking test me, Alex. I'm barely holding on."

When I don't say a word, he turns us toward my bedroom, my back pressed to his front as he forces me to walk down the hallway.

I can't do this.

I can't pretend that everything is okay. He can't just waltz back in here and act like everything is fine or that he has a say in what I do or who I do it with. Our whole relationship has been based on a lie.

Pulling away from him, I come to a stop, my arms banding around me as I turn to face him. "I can't do this."

"Alex, please," he pleads.

Please, what? Let him trample over my heart? Let

him have this one night and then walk away leaving me even more heartbroken?

"I can't pretend like you haven't broken my heart, Sebastian."

Tears spring in my eyes and I don't bother to keep them at bay this time. They fall down my cheeks, gathering on my chin before dripping onto my chest. It's time he saw the damage he's done.

When he moves to take me into his arms, I step back, an arm outstretched to keep him back. "I can't do this," I repeat, silently begging him to understand.

A pleading note, as if he's begging *me* to understand where *he's* coming from, fills his voice as he says, "You don't understand. I can't give you everything that you deserve."

My anger takes hold and I shout, "Bullshit!"

"Alex," he warns as if I give a shit anymore.

"No!" I scream, my voice hoarse with the emotions bubbling inside of me. "No. Don't 'Alex' me. Don't princess, queen or baby. Me." I tick them off of my fingers before pressing an angry finger into my chest. "You don't understand, do you? You broke us with your poison. I know you lied that night in your office, it took me a while, but I figured it out. Your actions have shown me everything I needed to know. Everything you've done for me has been *enough*."

I swipe at the tears falling down my cheeks. Finding strength I thought I'd lost, I continue, "Jesus. Sebastian, look at everything you did for me after my accident or the little things you did when we lived together. You are *enough*. You are more than enough. There are so many people in your life that love you and who you love back, so why can't I have your love? If you can't see how much you deserve to love and be loved then you should walk away. You should leave me alone, because if you can't give me all of you then you don't deserve all of me, no matter how much I wish you did.

"You might not want to admit it, but you have loved me, just like I've loved you." I pause, searching for the right words. "You've left me heartbroken, and yet, you stand there and ask me to give you another piece of me. Well, you've had it all. I've got nothing more to give."

My voice cracks and I pray that he decides to stay. That he truly hears what I'm saying to him. That he's enough and this is us getting our happy ever after.

"I'm sorry." His shoulders slump in defeat. "I shouldn't have brought you home."

And just like that he rips out my heart, throws it on the ground, and stomps on it, *again*, as he walks out. Ten-year-old Alex, who believed in fairytales and happily ever afters, would be heartbroken, but thirty-year-old Alex just got a stark reminder that happily ever afters don't exist. At least not for her.

I can't bear to watch him walk away, but when I hear the door click shut behind him, I collapse into a heap on the floor, my legs unable to keep me upright.

What I wouldn't give to have the strength to not care.

To not feel as if my world has been turned upside down because he walked away.

Somehow, I drag myself into my room, slipping off my heels and peeling off my dress. I don't bother taking off my ruined makeup, opting to climb under the covers as sobs wrack my body.

Maybe tomorrow I can start to rebuild myself. To fix all the pieces of me he's broken.

Maybe.

Sebastian

I fucked up.
Again.

Sebastian

It's early when I knock on Cooper's front door that morning. After I left Alex's, I went home and tried to sleep but it was no use. Every time I close my eyes all I see is the pain on her face as she bared herself to me.

Despite what she might think, I did hear her.

Something stopped me from stepping up and telling her how I feel, and I need help figuring out what it was.

"What are you doing here this early?" Cooper greets me, a frown on his face.

"Sorry, I should have called." I run my hand over my forehead, the beginnings of a headache making itself known. "Do you have time for a chat?"

"Uh, sure, come on in. You'll have to excuse the mess." He steps back from the doorway, signaling for me to walk in. "Coffee?"

"Sure, thanks. I didn't wake you did I?" I take in his

pajama bottoms and hastily tied up robe as I follow him to the kitchen.

Cooper chuckles. "Not at all. When you have kids you'll understand that sleeping in isn't a thing."

Will Alex want kids with me?

I scrub my hand over the back of my neck as I lean against the counter. "Well, either way, I'm sorry to come by so early."

Cooper busies himself making coffee, his back to me as he says, "So what's happened now?"

The weight of everything from this past week threatens to crush me. Cooper already knows everything, up until I went to Chicago last week.

"Alex came to the club last night."

Cooper turns to face me, his gaze assessing me. "Okay," he drags out the word, before asking, "Did something happen?"

"Yes." I look away, the images flashing through my mind fanning the flames of irritation burning inside of me. My jaw ticks as I clench it, fisting my hands at my sides. "She was dancing with a guy, and when she was about to leave with him I had Matt stop her."

"Right, because you love her. Then what happened?" He says it as if it's the most normal thing to talk about. Like he's just commented on the fucking weather.

"Then I took her home and she told me how she felt and I—I left. I feel like the biggest asshole for leaving, but I'm not the man she deserves."

"First of all, you are an asshole and you have some

serious work to do to make it up to her. Which I assume is why you're here. Secondly, who told you that you weren't the man she deserves? I assume it wasn't her."

Cooper hands me a mug of steaming coffee and leans against the counter, crossing his legs at the ankles as he waits for me to answer.

"I don't know why I'm here—"

"Yes, you do. Deep down you know, but that's not the point. I want to know why you don't think you deserve her."

"I didn't say I didn't deserve her."

"Yes, you did. When you say you're not the man she deserves, you're saying that you don't think you deserve her. Just answer the question. Why?" When I don't say anything he continues, "You're worse than trying to get a hostile witness to talk. Jeez, Seb."

"She deserves someone who has their shit together."

Cooper shrugs. "So get your shit together."

As if it's that simple.

"It really is that simple," he says, reading where my thoughts have gone. "Work on yourself, go and get to know the family you've found, see a therapist, do whatever you need to do to make yourself believe that you deserve her. God knows it helped me, and now I have everything I thought I never wanted. A wife that I love and who's blessed me with her love in abundance. I have a beautiful daughter and a son on the way. Nothing else matters to me."

He makes it sound like I can have it all.

Like I *deserve* to have it all.

"Wait here," Cooper says as he walks off in the direction of his home office.

While he's gone, I think over all of the things that he and Alex have said to me and how similar their messages are. Have I been wrong this whole time? I was wrong about George, so what else might I be wrong about?

Cooper returns, holding out a business card to me. "Here you go."

I look down at the card in his hand before taking it and examining it. It's for a therapist. I assume his own. Cooper hasn't shied away from sharing the fact that he sought therapy when he and Meghan split. He said it was one of the best decisions of his life.

Maybe it can help?

Maybe it won't but what's the worst that can happen.

Sensing my hesitation, Cooper reassures me, "You don't have to use it right away, or at all, but maybe it's something to consider if you think that maybe you really do want her."

"I should get going," I mumble, my focus on the card in my hand as all the time I've spent with Alex plays on a loop in my mind.

"You don't have to."

I lift my head, my eyes finding his as I push away from the counter. "I do. I've got things I need to do. Thanks for the chat, mate."

My gaze runs over the four story townhouse that houses the office of the therapist I have an appointment with in five minutes. As soon as I left Cooper's, I called them. They had an appointment this afternoon after a cancellation, and I accepted it without question.

My focus shifts to the time on the dash of the car, and I watch as another minute ticks by. I have to force myself to open the car door and climb out. The reluctance that I'm pushing against is borne from a need of self-preservation. I know what's to come is going to be ugly.

I need to do this so I can be the man Alex deserves. I *want* to be a better man for her.

Moving at a slow pace, as if I'm trying to move through quick sand, I walk to the door and press the buzzer for the office of Dr. Hunt.

It feels like hours before anything happens. The door buzzes back to let me know it's unlocked and I push through, closing the door behind me. A sign on the wall tells me the office I'm looking for is on the third floor. I climb the stairs and walk into a room just off to the right. A middle aged woman sits behind a desk in what I assume is the waiting area.

"Good afternoon, Mr. Worthington. Please take a seat, Dr. Hunt will be with you shortly."

Doing as directed, I take a seat on the gray couch

opposite the reception desk, scrolling through my work emails as I wait.

I'm not waiting long before a woman who must be around my age walks out of another door with a man following behind her. They talk before he walks off and she brings her attention to me.

"Mr. Worthington, it's nice to meet you. I'm Dr. Hunt, do you want to come through?" She steps to the side, sweeping her arm to the room behind her.

As I enter the room, I look around, noticing how bright and welcoming it is. There's another gray couch sitting along one wall, with two armchairs facing it and a coffee table in the middle. Bay windows on three walls allow the light to fill the room and a desk sits in front of one, sunlight streaming in across the light oak.

Dr. Hunt is still standing behind me as I come to a stop in the middle of the room. Her voice is soft, as if she's worried that I might bolt, when she says, "Do you want to take a seat?"

"Uh, sure." I move to one of the arm chairs.

I expect her to maybe make a comment about me being the patient and how I should lie back on the couch. Instead she gives me a soft smile, picks up a pen and paper and takes the empty armchair.

"Do you mind if I call you Sebastian?"

"Not at all." I lift my foot and rest my ankle over my knee as I relax back into the chair.

Another soft smile. "Great. So, what brings you to see me today?"

Isn't that the billion dollar question.

"I was referred by a friend. He said it could help me to talk to somebody about the..." I pause, trying to think of the right words. "I guess my feelings of inadequacy. I met the most amazing woman and..." My words trail off.

Dr. Hunt jots down some notes as I speak, before asking, "What has made you feel inadequate?"

"How long have you got?" I chuckle.

The corners of her mouth lift. There's a look of sympathy on her face when she speaks. "Why don't you start with the woman you met?"

My chest swells and a smile I can't contain spreads across my mouth at just the thought of her. "Alex came into my life like a freight train. Everything I've ever thought I wanted, she turned on its head. We actually met nearly three years ago, and I knew the moment she walked into my office that I was going to have her. I thought it would just be sex, because that's all I've ever done, but she made me want more."

The smile that was on my face falls as it dawns on me how monumentally I fucked up. I mean, I knew when I pushed her away after George told me about my parents. Just speaking about her has the knowledge of my actions pressing on me like a weight.

I sit forward and drop my head into my hands as I tug on the strands of my hair. Dr. Hunt doesn't say a word and I'm grateful she's giving me time to process. It's like everything has hit me all at once. Like it's gone from black and white to full on technicolor.

I need to figure out how to get Alex back.

Right now, I don't know how I'm going to do it, or if she'll ever forgive me, but I have to try. God, deep down I've known I felt more for her than I ever have with anyone else. That first night, when she barreled into my office, I knew it was something more than fucking. All of my actions the past few months should have shown me that I can love. *That I love her.*

I finish up my session with Dr. Hunt and make an appointment for the following day. On the car ride home, I play with Alex's ring, the one she left on my desk that now sits on a chain around my neck. Where it will stay until I put it back on her finger.

I just need to bide my time, work on myself, and then maybe I can get her back.

THIRTY-SIX

Alex

ONE MONTH LATER

I stand on the sidewalk looking up at a very closed restaurant as a cold November breeze blows through the block. The hem of my dress flutters around my thighs and I fumble around trying to hold it down while at the same time I dig my phone out of my clutch. Dark drapes cover the windows. Am I in the right place?

My fingers fly across the screen as I type out a message into the group chat.

ALEX

Are you sure this restaurant is open?
How close are you?

SAVANNAH

It's open. Just go inside.

MEGHAN

We won't be long.

Isn't this how people die in horror movies?

For all of two seconds, I contemplate waiting for them on the sidewalk, but I forgot my coat in my rush out the door. I'd have taken my time getting ready if I knew they were going to be this late. They were up my ass about how important it was that I was on time and I'm never late.

Ready to do battle should anyone try to attack me, I walk to the restaurant entrance and pull the door open. I half expect the door to be locked, but it comes away from the frame with ease. As I step inside, the door swings shut behind me, causing a draft to sweep through, flickering candles that cover the floor.

My mind can't comprehend what I'm looking at, or why the restaurant I'm supposed to be meeting my friends at is filled with candles.

Surely this is a fire hazard.

I take a tentative step forward before coming to stop at the sound of *his* voice. He's haunted my dreams for *weeks.*

"Hi, princess."

The deep timber rolls over me like a wave, and I close my eyes at the memories it evokes inside of me. It's been thirty six days, seventeen hours and a handful of minutes since I last saw him.

I don't want to be here.

I don't want to see him or talk to him. I'm not strong enough.

My feet move of their own accord, as I turn and walk

out of the restaurant and down the sidewalk. The cool breeze I wanted to get away from a moment ago is like a balm to my heated skin.

"Alex. Please, Alex, come back."

I keep walking until I don't know where I am, and I can no longer hear the pleading yet hopeful note in his voice. My phone buzzes in my clutch, but I ignore it. It seems I can't trust anyone. They betrayed me and sent me into the lion's den with a man they know broke my heart. Were they just willing to ignore how he left me? How he fucking broke me?

They might, but I sure as hell am not.

I walk until my feet start to hurt and then I take a cab home. A bottle of wine and a movie that will make me feel anything but broken are just what I need.

It's been hours since I left the restaurant. Goosebumps have formed on my exposed skin but I'm not really aware of them, my mind lost in having seen him again. Maybe it was stupid of me to expect him to leave me alone, but I certainly didn't expect him to be sitting on my couch when I walk through the door. He stands as I close the door, wiping his hands down the front of his jeans.

"I used my key." He looks nervous, like he's not sure how I'll react. *Good, let him be on edge.*

I guess that explains how he got in, but it doesn't really explain why he's here. My shoes get kicked off by the front door before I move down the hallway to my bedroom. He follows behind, averting his eyes as I pull my dress over my head and change into my pajamas.

"Why are you here, Sebastian? If it's to return the key, you could have given that to Cooper."

He leans against the doorjamb of the bathroom as I wash my face, his arms folded across his broad chest. I want nothing more than for him to envelop me in his arms. I turn to the rail, almost aggressively swiping the towel up to dry my face.

No. I don't want him to hold me.

Yes, you do.

No. No. No. God, I'm so mad at myself right now. Why can't I comprehend that he's not going to *ever* give me what I want? I need to get a grip.

"I wanted to make sure you got home okay, but I also want to talk to you about everything that's happened."

I round on him, my anger mounting at how cool and calm he can be. "And what if *I* don't want to talk?"

He looks defeated, and it deflates my anger slightly. I look at him, truly look at him. For the first time since I saw him in the restaurant, I see how tired he looks and how pale his skin is.

"Then I'll leave." He heaves out a sigh as he pushes away from the doorjamb. "When you're ready, you know where to find me."

With a final look at me, he leaves the bathroom, and it's like my heart is being ripped out all over again. I can't keep feeling like this every time I see him.

If anything, we should talk so I can move on. A lump

forms in my throat and I fight back the tears that blur my vision.

I amble my way to the door and call after him as his hand lands on the door knob. Even from here, I can see the spark of hope that ignites within him when he turns to face me.

"Let's talk." I swallow down the bile that rises as I say, "Then we can both get closure."

Moving back to my bedroom, I grab my robe from where I threw it over the end of my bed before I left earlier. With a final reassuring breath, I walk out to meet him.

Sebastian stands in the hallway, his hands in his jeans pockets, looking unsure of himself. He's nothing like the self assured man I've come to know these last few years.

But I didn't know him, not really.

I blink away the thought as I walk past him and into the kitchen to pour two glasses of wine. When I return, he's standing in the same position.

As I hand him a glass, I say, "You want to stand here and talk, or get comfy on the couch?"

"Couch." He clears his throat before continuing, "Let's get comfy on the couch."

He trails behind me as I take a seat on the couch. Silence surrounds us, the murmur of the heater the only sound.

"I wanted to say sorry." Without taking a sip, he puts his glass on the coffee table and turns to face me. "For so many things, but I'll start with pulling you into my lies with George. It turns out he isn't my dad like I thought, but my uncle."

My brow tugs into a frown as I take a sip of my drink.

His mouth quirks into a smirk, making his dimple pop. "It's a long story. But I had an agenda when it came to getting Sanctuary and I shouldn't have pulled you into it. Even though, in the long run, I'm glad I did. I hate to think what I would have missed out on experiencing with you if you'd outed me to George that first day.

"You know, that day I gave you the ring, I tried to convince myself it didn't mean anything. That it was just part of the plan." He looks away, shaking his head, "God, Alex, I loved seeing my ring on your finger. Knowing that it meant you were *mine*. I was like a fucking cave man when it came to you and that ring."

I can't help the smile that forms on my lips at the memories of him always checking if I was wearing it and what would happen if I wasn't. The smile is wiped from my mouth at the last memory I have of that ring, when I told him I loved him and he threw it back in my face.

When my whole fucking world crashed and burned around me.

Sebastian picks up my left hand and rubs his thumb over the bare skin on my ring finger. His skin tone pale, in comparison to my golden tone as he embraces my hand. Half of me wants to rip it away and tell him he doesn't get to touch me anymore. But the other half, the one that seems to be in control, is luxuriating in the feel of his skin on mine.

His voice sounds wistful as he says, "I hope one day you'll wear my ring again, but for now, I'd settle for us getting to know each other again. I know I fucked up, but I want to make it up to you because in the time I've been away from you, I've learned that I deserve to be loved. That I just might deserve your love if I work hard enough to earn it back."

I pull my hand from his and stand from my seat, walking to the window that looks over Lower Manhattan.

My back is to him as I wrap my arms around my waist. "What if that's not what I want?"

I don't know if I want everything or nothing with him. His words don't undo everything he's already said and done but despite all of his flaws, I still love him. I'm conflicted.

He doesn't say anything for the longest time, but I can hear him behind as he stands. I imagine him tugging on the strands of his hair as he tries to comprehend what I've said. I wish I'd turned on the living room light so I could see him in the reflection of the window.

Sebastian's voice is uncertain as he replies, "I just want you to be happy, Alex. And if that's not with me—"

It's not until he speaks that I realize what I truly want. *Him.* It's always been him. From the day I walked into his office that first night to the moment I walked out of it a month ago. It's always been *him.* I turn to face him, cutting him off because if he really has worked on himself and he's ready to explore this with me, then I'll willingly give him my heart.

He already has it because I never got it back.

"What if..." I swallow down my nerves, because despite what he's just said, this might be too much for him. "What if I don't want us to get to know each other first? What if I want it all with you?"

I don't want to pretend or waste any more time. Not when I've spent so much time trying to hate him both before I had him and in the last few weeks. I want it all with him.

He rushes me, his strong arms wrapping around my waist as he tugs me into his solid chest and dips his head to capture my lips. I match him in my level of urgency. It's been too long since I last tasted him.

He breaks the kiss, resting his forehead on mine as he cups my cheeks. "I'm sorry, I shouldn't have done any of the stuff I did. I was scared and it felt like I was floundering. I should have held onto you. Alex, I fucking love you." He drops my head, takes a step back, his arms falling to his side as he looks out of the window.

"I'm nowhere near a fixed man, but I've been working on myself to be better for *you*. Before we do anything, I need you to know that, and I will understand if you need to walk away. I don't want to hurt you again. I couldn't live with myself if I did."

"Bastian?" I call softly, drawing his attention back to

me. My tongue swipes across my suddenly dry lips as I give him a coy smile. "I love you, too."

I'm afraid he hasn't heard me when doesn't move or say anything for such a long time. I take a step forward, my hand landing on his forearm as I call his name again.

His voice is hoarse as he demands, "Say it again."

My eyes search his. All I see is his love for me and the wonder at the love I know is reflected back in mine.

"I love you."

I barely get the words out before he's devouring my mouth, breaking the kiss occasionally to whisper, "God, I love you." Over and over.

He picks me up and I wrap my legs around his waist as he strides down the hall to my bedroom, his urgency clear.

"I need you. It's been too long. I need to make love to my fiancée," he breathes against my mouth.

"I never said yes," I tease.

His hands tighten on my thighs for a moment as he stares into my eyes.

"But you would, right?" There's an almost boyish charm to him as he asks, and I don't miss the hint of insecurity he's not bothered to hide.

My hands cup his face as I rub my thumb over his cheek. "A million times."

This kiss holds all the promises that we will keep. Of a life that we will build together. Our own family.

Bastian sets me down on my feet at the end of the bed. His face is lit by the soft glow of my bedside lamp and the weight that seemed to be on his shoulders earlier is long gone.

We stand in the dim light, looking into each other's eyes, our connection building with each second that passes by. His hands reach for the tie of my robe, a question in his gaze.

When I nod in confirmation, he pulls it loose until the lapels fall open. He doesn't move to take it off and I squirm with anticipation.

"Bastian," I plead, a warning in my tone. He's going too slow. I need him now.

"I know, princess, I'm just savoring the moment."

I take a step back, pushing my robe off my shoulders and pulling my oversized t-shirt over my head, leaving me in nothing but a royal blue lace G-string.

"Fuck, Alex. I've missed you."

Moving toward him, I unbutton his shirt, my fingers fumbling on a couple. As the buttons come undone, I see the platinum of my rings. My fingers brush over them, as if to check that what I'm seeing is real.

My eyes dart to his. "You have my rings on."

"I'm just keeping them safe for you, princess. Until you're ready to wear them again."

I don't reply to his comment, instead tucking it away to analyze later. My focus moves to pushing his shirt from his shoulders. "I've missed you too. I feel like I might combust if you don't touch me soon though."

"Get on the bed," he commands, a gruffness to his tone.

I do as I'm told, climbing onto the bed, making sure to keep my eyes on him as he makes quick work of his jeans. When he's in nothing but his boxers, he levels his hungry gaze on me, his eyes flicking to my panties. I take them off, throwing them over the side of the bed.

As he climbs up my body, the anticipation of what's to come has me squirming. His hand smooths up my thigh, brushing over my pussy. A moan slips free from my lips and my hips lift looking for more.

"So impatient, baby."

"Bastian, I swear to God, if you don't—"

His finger swipes through my slit before dipping into my pussy as his thumb rubs over my clit. I'm so close to the edge, like I always am with him. He sets a pace meant to torture me but all it does it fire me up.

The tremors start in my thighs as a sensation of floating passes through my body. My walls clench around his finger as I cry out my orgasm. It's not big, but it's one all the same. When I open my heavy eyes, I find him staring down at me, his love shining bright.

Bastian settles between my legs, lining himself up with my entrance. He steals my lips as he slowly eases into me. It's slow and sensual, nothing like anything we've created together before. This feeling is brand new.

As he starts to move, his gaze bounces around my face and down my body to where I'm connected with him. I can't help but follow. The sight of us joined together, his cock covered in my wetness, is almost too much to bear. My eyes flutter closed as I give myself up to the sensations.

"Eyes on me, my love."

It's not a command, it's a request and I don't deny him.

I reach for him, my hands roaming over his shoulders as I kiss him. It's almost too much but equally not enough. "I love you," I murmur in the space between our lips.

He rests his forehead on mine, his pace steady and sure. "I know, princess, I love you too. With all that I am."

We get lost in each other for hours all night and it isn't until the early hours of the morning that we finally go to sleep. He holds me in his arms, his words reassuring me of his love as he slips the engagement ring he bought me all those months ago back on my finger.

Where it belongs.

Epilogue

SIX MONTHS LATER

Alex

B astian's arms are wrapped around me as I rest my head on his shoulder and we sway to the music. We're in the middle of the dance floor, swaying along to a cover of *Stand By Me* by Florence and the Machine. I've had the best day, all of our friends and family came to witness us say our vows.

In such a short time, so much has happened. We've rebuilt our relationship from the ground up, and I've been by Sebastian's side as he's continued to work on himself. About two months into our rekindling, I convinced him to take a trip out to see George and Miriam.

I could see all the work he'd put in, what with coming to terms with what George had revealed to him, and that Bastian needed to mend that bridge. It started with dinner and quickly escalated to a weekend at their house. They keep in constant contact now and it's really helped Bastian to let go of all the resentment and anger he had.

My eyes latch on to my dad as he sits talking to George and Miriam at their table. He wasn't pleased when I turned up to his house with a *real* fiancé he'd never met before, but he's taken Bastian in like a son. I'll forever be grateful to him for that.

Bastian's lips brush across the top of my head as he asks, "What are you thinking, my love?"

I can't help the small smile that slips across my lips at his term of endearment. Ever since he told me he loved me, he's slipped into calling me his love, and it's better than any endearment he could use.

"About the time I took you to visit my dad for the first time."

From my position pressed into his body, I feel the shake of his chest as he chuckles. "I thought he was going to kill me."

"Had I not been there, I think he might have."

We fall quiet as we take in the party atmosphere around us. The ceremony was hours ago and the after party is now in full swing. I look around at my friends as they enjoy themselves.

Meghan and Cooper are making the most of their first night out since they welcomed their baby boy. Noah and Savannah came together—although she's been insistent that they aren't actually together. They look pretty together, if you ask me. Ben came with a guy he's been seeing for a while now and although he said he's the one, I'm not so sure about that. He's giving me some really weird vibes.

Some of Sebastian's other friends have come too, one's I've only met once before, at our engagement party. Damien Houston and Jamison Monroe are intimidating men. They're hot, but they scream 'rich playboys'.

I tip my head back and look up at *my husband*. Instantly, he drops his head and brushes his lips over mine. We're in our own bubble, tasting each other like it's the first time. I want it to always be like this, both of us never able to get enough. He breaks the kiss first, his forehead dropping onto mine as he looks into my eyes.

"I love you," I whisper.

As with every time I say those three little words, a grin breaks out over his face. It's infectious and so I can't help the one on my face that mirrors his. My gaze bounces around his face, from his eyes to his lips, his dimple and even his nose. I drink him in.

"I love you too."

We're no longer dancing. Somewhere along the way, we got lost in our moment and now we're standing in the middle of the dance floor, vaguely aware of other couples dancing around us.

I want him alone.

My eyes are still locked on him as I whisper, "Do you think we can get out of here?"

"Are you sure you don't want to stay?" A frown pulls on his brow as he pulls away from me to study my face.

"I want you now, Bastian." There's no mistaking the urgency in my plea.

God, I can never get enough of him.

His eyes heat with need and without another word, he takes hold of my hand and walks me out of the room. I can't wait to start the rest of my life with this man as *my husband*.

Sebastian

I feel like I'm in a constant state of shock. My wife is amazing and has given me so many things and experiences I never thought I'd have. It feels surreal that we're married. That I get to call her mine. *My wife.*

There was a moment when we had broken up that I thought that was it and she'd never forgive me, and honestly, I wouldn't have blamed her if she didn't. I'm the luckiest bastard alive, and the fact that she chose me, that she loves *me*, well, fuck, if it doesn't make me feel on top of the fucking world.

She trails behind me as I drag her toward the exit. My focus is intent on getting us to the hotel room. Just thinking of all the things I'm going to do to her has me hard as a fucking rock. When her hand slips from mine, I pull up short. With a frown on my face, I turn to her.

She points to a supply closet, marching toward the door. "In here."

"You don't want to go to the room and—"

She cuts me off as she opens the door, turning to look at me over her shoulder. "No, I want you in here, now and then we can go back to the party."

I can't find fault in her plan, and I'm not about to start our marriage with an argument about where I take her. Following her into the dark supply closet, I close the door behind me. As I turn to face Alex, my hands land on her waist as I look down into her deep brown eyes. *My love.*

"How do we get you out of this?" I ask. The dress is stunning on her but I need it off.

Alex bends over and gathers up the skirt of her dress and pulls off her panties. "We don't take it off. I don't feel like you get the urgency of this need I have for you, Bastian."

It's all I needed to hear before I cup her face in my hands and devour her lips with my own. It's messy and rushed, both the kissing and our desire to touch each other. Her hands hike up her skirt as I find the back of her legs and lift her into my arms.

With her arms and legs around me as I press her into the door, I manage to free myself from the confines of my pants. Testing to see how ready she is for me, I move a hand to the heat between her legs. *She's fucking drenched for me.*

"Bastian, please, be quick," she mewls, her head thrown back in anticipation.

No more words are needed as I line myself up and slide inside of her. She feels *fucking* glorious. A heady rush takes over me as I begin moving inside of her. Her walls spasm with her need as she welcomes me.

"Savannah, stop," Noah growls. The sound of his voice halts my movements.

They must be just outside the door. My eyes lock onto Alex's and with a shake of her head, she tells me to not to move. We stay frozen, my hard cock still buried in her slick pussy, as we listen to our friends on the other side of the door.

"No, Noah, you stop! I'm tired of all o' *this*. Just leave me alone."

"You don't understand. I made him a promise," he pleads, a touch of desperation filling his voice.

Defeated, Savannah replies, "A promise you made thirteen years ago. Things change Noah, and that's okay."

Under the soft glow of the emergency exit sign, I can see Alex's eyes widen as we eavesdrop on the conversation. From what I can gather, something has happened between them and it seems it's been going on for some time. Noah calls out to Savannah again, but the conversation doesn't continue.

Alex and I listen intently for any noise on the other

side of the door, and when I'm certain he's gone, I ask, "You want to go back out there?"

She studies me for a moment before shaking her head, then pressing her lips to mine. It's all the confirmation I need.

I never thought love existed, let alone that I would get to experience it. For the longest time since I met her, I fought against the way she made me feel. I love this woman with my whole heart, and I'd do anything to make her happy.

Including making love to her in a supply closet at our wedding reception.

The End

Want a sneak peek of Savannah and Noah's story?
Keep reading for the prologue of Don't Make Promises...

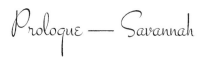

Prologue — Savannah

I'm walking down the corridor, trying to avoid the jocks and cheerleaders who always seem to

crowd around after the final bell has rung, when I see him. Even though I'm not one of the popular kids, I still know most people in this school, but I don't know him. He must be new.

My hand comes to rest on the latch of my locker as I stare at him unashamedly. It's like all the air has been ripped from my lungs as I take him in. A fluttering starts in the pit of my stomach as my body heats.

I've never felt anything like this before and I'm not entirely sure what's caused it.

He's the most beautiful boy I've ever seen, but I know I'd never stand a chance with him. Not with my braces, awkwardness, and weird reddish-blonde hair. I reach up and wrap a strand of it around my finger. As soon as I'm old enough to go to the salon alone, I'm going to dye it.

With a shake of my head, I turn my focus back to unlocking my locker and putting away my books so I can head home.

"Sav, come here."

I roll my eyes as I turn to face my brother, hating that he calls me that, but in typical big brother fashion, Jack does it all the time. He's four years older than me, and one of the popular guys in our school. He's the reason I know most of the people here, and why they also call me Sav.

"Come on, Sav, I wanna introduce you to my new friend."

My eyes land on Jack before moving to the boy that stands next to him. I swallow down the moisture that floods my mouth as his gaze connects with mine. The intensity in his green mixed with brown eyes forces me to break eye contact. The current of electricity in that one look is too much for me to handle.

Jack has an innate need to introduce me to people so that his friends become my friends. He hasn't quite grasped the fact that I don't mind doing my own thing. Or that I'm old enough to choose my own friends.

I don't really want to know who the new guy is, why he's here, or what he sounds like. From one look alone I know he'll occupy my thoughts and that he'll haunt my dreams at night.

With my eyes firmly on my feet, my heart hammers in my chest as they approach. Even when they're standing in front of me, I still don't look up. *Jeez, his feet are big.*

"Noah, this is my baby sister, Sav," Jack introduces me as he slings his arm around my shoulder, pulling me into his side.

Noah.

A swift elbow to the ribs makes Jack drop his arm. He laughs at me, a knowing smirk on his face when I lift my eyes to give him a death stare. *God, he can be insufferable.*

"My name's Savannah." I hold my chin up high as I look into the new guy's eyes, fanned by long dark lashes.

His voice is rough and far deeper than any boy I've ever met when he says, "It's nice to meet you, Savannah."

He holds out his hand, and because my mama taught me to have manners, I slip mine into his. His skin is smooth and warm as he envelopes my tiny hand in his far larger one. It feels like an eternity passes between us as we stare at each other. There's something hidden behind his dreamy gaze that tells a story of a lifetime of pain. It's hard to believe he's the same age as Jack.

The sounds of the busy corridor fade away, and I have an overwhelming urge to step into his arms and just hold him.

A frown pulls at my brow, and I drop his hand like it's on fire as I step back. He doesn't seem to mind, because he turns to my brother, an easy smile on his face.

"Should we get going?"

I look to Jack for an answer, unsure of what Noah

means because Jack's supposed to give *me* a ride home, not him.

Sensing where my thoughts have gone, Jack slings his arm around my shoulders again and says, "Don't worry, Sav, Noah's just coming to our house for dinner. Mama already cleared it."

Oh no, that's even worse than not having a ride home. I'd rather they left me here and went somewhere else. Jack turns me in the direction of the parking lot, too busy chatting away to notice my internal panic.

The feelings coursing through me are too much for fourteen-year-old me to handle, so I do what I do best and what I hate most; I retreat into myself.

The car ride home is filled with R'n'B songs as Jack navigates through Montgomery, Alabama as I try in vain to distract myself from the boy in the front passenger seat. I love this city and the familiar streets that pass us by, as the car eats up the miles home. There's so much history here, and when I move—my dream is to live in New York and make it big on Broadway—I'll be sure to come back and visit.

As soon as the car comes to a stop, I throw my door open and bolt for the house. My body is overwhelmed with feelings I've never felt before and I need some time away from Noah to sort through them. How I'm going to make it through dinner is beyond me. Maybe Mama will let me eat in my room.

Yeah, that's wishful thinking.

I race through the house and shut myself in my

bedroom, tossing my bag to the floor. Next off is my jacket and then my shoes, before I dive onto the bed and bury myself under the covers.

Later that night when I'm called for dinner, I drag my feet, wishing my earlier plea to eat in my room hadn't fallen on deaf ears. Especially as at dinner when I quickly realize that isolating myself in my room has done nothing to prepare me for seeing him again. It's been a matter of hours, and yet it's like I'm seeing him for the first time again. My legs feel like jelly as I walk to the table and sink into my chair.

There's no way I'm going to be able to eat, not with the way my tongue feels thick in my mouth.

My mama, always wanting to make people feel welcome, starts the conversation as she sits at the table. She's oblivious to the rushing in my ears when she asks, "So, Noah, how long have you been in Montgomery?"

"We moved right at the end of summer, ma'am."

Mama laughs as she says, "Please, call me Sadie. How are you finding it?"

Noah serves himself some of the salad from the bowl in the middle of the table, and I watch his movements from under my lashes. "It's different from New York, but I'm liking it."

He's from New York?

"You don't sound like you're from New York," I blurt out before I can stop myself. My cheeks flame as all eyes turn to face me.

My dad is the first to speak. "Now, don't be rude, Savannah."

I drop my eyes to the mac and cheese on my plate. "Sorry, I didn't mean to be rude."

When I'm greeted with silence, I look up into his stunning hazel eyes. One side of his mouth is lifted, and it's then that I notice how pillowy his lips are. "It's okay. I grew up all over, so was never in one place long enough to have just one accent."

"Oh, okay," I breathe, as if he's just told me the most fascinating fact.

He doesn't try to hide the smile that lights up his face and I drop my head as my cheeks heat again at being the center of *his* attention.

I spend the rest of dinner focused on eating my food until I can excuse myself to my room on the pretext of doing my homework. The reality is I did it hours ago. I just need to not be near him right now.

When he leaves, I watch through the slats of my blinds in my bedroom window as he walks down the driveway and to a house a couple of doors down. When his front door closes, I finally move and flop down onto my bed as I look up at the ceiling. Everything that happened today plays like a movie in my mind as I scrutinize our every interaction.

Laying in the darkness, unable to sleep, I vow to myself from this day forward I will be brave and bold. I won't hide anymore.

This is how I met Noah, my brother's best friend. It was the first day I fell in love and realized that you can't always have the one you want.

I wish I'd known when we first met what was to come, of all the heartache and pain that would follow.

Would I still have gone through it?

Most definitely.

Afterword

Thank you so much for reading my second book baby. If you loved Alex and Sebastian's story, be sure to leave a review.

If you're not quite done with the Breaking the Rules gang, you can sign up to my newsletter here (subscribepage.io/4kdNEJ) and get monthly updates on my books, enter giveaways and hear about some other awesome authors.

If you enjoyed Alex and Sebastian's story, be sure to pick up my third book, which follows the story of Savannah and Noah. You can grab your copy here.

If you haven't already done so, be sure to have a read of Meghan and Cooper's story here.

Acknowledgments

A huge thank you, first and foremost, to Allie Bliss, my editor who has been with me since book one and who I hope will be with me through to the end of my author journey. I love working with you and that you pull me up on everything I need to be pulled up on.

Thank you to Sarah from Word Emporium for your thorough work with proofreading Don't Fall in Love. I can't wait to work with you again.

Thank you to Riley, my PA, for supporting me with everything else that comes with being an author so that I can get the words down on paper. You're a star and this is just the beginning of our journey!

My beta readers also deserve a mention for all of the fantastic feedback and hyping that they have given me since I sent them over Alex and Sebastian's story. I hope they stick around for what's to come.

Tee, I finally got to put all of the advice and guidance you have shared with the Cygnets into these pages. I hope

I've done you proud. This book wouldn't have been what it is if I hadn't stumbled across your group. Everything happens for a reason and I truly believe you've come into my life to share your wisdom as I take on this still new avenue of life! I can't wait to meet you in July!

A special shoutout to my street team, thank you all for taking a chance with me and shouting about my book! It truly means the world to me as without your support I wouldn't be in this position.

Finally, a massive thank you to my boyfriend Ryan. For all of the support you have given me as I've hidden myself away to get this book written in a month and a half.

About the Author

KA James is an author of contemporary romance. She lives near London, UK with her partner and their Bichon Frisé, called Mia. Before starting her author journey, KA was an avid reader of romance books and truly believes the spicier the book, the better.

Outside of writing, KA has worked in HR for eleven years but has truly found her passion with writing and getting lost in a world that plays out like a movie in her mind. After all, getting lost in the land of make believe, where it's much spicier is way more fun.

 KA hopes that you enjoyed reading Alex and Sebastian's story. Be sure to follow along on one or more social media channels to be kept in the loop of all up and coming releases.

Printed in Great Britain
by Amazon